AMERICAN FERAL BOOK ONE

IMPRINT

DANIEL BECKER

D1501662

American Feral by Daniel Becker

First published 2022

Edited by Erik van Mechelen, Amelia Breamer, David Aretha

Cover illustration: Eric Buisson

Cover design: Paul Palmer-Edwards

CONTENTS

Fox, Owl, Rooster, Wolf

Eyes, covered. Hands, tied. Mouth, gagged. Ears, ringing. Smell, dusty. Location, unknown. The last thing I remember was: *Ugh, thinking hurts my head....* I was on my way to do something. Was I in trouble or was *I* the trouble? I swallow a wad of congealed spit. What is that weird taste? Metallic and dry. I wiggle my toes and count my fingers. All ten accounted for. My ass itches as if mites are digging in for a new home. The floor feels like carpet. I listen, hear the hum of a motor below me, then the flip of a page. Other people are with me. Who?

From my left, I hear a female's voice. "How is your leg doing?" she asks insincerely.

From the right a deep male voice. "Better. I had a bit of a hard time landing after jumping a fence."

I know that voice. I heard it before I fell unconscious.

The left entity makes a sound like glass placed on a counter. "That's just you getting old. Guess I'm going to have to put you down soon," she comments with a chuckle.

"My own bullet will put me down long before I get to that point."

Come on, think. Why can't I remember anything from this morning to now? I think I was walking, had to be in Detroit, walking in Detroit to somewhere to do something. Something important... someone was waiting for me. I feel like I just woke up from anesthesia. Did they give me something to make me forget? The room feels like it is spinning and I don't know if it's my panicked mind or the drugs. No, I need to calm down.... Deep breaths. Maybe if I listen to them, I can find out more about where I am.

Left sighs and a creaking sound. "Well, if you need some physical therapy, I can get you set up with Claud if you need me to."

Some more rustling of paper. "No, I just need to take some time off of my feet, maybe call in sick for the next mission like Feather."

"I don't know why he didn't want me to do his kid's surgery. I could have done it faster and better than any surgeon," she says.

The paper stops rustling. "Knowing him, he didn't want to bother you."

"It was just an inaugural hernia," she points out. "I've stitched a man's balls back on the field during a lunch break. I could have made time."

"Well, in his mind, you were heading to Detroit. He knows that you always put the mission first."

Mission? Are they some sort of organized group? Wait... could this be the Detroit Hunter's Lodge or the Chinese Fangs?

"Yeah, but it's his kid I would do anything for Talon. Speaking of birds, Gores is going to skin you alive when you don't come back with the crow, and you decide to kidnap this kid instead."

I have a surgeon and someone else.... I get a whiff of smoke from a cigarette, or is that gun smoke? He has a gun. They both were on a mission to take someone was it me? I doubt they are organ harvesters, and wouldn't target someone directly. Could they be terrorists taking me for ransom? No, why would they? I have no money and no one would pay for my ransom.

"When he wakes up, I will show you why."

I can hear the woman get up from sitting down, and her feet approach me. "Well, I am just going to make sure he is still alive. He hasn't moved much in the past hour."

Shit! Just play it cool, don't move, and don't flinch! I can feel her breath; it smells of mint gum. I feel a sharp point pressed against my neck, and I immediately jolt out of instinct. Must have been a pressure point.

The hazy outline of a figure through the blindfold turns back, and there is a rustling of metal and plastic. *Don't pull off the blindfold. Please don't pull it off.* "The midazolam should have had enough doses for at least forty-eight hours." She approaches me, and I feel a hand reach around my neck. A leathery felt finger wraps around my Adam's apple and presses against my pulse.

6

The blindfold comes off, and a blinding light pierces through my eyes. My captors are revealed.

She is a Prime, a half animal hybrid solider, created by the US government a half century ago to fight China in World War III in the place of human solders. Blue human eyes fitted into an anthropomorphic fox face, crouched down, and a face juts out from the blinding halo in my eyes. A muzzle is short and narrow, with morning orange fur traveling down to a coal snout. Her coat is tinted crimson as if highlighted, and it covers her arms up to her snowy vest and a black T-shirt. Her feet are placed in tip-toe formation with her heels in the air up to her white pants; these are also dotted with past stains of red. Her blue eyes and their concave irises focused on mine. "Hey, he's awake." She turns her head. There is no hair, but instead, a long mane that goes down her head. It's strange to see a Prime without a collar. She must not be from the US.

I hear a paper being crumpled and the sound of a giant approach. "Oh good, he's up." The fox Prime steps aside to reveal a titan. As the figure steps out from the smoke in the room, I notice the glaring eyes of a wolf, the muzzle of a canine, and fur the color of the metal on his gun on the edge of a table. From what I can make out, his face resembles a wolf's face molded into a human head. His eyes glaze with a teal hew that shines in the shadows. A small cut in his cheek stretches down from the bottom of his left eye to the tip of his nose, where his mouth opens, revealing a set of fangs. His hair is much darker than his arms, and his ears blend his body and facial tones. His ears are down, in a state of control.

A cigarette hangs from his damp, gray, protruding muzzle as ash specks float onto his ashen fur. He wears a snow-white jacket with the front unzipped, revealing a white T-shirt that is stained with darker red splotches. His legs are much like the fox Prime except they are much longer, and his feet could crush me like an ant. On the front of the jacket is a badge resting on his left shoulder depicting a lion consuming a bald eagle and the words "PRIME LIBERATION FORCE" embroidered in an elegant gold thread. I haven't done anything to hurt Primes and have actively supported them. I vote for pro-Prime politicians. I post pro-Prime arguments on websites. I am not a threat to them. Why is the Prime army after me?

"Just give him another dose of versed," the male says.

I blink furiously to convey my distress and try to moan *no* as loudly as I can. The tape makes communication nearly impossible. I glance around for an exit route. I'm in a gaudy trailer from the '30s that has been refurbished into some sort of military supply van. The blinds on the windows are taped shut, carpet torn up to serve as another spot to store God knows what. There is a repurposed couch on either side covered in cigarette burns and torn up fabric on the cushions. A door is behind me, leading to what I assume to be the bathroom, an exit door to the right side, and a straight compartment head that is closed. There is no escape and worst of all, we are moving somewhere, so I can't leap out the window.

The fox turns around and starts rummaging through a medical bag that is opened up on a small coffee table in front of a refurbished plush sofa set against the left wall. "Those doses you gave him were doses for a Prime. If we give him another he might not wake up."

I breathe a sigh of relief that she knows what she is doing. The wolf Prime must have made a stupid mistake, giving a Prime dose to a human. How many did he give me? I still feel groggy and confused. I am glad I am still alive.

He looks at me and reaches down. I suspect he plans to hit me or knock me out again, and I wince in anticipation. Still, he only pinches the duct tape over my mouth, and, in one motion, a painful motion rips the tape off along with hair from my lip. Tears fill my eyes from the immense pain, and I spit out a small cloth gag. It's a relief to have my airway free. The gag tasted foul.

He kneels to my eye level and clutches my chin before I can utter a single word. The feeling of his vice is unmatched; as he pinches my chin with just two fingers. "Unless you want the tape back on your mouth, you will answer the questions I ask you. Understand?" He speaks sternly. I know I need to answer every question he asks me. I don't know what they want, but I don't want to end up dead.

I nod yes, looking directly into his fixated eyes.

"At least one American has some goddamn common sense around here." He lets go of my chin and frees my bound hands. "Last name?"

"Sparrow." I need to answer him swiftly and directly. Quick answers, and I might get through this. They obviously couldn't want a ransom. I have no money, I have no influence, I am only a high schooler. Or I was. I got kicked out of Raiden Academy today. Yesterday? What day is it even?

The fox Prime interrupts the wolf as soon as she realizes what he is doing. "Why are you letting him go? He is..."

"Not now, Kit."

Her name is Kit then.

"Now Ghent," the male says.

How does he know my name?

"Where did you come from?"

I rock my butt back and forth to notice my wallet and wallet chain is missing. He must have taken it and seen my ID. "Detroit Midtown." My phone in my left pocket is missing too.

He looks at me like I am stupid. "I know that. Where were you born?"

If only I knew. "Some camp in South America the name is Oasis. I don't know where."

His dog ears perk up. "Why were you in a camp?"

"I don't know. I was just born there. A fire happened, and I escaped. I ended up in a hospital in South America. I was sent to Detroit to live in an orphanage, The Children of War Orphanage off of Seventh Street."

"Your parents were human, right?"

"I don't remember them." Why would he think they weren't human? "I've always looked like this. I'm human."

He sighs and figures this is going nowhere fast; I must not have answered his question somehow. "Ghent Sparrow, why did you attack that asshole back in the alley?"

The last thing I remembered about school was the principal telling me I couldn't come back, but my memory of that day was patchy. What had I done? I poke my canines with my tongue and can taste something strange, metallic. "I don't remember attacking anyone. I don't remember anything I swear!"

Kit pauses for a moment as if she remembers where her keys were left. "Hey," she asks the wolf, "do you have that vial of versed I gave you?"

He reaches back behind him to his coat and takes out a small amber vial the size of his upper ring finger. "Here." He hands it over.

She holds it up to what little light the above ceiling fan provides. She tilts it to the side and her face drains. "It's empty."

9

"Yeah." He goes back to me. "I administered the doses to him just like you said."

The vial is clenched and she shoves him over, causing him nearly to tip over. "You must have spilled some."

He puts his palms up; they are worn and tattered with scars. "Hey I'm not the doctor around here that's your job." The wolf digs in his pocket for a silver and gold pocket knife.

Who did I hurt? And what is she saying that I was given a dose meant for a Prime? Was that why he was asking who my parents were? Am I okay now that I've woken up, or am I still in danger of dying from an overdose? "Am I going to be all right? What do you guys want from me anyway? I am a Prime advocate in high school!"

The wolf Prime slaps me hard against my face left to right. I immediately fall to the floor hunched over. "Listen." He grabs me by my Raiden Academy-branded, marble-colored sweater and pulls me up. "You are to listen to me, and me alone. If you do this, you will survive," he tells me forcefully. "You are going to be put in front of Pure and the Zodiac; you need to get a hold of yourself understand?"

No, I can't meet him. Nothing good comes out of meeting him. "He is the leader of the PLF what does he want with me?" My head moves less than an inch closer to his face. My eyes start to water again as the pain from the cut radiates up my arm. "I don't want to be tortured or put in prison. I know nothing and-"

They must have kidnapped me thinking I was someone else, someone important. "Sorry." I begin to sniffle and try to hide the tears. "I... I just want to know what's going on."

He sighs heavily and lifts me back up by the cuff of my shirt and stands me up along with him. He has my entire body lifted off the ground by one hand. He sets me on my feet. I am at his shoulders and am staring directly at his stone-cut chest. "My job right now is to keep you alive. Listen to me, follow my orders, and most importantly, stop your crying. I will get you out of this with your skin still on what little meat you have on you."

I feel him move his left hand to my arm and press the blade across my fingertips. My blood flows onto his knife and drips onto the floor. My body clenches at the pain, but for some reason it doesn't hurt as much more than a paper cut. Must be the drugs.

10

I guess I have no other option than to listen to him at this point. I can't really go anywhere and I can't fight them. I sniffle and wipe my eyes on my sleeve. "Okay... what do you want me to do then?"

He pats my arm. "Good boy." He turns around to Kit, who is digging in her bag. "Kit, get that blood thing that spins."

From a cupboard, she pulls out a bulky metal medical case and rolls her eyes. "Blood thing that spins..." She whispers under her breath. "Why?"

He looks right into my eyes and lifts up my bleeding finger and presses it against his blade. "You will see."

Kit digs into her bag and pulls out a thermometer-shaped object with a screen attached to one side and a tray on the other. He hands her my blood sample, and she places it into the dish and flicks the on-switch.

Is there something wrong with my blood? I've never seen anything like that before, I've watched plenty of investigative crime drama's but never seen someone use something like this when they are identifying blood.

It buzzes and beeps several times before a high-pitched beep rings. She taps a few selections on the touch screen. With every tap, her face becomes more confused, and with every swipe, her face's pensiveness intensifies. That can't be good for me if *she* doesn't know what's on the screen.

"Did it work?" He peeks over the screen. While he looks away, I manage to see more of the badge he has on his shoulder; it reads *Lupine Canidae: Sagittarius Beta*. Beta... is that a rank? If so, he's not their leader. Could the leader be driving?

"Shut up for a second." Kit wipes more blood from my fingers and applies it straight into the machine using a tiny vial placed in a centrifuge. I glance at her shoulder and notice no badge, but her coat sitting next to her has a badge peeking out, which I can see reads *Gamma*.

Lupine hands me a bottle of peroxide and a couple of large bandaids to put over my finger. He tells me to go to the sink and make sure the cut is cleaned and sterilized before putting the bandaid on. I obey his command. In the toilet adorned with baby blue plastic, I rinse my hands in the sink engraved with "Made in Africa." I clean my mouth of the tape residue. I keep hearing Kit pressing the buttons on the device that is now hooked up to a tablet through a USB drive. I've never had my blood drawn or tested for anything. I had thought they were not organ harvesters, but with them testing my blood, maybe they are just printing out a label to slap on my kidneys or liver. I don't really know what Lupine is testing me for. Maybe they are making sure I am okay from the versed dose.

The peroxide stings when I put it on and foams, I am tempted just to wash it off but I don't know what that knife could have cut before, so I just wince and grind my teeth to get past the pain. I finish up in the bathroom, but before I can take a seat back on the floor, Lupine motions me to sit on the couch I was on before behind a table with an ashtray and a folded newspaper dated March 24th, 2054. The date that I remember before being kidnapped was March 30th, so that newspaper is almost a week old. I don't feel too hungry or thirsty, so it couldn't have been too long since I was unconscious. I take a seat close to the middle while he sits on the left end.

Kit continues to pace back and forth in a meditative state. She throws the tablet back into its bag. "This is impossible there is no way. This piece of shit is broken, or you must have not cleaned your blade from the last Prime you cut. It's reading as Prime blood."

He motions over to me with his thumb. "He's part Prime."

She is blown back. "What? How do you know? That's never been done it's impossible. Humans and Primes cannot breed-"

Wait, are they saying that I am part Prime?! "You're saying I am a Prime?"

He takes out a lighter from his pocket. The lighter is silver with a wolf's head engraved on the top. It opens up with a rusty hinge that squeaks as it is lifted up. "I saw him attack a man twice his size and pin him to the floor. When I intervened and pulled him back from killing the man, I saw he was not completely human." He pulls a cigarette from behind his ear.

I attacked someone as a Prime? No, he has to be lying this isn't real. He has to be making some sort of excuse to kidnap me for another purpose. There is nothing about me that is like a Prime. I am a human I've always been one.

She drums her claws on the screen. "You've been sleep-deprived for the past three days. You were probably seeing things."

"I know what I saw," he confirms. "This kid is a Prime and we are going to go to Kingdom and confirm it."

Kit looks over at me, then to a smartphone on the table peeking out from under the medical bag. "If, and it's a big 'if,' this kid is a hybrid, that means that someone was experimenting with Prime genes that the PLF doesn't know about. This could be an international nightmare to cover up." Ever since World War III ended, genetic engineering with the Prime strand was outlawed internationally.

Lupine rests his head on the right sofa. "Exactly, which is why we are taking him to Fawn to confirm that he's a hybrid, then to Pure to deal with the international ramifications of this."

She takes her smartphone and grips it tightly. "Then maybe we will track down who fucked to make this kid."

Wait... if I am a half breed, one of my parents might be a Prime. Then could it be that they were separated at Oasis from me because they figured out what I was? They had a child and panicked because they didn't know where I would belong? There have been stories of Primes falling in love with humans, but they've been mainly affairs with Primes that were contracted or owned by the wealthy. If I did find them, all I would want would be to ask them why they lost me and never went out to find me. From their answer I could then decide if I would call them family or never speak to them again.

Kit refuses to take this lightly as she takes me aside and gets another sample, some of my saliva, while Lupine appears to be near to sleep, lazing out on the couch. I take this opportune moment to speak with a swab in my mouth. "Umm, can you please fill me in on what happened back in Detroit?"

Lupine starts taking off his shoes, which are clown shoes compared to mine and latched several times up the heel and to his ankle. "Came across you in a brawl with some guy in an alley. You managed to pin him down. I separated you two. He pulled out his knife to attack me, so I rushed him, put my barrel to both his balls and blew them off."

What?! I tighten my legs to hide my crotch. "Did you get his name?" If I get a name from the man, I might remember why I'd done it.

"No point." He pops his shoes off with one tug, and the smell of his feet is rancid, like wet dog fur coated in sweat. Christ, even his feet are toned like marble.

Well, that could be anyone in Detroit if they sound like that. Man, I wish I could remember what happened; maybe Kit knows if I will remember eventually. "Hey Kit, will I remember who I hurt back at school, or anything of that day?"

13

She is centered on the centrifuge, taking it apart and cleaning out every speck on the machine. "It's made not to. When you get your wisdom teeth taken out, you are not supposed to remember it. You might get snippets but nothing concrete."

Well, do these memories actually matter at this point? I mean, if I don't ever return home, it's not like anyone can reach me if I'm in the PLF.

Lupine rises from the table and throws his shoes right at the door to the driver's compartment. "Hey, Hoots, park the van and get over here!" Hoots? I imagine he's an owl Prime. I know that Primal naming conventions are mainly based on nicknames as most of them were born in test tubes and were not really given names. They mostly just made them up on their own or were given to them by other members of their division. I can't see an owl Prime being an alpha in this group, especially with how Lupine and Kitsune seem to act, and if he was their alpha, I think he would have been alerted of me as soon as I woke up.

"What do you want?" The driver speaks with a heavy Asian accent. "The god damn road is hard enough to drive on!"

Half Prime... Like what kind of Prime am I? "Hey, um, Kit, is it?"

She keeps looking at the scanner with one eye and keeps the other on me. "It's Kitsune, and what do *you* want?" She speaks to me like I am inept.

"What kind of Prime am I?" I ask hesitantly. Before I didn't know what I wanted to *become*; now I am a step back asking myself what I *am*.

Her hands creep toward the scanner in the bag. "I can't tell you. It's too difficult to say here."

Well, I guess I've been waiting for my whole life to figure out who I really am, so waiting a couple more hours till we arrive in Kingdom wouldn't hurt.

I know very little about Kingdom. The U.S military lost Seattle to a siege by the Primes at the initial revolt triggered by years of discrimination and several tense race fueled standoffs with the US government. The Primes decided that the first city they took would house their defenses, which eventually transformed into their capital and was renamed Kingdom. After they took Seattle, the PLF. preceded to snatch up any land it could. The PLF pushed people out of their homes and sent them to flee east to the Mississippi River. They took land up to the Mississippi before running out of money, Primes, and overall morale, then the U.S shoved them back to the Rocky Mountains before running out of steam itself, and that's where the P.L.F. border stands today. The De-escalation Proclamation was then created, which installed the PLF-United States Ceasefire Buffer Zone, or as everyone calls it, Wasteland, a buffer between the Prime Liberation Force and the United States. It stretches from the Mississippi River to the previous border of Colorado. Both sides hoped that one day things would cool off enough so that peace could be made.

I've never been out into the Wastelands. I heard land past the Mississippi River had been fertile farmland and countryside that spread for thousands of miles. Still, after the invasion from the Primes, the property was turned into a warzone. Bombshells, bunkers, and farmland were destroyed by chemicals and debris that rendered most of the ground a barren wasteland. Now it's only uses are to house criminals, those stubborn enough not to leave their homes, and fringe terrorist groups, including the Hunters and Evolutionaries.

It feels awkward, leaving the conversation there. I have so much more I want to ask, but I am also unsure I'll be answered if I do. I mean, I was just some freak of nature that Lupine picked up in an alley. My desired life of excitement didn't include being held hostage by P.L.F. soldiers and learning that I was the only half-human, half-Prime hybrid in the nation maybe the whole world. I didn't feel special. Maybe they really have confused me for someone else.

Right now, I am a trophy to be presented to Pure, the powerful dictator of the PLF. The world doesn't know what to do with me and neither do I. Will I be put into a zoo for Prime kids to look at, or am I going to be placed on an examination table and taken apart to see what makes me Prime? Kitsune is pressing more buttons on her scanner. On occasion, she looks at me before pawing more controls. I get the feeling she wants to dissect me.

I feel the trailer come to a halt and the ruffling of metal and cans from the front compartment. Out of the driver's seat comes an owl Prime. He has the body of a stunted human, but he is covered in feathers from head to claw. He looks at me with irises that eclipse a fading sunset, his eyes wide and unblinking. "He doesn't look half Prime to me. Looks like any old human." His mouth makes a low click when he shuts his mouth. He pokes me in the arm with a claw from an unfolded wing. "He feels like a human too. No scales." He peeks behind me. "No tail." He grasps my hands, and I let him examine me because, at this point, they've tied me up, gagged me, taken my blood, and injected me with dangerous sedatives. And this might be just the beginning. "And no feathers. Some Prime."

"If you don't believe Lupine, then look at this." Kit tosses the scanner at the owl Prime.

He looks at it, thinks for a second, and then looks at it again. "You think I know what this shit means?"

I hear Lupine calling from the front. "He's half Prime. She says so; I say so; hell, even the kid says so right, kid?"

I do not know what to say, so I say nothing.

He answers for me. "I didn't hear a no, so that must mean a yes."

Hoots refolds his wings, scans the area, then struts down to the spot where I was tied up. With his foot, he throws the ropes into an empty cargo box. His head is swiveling around, even when his body isn't facing me. It hits me: I know I'm no longer among humans.

. . .

I am unsure how long I am sitting here with these Primes, but the more I sit on the couch with Lupine, the more I hate the way I smell. I noticed a shower and bathroom at the end of the trailer, and I asked the wolf if I could use it. Lupine informs me I can only take a shower if he is watching; he doesn't want me to escape through the window above the sink. I politely decline.

Kitsune watches me while Lupine sleeps with a hood over his eyes. Lupine was texting and calling a few people, and although he spoke in some Asian language, I heard my name come up at least five times. She continues to fiddle with the scanner for what seems like an hour before giving up and stealing a cig from Lupine's box and lighting up a smoke. I avert my eyes to the brightness of the lighter.

Lupine sniffs. "Those are mine," he murmurs.

She lobs an empty pack into the trash. "I need it more than you."

She needs it, and even though I don't smoke, I am tempted to grab one from the table near Lupine.

"You should know those aren't good for your health," he comments.

She strikes his lighter on the table. "Bullets aren't healthy for you either, and yet you take them."

He sighs and looks over at me. "Are you bored?"

Unimaginably. "Yeah."

"Want to have a project? We got some jerky for you to eat and a water bottle if you do it."

I can't imagine what he wants me to do, but I am hungry and my mouth is still dry from that gag. "Sure." I mean, I am dreading meeting Pure, but at the same time, I just want this to be over like ripping off a bandaid covered in barbs, and some menial labor can make time pass faster.

He reaches down below him and pulls out a large crate full of rattling metal inside. He places it on the ground in front of me and opens it up. Inside is a pile of bullet casings that go up to my knee. There must be thousands of empty shells stacked in a golden pile like a treasure. "We need someone to sort these casings by size." He reaches down and pulls out a couple and shows them to me. "Just pull them out and sort them into a couple of empty bins." He throws them back into the pile and gets a couple of empty gray metal totes from the other side above Kitsune, as well as a plastic unmarked water bottle and a couple of bags of what look like emergency rations out of an overhead bin.

It's something to do, I guess, and besides, I should do anything to get them on my side. "What do you do... say, why do you have totes of empty casings anyway?"

"Bandits on a highway thought it was a good idea to raid us. It's salvage from their stash. Worth their weight in gold around here." He hands me a water bottle and some jerky before crashing on the sofa.

Truly is the Wild West brought to life, gold coins replaced with simple brass bullet casings.

. . .

About a quarter of the way through the pile, the trailer slows to a stop. Hoots parks the trailer and opens the door. "Lupine, we need to stop for gas at Maurice's and Bella's. We can also get some more food for the kid and supplies empty out the waste tank as well."

Lupine wakes up from his nap and stretches out, nearly tipping over a tote I have placed right at his feet. I manage to catch it before it falls over onto the floor. "All right, just don't park near some mortar gang just like Tucker did a couple months ago." He gets up and stretches while getting his boots from the closet.

Hoots leans against the door. He seems pretty worn down after driving for all this time. "He probably just wanted to lift some parts from their bikes."

Lupine just shrugs his shoulders. "Maybe he didn't see over the steering wheel."

Kitsune finishes up a nearly empty plastic water bottle. She's been keeping an eye on me the entire time. I've been managing to avoid eye contact with her while she writes down notes in a small journal as if she is observing me like a monkey in a cage. "You want me to watch the kid?"

Lupine takes out a long rifle from the closet and straps it onto his back. "No, you are going to guard the van, Hoots will keep an eye in the sky."

Wait, I am going to be left alone in the van with Kitsune? I don't want to be alone, especially with her. "Umm... Lupine?"

He tightens the strap on the rifle to his chest and looks at me. "What?"

"Can..." I twiddle my thumbs between a casing. "...I come with you?"

He seems dumbfounded as he cocks his head to the side. "You know it's dangerous out there, right?"

My life is already in danger. "I just...don't want to be left alone." If there is any chance I can escape it's going to be with Lupine walking around outside. I doubt this will work, though.

He rolls his eyes and looks down at his rifle and drums his claw on the magazine. "All right."

Kitsune's mouth turns agape. "Are you nuts! Why the fuck would you bring him out to an outpost!"

But I want to go. An outpost in the middle of Wasteland. Lupine better bring some serious heat to deal with the bandits and elements that live there. Well... come to think of it, can it be any worse than Detroit? I mean where I live... or well *lived*... had its bad parts of town, but Wasteland is an entire half of a continent of desperate people with guns and high tensions. I guess if I am with a trained PLF soldier and he has enough firepower to take down a tank then I guess I will be okay, and if I can somehow manage to free myself, I should be able to find someone, or some way back home.

He takes a couple of magazines and loads them into his pocket. "If he is in my sights, I know that he won't escape." He inserts one into the slot at the bottom of the M-16 style rifle. "Besides, I want to test something out anyway. Lastly, he's much safer with me than you."

She gets up and heads to the same closet to take out a shorter submachine gun and ammo. She bumps Lupine out of her way toward the door. "He is going to get killed."

He nudges her out of his way to reach up to grab a metal latched case. "Well then, you can dissect him and tell me I was right." He sets it down next to his feet and continues to reach in and pull out a knife, a longer blade that he wraps around his back, and several more magazines for a smaller handgun. "Because he will be a good puppy and stay on his leash." He looks over at me. "Right, boy?"

As he loads more guns and mags onto himself, I feel safer and safer going out with him. I nod my head yes at this one-man army.

"See. Now let's get you a leash to wear." He turns around by throwing his gun strapped over his shoulder and then digs under a drawer under the couch.

I move out of his way and move the totes so he can open the drawer up. "I don't need a leash; I can follow you."

He pulls out a long section of hemp rope. "It's not to keep you close, it's to tell everyone else that you are mine." He hands me one end of the rope. "As an American you should know how that works, right?"

"Yes, sir."

He ruffles my hair like a dog. "Don't worry, I will get you a treat when this is done."

. . .

I get tied up around the waist with a knot tighter than a vise by Lupine; at least it isn't by my neck. He finishes arming up by taking out a handgun and loading a couple of mags into his coat pocket and a single mag into the slot of the pistol, which looks familiar. I take a closer look at it, and there appears to be splashes of blood on the barrel of the gun. Wait, that is the gun he pulled to shoot my attacker.

"All right, Kit, you watch the trailer." He heads down and pulls me along to the door of the trailer. "Hoots, find somewhere to perch for a shot, just let me know over coms."

Hoots heads over to the middle of the trailer and pulls out the carpet on the floor with a hidden tab that unzips to reveal a cache underneath with a long rifle. It is about my size long with the barrel being half of its length. It is equipped with a substantial scope on top and a shoulder brace at the butt of the stock. "Understood." He takes out a mag with middle-finger-long bullets and loads it into the gun and then follows behind me.

As he steps out into the dry, dusty air, he turns back and tightens a set distance between him and me. "All right kid, stay this close to me at all times."

He is out of arm's length. I think he doesn't quite trust me that I won't grab for his rifle on his back. Speaking of which, what would happen if he needed to use it? There might not be people crazy enough to attack a Prime armed to the fangs, but my anxiety likes to be calmed by knowing the plan of action. "Okay... umm, Lupine?"

He ties the rope around the strap on his duster. "What?"

"What... happens if I get attacked by bandits?" I ask concerned.

He tightens the knot. "You won't. People know who I am here."

He must have done this before. I am not his first kidnapped person. "Is it normal to bring kidnapped people here?" I heard of plenty of sketchy things happening in Wasteland: kidnapping, sex rings, drug lords, and gun-running. It's supposedly commonplace around here.

He turns around and pulls me down the stairs. "Stop talking."

I nearly fall forward.

"The more you talk, the more chances you have to piss someone off," he tells me, agitated.

"Who?"

He reaches for his rifle and equips himself with a click of a switch and a cock back of the top of the gun. "Me."

Wastelander

The trailer is parked at the side of a cracked and discarded asphalt road that curves to an outpost guarded by a barbed-wire fence and six feet worth of bricks, cement, and stone cubes that are piled on top of each other. Small slits shine light through the unmatching brick and mortar spaces, creating a pattern of what once was around here. A small town ripped apart and cannibalized to form a monstrous series of slums and three-story buildings made of metal scraps, reused wood, and any other bones from buildings they could steal. The outpost expands at least three miles down the road toward an empty vastness that would bring me home. I can't imagine I will ever be setting foot back home, and in fact it might be the last time I am ever this close to home. Even if I were to escape right now, what would I do? I would be running from the PLF and from a blood hound that has my scent. The more I realize how far gone I am from home the idea of escape is fading away. Along the road is a green landmark sign that is dug into the ground and is being devoured by the earth below it. The number below it has been etched out and replaced. "Bismarck: population zero."

A lone steel plate gate stands at least three cars wide and is patrolled by several armed guards stationed on a balcony above the entrance and along the top of the wall. Both men and women are tanned to match the dirt being kicked up on the ground below. As we approach, they immediately take notice of our advance, and a woman with brunette hair and a bandana over her face calls down to us. "Name and purpose?"

Lupine tilts his head up and takes out his PLF badge and flashes it at them. "PLF, and none of your goddamn business."

I slide behind him, ready for him to be shot for saying that.

Instead, she just smiles and makes a swirling motion with her hand, and the gates begin to open up. "How's it going, Lupine?" Two massive metal plates—one shifts left and the other changes right to allow us to walk in.

"Same as ever," he relays back to her.

Inside the outpost is a series of small homes sprawled beside market stalls. The air changes to smoke as we walk inside to see several campfires and grills made from metal and a massive collective fire that people gather around while cooking various meat. I don't care what animal it was; it smells amazing right now. I notice that when Lupine breathes in the aroma through his nose his tail starts to wag, but it seems to wag only halfway.

There are not many children roaming around as the majority of the small town-sized crowds are adults, mostly armed with multiple forms of guns. Even a pregnant woman armed with a shotgun watches us come in from a porch chair, while watching the meat grill beside several grizzled men.

There are several arrays of cobblestone paths that create roads for smaller vehicles, such as mopeds and smaller cars and golf carts, to slowly move through crowds of gathering people. Despite the vast array of guns in front of me, I feel safer in my slum in Detroit.

Lupine immediately tightens his grip on the rope as we walk to the left, proceeding carefully, and go along with the grain of people walking with us. For living in Wasteland they look relatively healthy and content. I was thinking of more destitution than the relative sense of "okay." Lupine seems to be getting more looks than I am. I guess even though he is PLF and this is Wasteland, he still has authority here as several people seem to move out of our way. Some don't even realize I am behind him and crowd back together, only to separate after noticing the rope between us.

The haze of the cooked smoke fades away and I recognize the smell of homeless people who haven't been washed since the last rainfall. I see that water can be collected on rooftop basins. The feeling isn't that of Detroit on the path we walk; it's a more wholesome feeling as everyone seems to be quite content with where they are and what they are doing.

Conversations of bandit raids, weather, and farming life are the majority of what I can pick up between the sound of stoking fires and the stomping of boots against the cobbled road. These are simple people wearing decades-old clothing, with decades-old tablets used as dinner plates, and empty cans from discontinued pop cans condensed down into bricks kept together with phone charger wires, and decades-old vernacular that faded long ago during the Exodus. It's as if time stopped for these people and started devolving back to the days of western expansion and Manifest Destiny.

We reach the edge of the town where a thin river breaks into the ground, a small bridge that would not even pass a test in a third-world country, more set aside than built into the ground. As we walk across the shaky planks, I can feel the bridge shake and creak. At the edge of the bridge, a dirt path stretches up to the home, sitting on top of a mound up in the corner of the facility right against the wire fence.

The sun is setting down across the outpost as the shadow of a one-story shack home with half a trailer home stitched onto hammered two-by-fours creates a shadow over us. On the right-hand side appears to be what remains of a rust-colored aluminum barn with the top bisected by a tin roof. The door to the barn is secured with a lock and several chains binding the handles together. Around the property there appear to be several worn-down shacks that I can see have tools, garden supplies, and stacked wood piled against the windows. Several windows are also broken and replaced with wooden panels. A well is surrounded by a barbed-wire fence, and a mechanical pump is reaching down into the well. There looks to be several sets of tools scattered around the pump.

A sign made out of a wooden post and a baking tray reads "Maurice and Bella's" on the front, written in red paint, the same red color that covers the trimmings on the shack.

Lupine approaches the shack's porch jutting out from the house. A swinging bench is cut off at one end and propped up by a wooden box. Two chairs, along with a box of shotgun shells, are placed on a small barstool beside the chair. The windows are draped over from inside and have bars inside the house behind the glass. I know that several outposts in Wasteland are scattered around as tales of bandits raiding them become stories to tell from refugees that manage to sneak into The States. I've read several stories about what people experienced in Wasteland, but it's hard to tell whether their stories are overdramatized or if this land is as cruel and unpredictable as people have claimed.

He knocks on the door, and a slit in the iron-scrap reinforced door opens up to a blue set of eyeballs peeking through. The slit immediately closes, and several locks are undone before there is a knock back. Lupine waits several seconds before opening the door, then leads me in.

A homely living room and kitchen are spliced into this one room, which smells of fresh-baked bread and bacon grease. A haze of dust covers the light beams that come from the back porch glass door, which is covered with long, horizontal white shutters. A living room set consists of a couch that is well worn and past its time and a loveseat which has a man sized depression molded into the cushions. A single radio plays classic-retro rock, Green Day, from the speakers. The floor is hardwood and cement square slabs. The trailer on the left-hand side is connected, and a bedroom resides inside the van—a bed along with a small closet with clothes stacked inside. On the bedspread rests an open suitcase with papers spilling outside. It looks like US money, but it's a different shade of green that I don't see on our money since The States changed it to prevent Primes or people from Wasteland from buying things in The States.

In front of Lupine is a bulky man with his thick, hairy arms covered with grease with hairs standing upright on their own. He wipes his hands down on his stained and hard-worn denim jeans and slips on a pair of tan slippers. His white T-shirt is stained like a Jackson Pollock painting with just as many colors. All of his hair from his head has gone to his mustache and beard, which creeps down the stop of his sternum and is only as white and stained as his shirt. He reaches out to Lupine for a hug, and I can see many scars and healed scabs on his hands. "Well, I'd be damned—look who it is! Bella, it's our favorite wolf friend!" he states with a heavy twang of hillbilly politeness and homeliness. I guess he is Maurice.

From the kitchen, a woman approaches who seems just as hearty as the man and with just as much muscle and bulk. She is wearing a set of jeans suspended with suspenders and a plain white T-shirt under it. No makeup or jewelry on her rounded face, just a small hairband wrapping her brown, graying hair back into a bun. "He better not be tracking in blood onto my God damn floor again. If he does, kick him out!" she jokingly shouts while wiping down a blue china bowl in her hand with a gray rag.

He turns to what I assume to be his wife. "Nah, hun, he just has a human pet!"

I squirm at the notion of being a pet, but it's best not to say anything to upset Lupine.

Lupine lightly hugs him and immediately wipes off his coat with the fur on his forearm. "We need fifty gallons of gas, two days' worth of food, and—"

He slaps Lupine on his back and moves him to take a seat. "You come in and just ask for this and that without even saying hi?" He motions behind Lupine to me. "Or introducing me to your friend?"

Lupine glances down at me and sniffs. "He isn't my friend, and I am kind of on a tight schedule."

He reaches down to pick up a silver thermos on the floor. "What schedule could you ever have?" He undoes the top and walks over to a rusty steel sink centered on the white marble kitchen countertop. "PLF isn't expecting you back with the crow's head for a couple more days, and you've decided to bring something a little extra to Gores."

"I didn't kill the crow," he mumbles and puts up his shirt over his nose. I don't smell anything weird here. "It's been put on the backburner for now."

He nearly slams his thermos down onto the countertop, causing his wife to jump. "You did not complete your mission?" He gives a hearty laugh. "Well, that gives you all the more reason not to go back so fast if you value your hide!"

Lupine wanders toward the sliding glass door. "The kid is more important right now."

Maurice flips a light switch next to the sink, and a motor hums before water comes out of the tub in a small stream. "Who is this kid to you? He better be Graft's kid if you think he's worth more than the crow."

It's nice to know that I am worth more than possibly a high-priority target for the PLF's infiltration squad. Especially if Lupine truly believes it and risks his job on it. That will only ensure that I will be delivered safely to the PLF. From there, however, I don't know where it will go.

Lupine attempts to open the sliding door, but it's locked. "He's *special.*"

Maurice puts his thermos under the sink, then heads over to press a button on the bottom of the sliding door with his severely uncut and bent toe. "He better be if you want to keep your job."

Lupine flings open the door and puts down his shirt. "How much for a full refuel and rations, waste tank removal, and maintenance check?"

Maurice turns off the switch and screws back on the lid. "Is Borne with you?"

"No, he decided to take the week off." Lupine mentions looking outside at the backyard.

Maurice ponders for a second and drums his fingers on the thermos. "Two hundred and eighty then."

Two hundred and eight dollars seems pretty cheap for everything Lupine is asking. Taking a look back at the stack of cash on the bed I imagine they make plenty of money being what I can assume to be vendors for basic necessities for the people living here. He must have a lot of sway in this town if he has this much money and supplies to sell to the PLF.

The woman comes over from a pantry built into the far-right bottom corner of the kitchen and places some canned food on the counter. "That boy sure eats me out of house and home. Man, when he came over for dinner two years ago with Borne, Feather, Kit, and you ate that entire fucking hog."

Lupine stretches his neck out and takes in a deep breath like he is suffocating. "He is a bear."

The man heads over to Lupine and leans against the glass. "By the way, I don't know if you encountered the raiders coming here, but I've heard they are on the move close to the mountain border. A couple of my trucks have been pulled over and robbed the past couple of days. Best look out."

Lupine drums his fingers on his sidearm. "Got it."

He tilts his thermos to Lupine. "I mean, unless you want to deal with them, I will pay you. The next three refills would be on me!"

His dog ears twitch and his tail begins to sway. "Well, I don't have the manpower for that. I got me, Kit, and Hoots." Lupine walks back over to me and sits on the back of the sofa. Even though that sofa looks like it has been through a couple of wars on its own, I could sleep on just about anything right now. My body feels too heavy, and getting up is an exercise on its own.

"Man running on the skeleton crew on this mission."

"I went alone." He strikes a stern tone.

The man pauses as he takes a sip from his water. "I understand." He presses off the glass and begins walking outside. "Speaking of Tucker, next time he comes by, I will pay you guys to fix my shitty water pump out back."

I wonder if some of the larger towns and outposts in Wasteland have running water. It seems like this place sustained too much damage to sustain a system where water can be equally distributed.

Lupine tugs me outside with the rope, and I move through the kitchen and outback. "Do we look like a plumbing service?"

It sucks being degraded like this in front of these people. I mean I know Lupine just wants to keep me close but I don't have any intentions of running because I know it will only get me beaten or tied up again. I guess the more I follow his orders, the laxer he will be on the rope. Anything to get a little more freedom.

Outback is a spacious backyard that reaches as far as the fields behind the outpost. I can see two other barns with the same roof and siding placed across from the right barn and then a more extended barn situated between them. Stacks of metal, boxes, cardboard piles, and steel drums are set against each barn side. It looks like this guy has a lot, despite looking so miserable. I can only imagine that he is a merchant in the Wasteland, but protecting all of this stuff from bandits seems almost impossible with just him and his wife.

He walks over to the well on the side, stepping over some barbed wire that was cut to make a small dip in the fence line. "No, but I know Tucker could fix it and fix it well. The last couple of chucklefucks I had come to fix it just slapped a bandaid on it." He picks up a toolbox of tools and tosses it on the ground, spilling them all over. "I can't live without my pump, and I have had to buy my water in the last couple of days." He points over to a stack of blue plastic drums sitting on the back right side of his house. They're connected to a smaller pump than the one placed at the well.

"Well, you should tell them to fix your fucking pump right, and if they don't, don't pay them," Lupine suggests while stepping down onto the long, uncut grass.

Maurice reaches inside the well and starts pulling up a chain. "It's more than about my pump..."

I hear the window to the kitchen open, and her head pokes out to look for her husband. "You talking about that pump?" She turns to Lupine. "Can Tucker fix it?"

Maurice hops back over the barbed wire fence. "Tucker isn't here today, hun."

She pulls her head back in. "Well, you tell that aramadick to come over here and fix it right."

Lupine's feet scoot across the ground backward. "Fine, we will fix your pump next time we come over, for two free refills."

Maurice goes over to Lupine. "One, Borne might be with you."

"You want running water or no?"

Maurice grunts and reaches down and picks up a rusty rail spike from the ground where Lupine's foot went across. "Fine, two. But he better fix it for good."

Lupine starts heading back around the trailer. "Knowing him, he will fix it and strap a 125-calibre turret on it for you."

I see Bella appear at the sliding door. "Good, maybe that will scare some of those chinks off our property." She looks at me and waves me to come into the house.

"Hun, you need to stop calling them that." Maurice heads back inside along with me to head over to the suitcase on the bed and shuffles papers around to find something.

She guides me over to a seat on the sofa. I sit down, but as I sit down, I can feel the loose fibers and broken spring go right into my tailbone. "I will stop calling them chinks when they stop coming over and trying to break into our shed."

Lupine opens the front door and heads over to Maurice. "Just give me clearance to drive my trailer in."

He pulls out two slips of paper and grabs a stamper on the bedside table. "Here." He holds up a sheet of paper to the wall and stamps it with his name and insignia, which is a wagon from the days of cowboys and Indians. Now I guess it's just Americans and Primes here. "That will show proof of payment and this..." He hands him a set of keys. "...will get you into the yard."

Lupine reaches down and picks up the rope on the floor that I was dragging with me. "We will be back."

Maurice steps on the rope. "Why not leave the little scamp here? We can watch him."

These people seem pretty kind, a little robust and slightly racist, but welcoming to me. Wouldn't mind hanging out with them for a while and resting my feet.

Lupine takes a look around the room and then tosses the rope over to him. "All right.... But if I come back and the kid isn't in this room, I will have Tucker build you guys your coffins instead, understand?"

Maurice picks up the rope and tosses it over the back of the sofa. "Pfft, what will he do? Run out into Wasteland by himself unarmed?"

Before Lupine leaves, he turns back and remarks, "No, I just want one escort mission where nothing goes wrong."

Maurice plops down on the sofa next to me and puts his elbows on his knees. "Well, kid, what's your name?"

If Lupine trusts me with these people, I guess I am as safe as I can expect to be. "Ghent, sir."

He waves his hand. "Oh, drop that sir shit. You're not around PLF anymore."

"So," what can I talk to them about? I mean, I have a million questions, but I don't know how many they want to answer. "you guys run an outpost?"

He reaches over under the entertainment set that holds the radio and finds a series of photographs clipped together. He removes the clip and sets it on the table and begins to page through the photos. "Since the Exodus when every human was fleeing the PLF eastward, we decided to plant our feet here and start a depot to help anyone that comes to us for help."

I peek over to the photos and see him along with his wife standing in front of less developed outpost interests and a group of tough-looking men standing with them. They aren't that much younger so this couldn't have been less than five years ago. "What's it like living in Wasteland?"

He moves over to another photo. It's them working on the construction of a building. "Hard."

I can see the scars and feel the sandpaper touch he has slid over the photographs.

"But we don't have to worry about some bureaucratic dickhead knocking at our door asking for taxes or our guns."

The United States, in regards to Wasteland, remains completely hands-off minus a couple of miles past the Mississippi River. They remain autonomous, act independently, and function as their own state as long as they did not take sides on either side. Pure and Graft agreed that the land in between should forever remain a buffer between the United States and the PLF, and any advances would sound the alarm of war. The actual reason behind the particular length of Wasteland and all the land that is wasted by both sides remains a mystery.

Maurice explains there is a lack of government or law. It's really anything goes outside of its capital of Paradise, which is a hollowed-out Oklahoma City.

From news stories and movies back in The States, we are always taught that Wasteland is a lawless land reminiscent of the days of the Wild West. "We were always told that Wasteland is the Wild West come to life—is that true?"

He flips to a photo of them standing in front of what looks like a burning campground with their guns in the air and celebrating. "Pretty much. I mean you got raiders, shootouts... Everything is free for the taking. Food, money, water, gas, lives—it's all the same." In a photo, he points out a man standing next to him who looks similar to him. "My son got at least four kills from a Prime gang called the Hyenas one day when they attacked the outpost."

At school, we were always told stories of these groups of bandits that roam Wasteland. US citizens were given the opportunity to return to the US, but they still refused as a majority of those who stayed in Wasteland were Chinese citizens or other minorities who preferred a free life away from what they saw as organized racism orchestrated toward them.

I probably shouldn't ask where his son is now, since he's not around here. I assume he's either out on his own or dead. But I don't want to bring it up while in my current position.

"You from The States?"

"Detroit."

He collects and organizes the photos and sets them down on the coffee table in front of him. "Not so different from here."

I recall rampant burglaries around the orphanage and living in an underfunded apartment building run by a man who might be using the basement for an underground fighting ring—great talent wasted on a lack of opportunity and chance to succeed. "No, not really."

He leans back and rests his arms on the armrests. "Tell me, son, why did Lupine decide you were worth more than a high-threat target?"

I don't know if I should tell them, but Lupine didn't say I couldn't. "He thinks I am a Prime."

He gets onto the edge of his seat. "What? Really?"

I fiddle with my hands and look down at them. "Yeah."

"Fuck me...." He rests back and looks closer at me. "Do you think you are?"

"I don't know..." I slump further into the couch and feel the spring poke my back. "With everything going on, I am not sure what to think right now." I am glad to sit down, and glad that Maurice seems to be kind, but I don't know what sort of answer he wants me to say, so I stop there. I have no idea if this Prime thing is good or bad news. I might end up king of the Primes, or maybe I'll be dissected alive for whatever passes as science.

"Well, let me give you the word of advice right now." He moves over to me and puts his hand around my shoulder. I can smell the grit and sweat on him as it seeps into the back of my sweater. "Just stay with Lupine and only concentrate on living. Your stuff, your past life, your ideas, ambitions, don't even think about them." He pokes me in the chest with his sausage pointer finger. "Focus on what matters right now, and that is being a man and staying strong no matter what is presented to you."

I can't just grow up and be a man like that, though. I am just a kid who just wants to know what I really am, or where I came from. "Am I that much in danger?"

He softens his tone. "I don't want to say it, but you need to hear it. Yes, you are going into a world where humans are not allowed, a world hostile to your kind, but you will make it out of this alive," he encourages.

How is he so sure? "How can you say that?"

He strums the rope around my waist. "Because you have Lupine protecting you. I would have no other person on the planet to protect me from going in there than him."

So far, he seems like any other PLF soldier. What makes him unique?

"Primes might be part human but still remember that they are still animals. They judge based on how strong you look. If you are slouched, cowering, and avoid eye contact with them, you are going to be judged as weak, and you will be preyed upon."

I'm a human so I am automatically weaker than them.... If that's the case, I stand no chance surviving in the PLF. "Thank you... I just..." I begin to curl up on the couch in the corner of the sofa. "I don't know what's going to happen to me."

I bite my lip to hold back the emotion. I hate showing sad orphan eyes to anyone.

I feel a hand rest against my head and see Bella sit on the armrest.

"Hun…" she consults me, "if you need to cry 'cause you're scared, it's best to do it right now when Lupine isn't here. It may be the only chance you have for a long time."

With a couple of tears, I can feel the dam give way, and I dig myself into her arms and the couch corner and begin to sob helplessly. I can't remember the last time I cried this much…. Maybe it's a long time coming, but I can't keep crying like this! Not now, but it feels so good to cry in someone's arms instead of by myself or in front of a disinterested therapist.

She strokes my hair as I let a dam break on her denim jeans. "It's okay, hun. You will be all right."

Maurice gets up from his chair. "Umm. You want a glass of water or something to drink?"

I dry my eyes on my hood and look over at him. "Water would be fine…" Then I remember this is Wasteland water…. You know what, I don't care if it kills me at this point. The water has less of a chance than Pure at this rate. "Thank you."

She leans over and puts my hood back. "Sorry we didn't get you one before. Lupine never likes us interfering with PLF matters. But you seem like a good kid who is just caught up in all of this."

I turn to her and blurt out, "What do they want with me?! I am just a kid!"

She moans and then thinks for a moment before calmly resting her hand on my head. "How about you think of it this way? If it's true that you are a human Prime hybrid, they will want you alive. It does them no good to kill you."

Maybe, but it doesn't mean I am safe. Being alive is one thing; being safe is entirely different. "Unless the PLF dissects me, or keeps me prisoner, in a camp."

She laughs. "You sure have a wild imagination. They might just want to ask you a couple of questions. What makes you think that they are going to hurt you?"

I take some deep breaths and regain my composure, or at least try. "Because every human that goes there ends up mauled or…"

Her calloused hand sets down on my hand and squeezes lightly. "That's just fake news trying to scare you. You are an innocent child."

Am I, though?

"You've done nothing to deserve it. Trust me when I say that if you had a beef with the PLF...sure, they might rough you up a bit, but you seem innocent. The PLF will not harm you—they have no reason to."

She's right, I guess. I mean, I am nothing to them hurt or dead. They might just take a couple of samples of my blood, maybe some hair, do some tests, but will they let me leave? "I guess, but what happens after?"

"Well..." She puts her thumb to her chin and thinks. "Maybe they will just ask you to go back home to your parents."

I know she doesn't know I am an orphan, but it still hurts like a broken bone that didn't entirely heal right in my chest. "I don't have any parents."

Her face goes red. "Oh, um...sorry about that."

I wipe the rest of my snot on the sleeve of my sweater. I am used to it. "No, it's okay." I do feel better, not entirely stable, but safe from tipping over the edge. Even my movements seem a little lighter. "Thank you for telling me this."

She hands me a glass of water from Maurice. "You feel a little better?"

I take some tiny sips from a mason jar. "A lot, actually."

She claps her hands in joy. "See. You just needed some time to think and let your emotions out." She reaches over and corrects my hood again. "You have a long road ahead of you, and you know what I think you need." From the couch, she goes over to the kitchen and into a cookie jar. Then, she takes out a thin plastic bag, puts some cookies into the bag, and ties it with a twist tie from a bread bag. She then hands six peanut butter cookies over to me. "Now, don't let the big wolf eat all of them."

I graciously accept them, tearing up again at the kindness. Nobody ever did anything like this before. "I don't know how to repay you."

She giggles and straightens my hair. "If you see a small pangolin Prime named Tucker, tell him to come to fix our fucking pump."

I crack a smile at her. "Got it, ma'am."

The front door opens up, and Lupine strolls in, springing his keys on this finger. "Trailer is parked out front and..." He stops, eyeing us on the couch. "What are you doing?"

She wipes her hands on her denim jeans. "Giving some well-needed advice."

He tilts his head and sniffs. "Those cookies for me?"

33

She smiles at him. "No, they are for Ghent." She gets up from the couch and walks over to him and pokes him in the chest. "If you want a cookie, I have some dog treats in my pantry." The guts of this woman to poke him like that.

A growl comes from Lupine, and he throws the keys at Maurice, who catches them in both hands and then heads outback. "All right, Ghent, let's get going before they adopt you."

Who knew I had to go all the way to Wasteland to hear that, and from a PLF soldier to boot? I know I couldn't live out here with them, despite how much I want to stay. I feel like they actually mean it when they say that I am safest with Lupine at my side.

Maurice turns around before heading out the porch door. "Have a safe trip, kid."

Bella tugs on my sweater as I get up and head to Lupine. "Stop by whenever you get the chance."

I turn to her and give her a little hug. "Thank you." Then I let her go and head over to Lupine, who rolls his eyes as he reaches down to grab the rope that is still tied around my waist.

. . .

When we are earshot out of the house, Lupine stops and turns around and squats down to me. "What did you tell them?"

Shit, I didn't know I shouldn't have told them. "Nothing...they just..."

He pinches my chin with his fingers. "You are a shit liar."

"Isn't that a good thing for you?"

He thinks for a second and then releases my chin with a quick swipe. I can feel his claw scrape the epidermis of my skin. "Fair." He continues to pull me along back into the heart of the outpost. "While the trailer is getting stocked, we are going to make a quick stop."

"Where are you taking me?"

"A Prime that owes me a second opinion." He tugs in a couple feet of rope. "Now, stick close to me." Seeing that we are going to go deep into the outpost, I adhere to Bella's suggestion and get right beside him, close enough to feel his tail swipe behind me. He notices my advance and puts his palm to my head and pushes me back to arm's length. "Too close."

Concussed

Lupine keeps on moving me forward, deeper into the crowd of Wastelanders toward the town square, which is a block of squat, one-story homes made from scrap and broken downtown buildings. Not one person we pass by, Prime or human, is out on their own. They are all huddled in small groups of at least three, conversing among themselves. However, there don't seem to be any Primes in human groups, or vice versa. They don't seem to pay us any attention walking around by ourselves. It must just be a normal...day for them I guess. We stop by a small market stall selling hemp bags and woven baskets and other containers made from straw and plastic, Lupine asks me to give him the cookies Bella gave me back at her and Maurice's.

I take them out of my sweater pocket in front. "Are you going to eat them or something?"

He grabs them and then opens his jacket. I can see a submachine gun poking out from inside his inner pocket. "I might have one, but I gotta keep them from being stolen."

"People really would steal someone's cookies?"

He shuffles inside an empty coat pocket. "People have stolen less."

I take a seat on one of the empty boxes next to this old white-bearded gentleman's stall. "So how dangerous is this place?" I take a look past Lupine and see several armed men walking around with full automatics, while several members of the group go around and play cards, talk with shopkeepers, or eat and drink at tiny restaurants. There seems to be always one person that is keeping an eye out. "Looks like this entire outpost is ready to go to war."

He takes out a cookie from inside the pocket. "It's more of a show of force than anything. People around here like to show each other they are armed as a deterrent. I've heard of only a couple of instances of a full shootout in this outpost since we've been using it. Once over a woman and the other was over some deal that went south fast between Primes and humans." I guess if someone wanted to start something they better be ready to die fighting for it.

He finishes a cookie and then tugs me toward the western section of the outpost. As I shuffle behind him my eyes wander over to a set of muscular thugs covered head to toe in tattoos and armed with hunting rifles. One of them, a more lean and agile-looking man with a shaved head, nudges one of his buddies and whispers something in his ear while motioning to me. I reach down and grab the rope to tug it to make Lupine aware of them. I lightly tug the rope several times; Lupine turns around and I tilt my head over to them. He turns his attention to the group and sees them eying me up like a piece of meat. Once Lupine stares at them and growls at them and bears his fangs at them, they scatter into the alleyways.

I scoot up to him. "That was so cool!" To scare them away with just a growl and a stare!

He turns back to me and holds me back to get more distance on him. "What did I say about being close?"

"But should I want to be close to you, so you can protect me?" I mean the closer I am to him the safer I am, right?

He takes the rifle from his back and extends it out to my feet. "I need this much distance between us at all times so I can take my rifle out and shoot at anyone without you getting knocked out or shot at."

Ah, that makes more sense. "Sorry, I didn't know."

He throws the rifle back over his shoulder and reaches into his coat pocket. He pulls out a handgun and flicks a switch on the side. "They won't shoot at you; they are going to fire at the guy with the guns. If you are next to me, you are going to get shot. Understand?"

"Yes, sir." I shuffle back a couple more inches from him.

He loads a fresh magazine into the grip of the gun and slides back the top and clicks it back. "Do not worry about everyone around you. I can smell gunpowder from some distance away. I know at all times who is armed and who isn't."

Seems like a stretch. "I don't believe you."

He takes a heavy sniff in through his nose and looks around him while sniffing. "Starting from the guy to our left wearing a wifebeater and gray cargo pants going right." I look over to see the guy he is talking about. He is sitting at a bar with several of his comrades in a line. "First guy has a Beretta, second guy has a .22 submachine gun, one has a sawed-off shotgun, and the last one has an M-16 that was repurposed to fire 5.7-millimeter ammo."

Holy shit, that is so fucking awesome!

We continue to walk down the center of the road as Lupine splits the crowd into two, like Moses. I do notice that while we are walking he is constantly sniffing the air and looking at each person who walks by us.

I keep my distance from Lupine as we make our way down the street. I keep my head up so as not to look weak, and keep my eyes on Lupine's tail, which is poised up and straight. It's best if I just do what Lupine tells me...keep calm and walk on. I feel a little bit better as we move through the crowd as hardly anyone looks at me.

The crowd begins to thin out on either side of us. I peek behind us to see several younger men poke their heads above everyone else and they are tailgating us. They notice me watching them and start to get up close, right behind me. I immediately look away and keep matching forward. I grasp onto the rope a little tighter. I want to go to Lupine but I know I have to keep my distance. A looming shadow of an internet tower spans up ahead of us. Despite the destitution around us, the structure is still standing strong. Along the top of it sits several birds and crows roosting inside the panels.

A greasy fleshbag oozing sweat from his brow passes by me and then keeps pace with me on my right. He is wearing a dust coat and some winter boots with holes punched in them to let his stinky feet waft in the air. He paces over closer to me. "Well, would you look there." His breath mixes with his bio and is just as nauseating as his looks.

I feel Lupine reel in the rope closer to him by wrapping the rope tighter around his hand. He knows what is happening without even looking back.

Another sleazy younger adult with a dead skunk stench and matching haircut comes up on the other side of me. "Hey, kid, you want us to rescue you from the big bad wolf?" His voice even sounds like roadkill, inflating and deflating.

With a swift movement covered by the dust kicked up by a heavy breeze, the bandit pulls a blade from within his sleeve and he wraps his sweaty arm around my neck and begins to chokehold me with the knife to my throat. As soon as he grabs me I see his other two lackeys cut the rope between Lupine and me before pointing crossbows made shoddily at Lupine.

Sleazy aims the hunting crossbow right at Lupine's head. "All right, PLF, hand over the money and we will let the kid go."

The knife is cold on my neck. How has Lupine not even noticed the commotion? *Lupine will help me...don't struggle. If I struggle it will make it harder for him to save me... just keep calm.*

Lupine finally stops about ten feet apart from me and the bandits. He slowly turns around. I do notice that he has shifted something in his coat before revealing his open jacket and his wad of bills swinging by a cord in his hand. "Really?" He extends his free arm at one of the bandits with the crossbow next to me and looks at the nearby internet tower, his wristwatch flickering in the sun. "Do you really think I care about my slave?"

I tell myself he has a plan. He has to. Why bother to kidnap me and take me here just to let me bleed out on a street with no name?

The knife gets held closer to my throat. "He has to be worth more than the bills you have in your pocket."

The bandit that cut the rope sounds like a hyena and is jittering like a crack addict. "And your guns."

The greasy bandit points the gun at Lupine's badge on his shoulder. "And your badge."

Lupine stops fiddling with the folded wad and takes off his PLF badge with his other hand and takes out the handgun that he had out before. He quickly does a quick take behind him to the internet tower. "All right." He holds the pouch in his outstretched hand and from my angle I notice him dig deep into his coat pocket with his obscured hand. "There is my money." He tosses the wad right at the bandit holding me.

The bandit reaches out with a hand holding my arm back. As he reaches out I glance around to see the crowd just simply watching in anticipation as if they know what's about to happen.

"And I will give you my guns." He looks up to the sky behind us and his ears perk up.

The bandit catches the wad of cash in his hand. "Give me the gun." He chuckles.

Lupine laughs, cracks a smile, and then nods his head. "As you wish."

The next thing I hear is a deafening ring in my ears as a rifle shot from a great distance skips through the air and impales directly into the skull of the bandit standing beside me. Blood and skull fragments burst out from his face, and the viscera spills out and lands on me as Lupine pulls out his handgun and fires a bullet directly into the head of the bandit holding me. As the gunshot rings from his gun I can feel rain fall onto me as we both fall forward. I fall to the ground but don't hear myself land. My ears are ringing and my heart feels like it was shot out with that bullet. I am soaked as if I took a shower. I shakingly reach up to my head and touch a fragment of bone. This guy... His brain is all over... I immediately feel sick to my stomach and gather enough strength to escape from under him.

As I free myself, I press my hand against a hot bullet that has planted itself into the ground. I jump like a cat with tape on his paw and sprawl to my side. I roll onto the ground to try to get this shit off of me, but no matter how much I rub myself on the soil nothing is getting it off of me. I start to feel numb and the only feeling that comes up is the acid in my stomach as I vomit on the ground. My bile pools with the blood rushing out of the decapitated bandit beside me.

I can feel Lupine's feet approach and step by me as he pulls the trigger again. "You have my money." He reaches down and loots the dead bandit for his pouch. "Your friends have my guns." Another bullet is fired. "But you are going to have to take my badge over your dead body."

The bandit begs for his life before a final hollow bullet is fired.

I begin to curl up into a ball in blood and vomit.... This is not what I wanted when I said I wanted to see the Wastelands.... I feel as if my skin wants to crawl out from me to be with its own kind. I'm shivering, and the blood on my face is starting to cool. I feel a pair of giant's feet approach me.

Lupine's boots are shadowed by his hand as he reaches down to pick me up. "Let's get you cleaned up."

I hug onto Lupine's jacket like it's my skin under all the blood and bone flaking off my body. I forget I need to look strong. I hold tight to his shoulder for any sort of comfort. I keep my eyes closed so as to not get...anything in my eyes and to stop looking at the bits and pieces falling off onto Lupine's coat. I've buried my head into my hands, which I scraped off the debris from, the only part of me I know for sure is clean of gore.

He walks, and so I walk with him. I want to be clean.... I keep gagging, trying to hold my mouth shut so as not to taste anything else that might be on me. I have nothing left in my stomach to puke up.

Peeking through my fingers, I see the light start to dim as Lupine enters an overhang of a jungle gym of boards and walkways that intersect each other on multiple levels. Piles of debris and wood pile up on towers of scrap iron, construction material, and concrete slabs that create the foundation of this slum. Lupine turns and ascends up a staircase full of nails protruding. He climbs to the second story and approaches a door made of a flatbed overlayed on a flat, wooden square sheet.

"Don't worry, I'll take you somewhere safe. We'll get you cleaned up." He knocks on the door.

About two minutes later he opens a crack and a golden muzzle pokes out of the door. He takes a sniff, then closes the door. A series of locks and bolts unlock and the door swings open.

A golden retriever Prime emerges from the dusty void beyond. His ragged golden fur is covered in dust like a duster, and there are knots all over his fur. On his head he has his fur combed back and bunned up. He looks at Lupine with wide golden eyes that are ocean blue, and so is his Hawaiian tsunami blue shirt with white shorts, which are just torn khaki jeans at the knees. He is barefoot as he steps into the dusk light, as his feet are similar to Lupine's but much skinnier and shorter. "Well, look who it is bringing another corpse to throw on my pile," he complains as he leans over to me and Lupine backs off.

Lupine budges his way in and sets me down onto a chair beside a table with two of its four legs broken and sitting on cinder bricks. "Fuck off. He's alive and needs a shower."

I take a peek out of my hands and coat to see a hovel of a home. A hammock sways in a room not larger than half the trailer and as high as Lupine and a half. The floor, walls, and ceiling are all a mismatch of broken planks, plastic tubs, plaster, and metal plates that are all fixed together with nails, duct tape, and welded metal. The ground is uneven. I can rock the chair back and forth as I sit. A small kitchenette leads on the right-hand side to a bathroom, which strangely is the largest room in the home. I can see all of the bathroom from my seat at the table. It's a large room with porcelain tiles of different colors and shapes. The ceiling is covered by enough planks and junk to just cover about eighty percent of it. A rusty showerhead and a toilet are placed in the room that takes up the other half of his house. I hope I'll be allowed to clean up there.

I glance at the kitchen, which has a stove that has been repaired several times over and replaced with parts that were obviously not made for that type of stove. The fridge is a standard stainless steel fridge hooked up to an AC unit on the top that is humming. It is the only background sound in the room besides Lupine and the dog Prime. We are alone.

The golden retriever looks out, scans the stairway, and then closes the door. "What the fuck happened to him?" His voice quivers. Lupine walks around the room, turning over some newspaper on the kitchen counter, and then moves to the table and rattles some empty cans and pours out a couple of chicken bones. "Some newbie bandits obviously not from around here decided to fuck with me."

He collects himself and stands up, placing himself between Lupine and the table before Lupine can knock anything else over. "Well, why should I help you? Don't you think I forgot what happened last time I *helped* you?" He is still scared of him but he is trying to act tough, a kitten standing up to a lion.

"You aren't helping me—you are helping this kid." He pulls off the coat and reveals me. "He's been through a lot today and needs this. Let him clean up in your shower. He isn't injured. Well, go as soon as we're done."

Golden Boy reels back as he looks over me. "Who is the kid anyway?"

"Yip Canidae, *ex*-PLF," he reminds him. "Does it really matter to you anymore?"

He pounds down on the table. "Just because I am not with the PLF anymore I still have a right to know why you bring people covered in blood to my clinic!"

I take my fingers away from my face and try to keep my eyes straight into the back wall near a window. Three window panes are broken, letting in a breeze of garbage and dust from outside.

Lupine opens the oven with a shower railing handle and looks inside. "I'll show you later, but now we need to get him clean before he pukes all over your floor."

He looks over at his shower and then back at Lupine. "Ten bucks."

"For a shower?" He slams the oven, nearly breaking it off its hinges.

He reaches over and picks something off my head. "Wasteland's water isn't free."

Lupine growls and reaches into his pocket for the coin purse that is still covered with specks of blood. "Fuck, this kid is going to bankrupt me." He throws him the coin purse.

Yip barely catches it in his open hand and takes ten bucks out of his money clip before setting the ten on the table in front of me. He then tosses the clip back at Lupine, nearly missing him and landing on the floor before Lupine catches it with his foot. "All right, bring him in."

. . .

Lupine picks me up and brings me over to the shower. Once inside, I quickly realize what this room is for. There is a cart pushed to the side with a light cloth over it. From under the bottom of the cloth I can see a sharp scalpel poke out from under it. There is also a dentist chair that has stains of red that is in the center left of the room while the shower is attached to the wall on the right. There is a broom, mop, and bucket stacked in the corner along with a cabinet above with cleaning supplies in a plastic bucket. He turns on the water, which is as hard as river water, and as the splashes of drops hit my tongue I can taste the rust and grit.

The dog takes off the head of the shower and drags it over to me with the water running, then rinses the majority of bits off my clothes and hair. Lupine's claws dig into my scalp and beat off the chunks of...brain...off my shoulder and sweater, which is now dyed with crimson. As the blood washes off me and is sent down the drain, I still feel like the blood is on me. The bits of skull and face are still sliding down my face and arm.

"Okay, Ghent." Lupine tugs on my sweater. "Take off your clothes so we can get everything off."

I rip the bloody sweater and T-shirt off with my eyes closed. I don't want to see anything. I don't want to think about the sharp bits that are digging into my palm as I lift my shirt off or undoing my pants and taking them off and handing them to one of them. The water is freezing and I'm shivering. Looking for any sort of warmth, I curl up in a ball and tuck my knees into my chest. Lupine asks me to finally take off my boxers. At least my blush warms my face, but I feel ashamed being seen like this. I want to be clean. I want this all to be over.... I want to go home. I feel someone's hand move my arm up and wipe down under my arm and then my back.

Yip seems averse to looking at me or getting near me. He lets Lupine do all the washing. "This kid from Wasteland?"

Lupine stops and I can see a glimpse of his head turn to Yip. "Detroit."

The blood should have gone away now. I look up and open my eyes to see Lupine crouched down in front of me. "You okay there, bud?"

"No," I chitter through my teeth, "but better than I was...thank you." I take a look down at my hands on my knees to see my entire body shaking, but clean.

Lupine approaches him and he immediately backs off. "Go wash his clothes while I finish up here."

Yip scampers away with my clothes out to the kitchen and I hear some water being run from a sink.

Lupine turns off the water with a valve under the showerhead and places the showerhead back into its cradle. He then walks over to a small cabinet and takes out a white raggedy towel. "Hey, you can use this towel to dry off." He hands me the towel, which looks like it would disintegrate in my hands, and I begin to wipe myself down.

As I grasp the frail ends of the towel and begin to rub my arm, I can feel the flakes of the towel start to come off. Despite how much I try to dry myself, I never feel dry. Come on, I just want to be dry! I look for another side that is thicker but it's all the same shitty fabric. Everything starts to slow down in my mind through my frustration. *Why?! Why am I the one who had to be here!* Tears drip down my face as I can barely hold myself together while I grasp at this rag for all the dim warmth it can provide. I want to be home! Even my shitty life back in Detroit is not worth this.

Suddenly I feel the towel be taken from me by Lupine, who hands me a white undershirt. I gaze up at him and notice he took off his white undershirt under his bulletproof vest. "Here. This should be better than that."

It feels like cotton picked from clouds in heaven compared to the cold floor and the rag. It's about half my size and twice my width. The only person to show me humanity isn't even human. When I was living in Detroit no one gave a shit about an orphan. "Why are you so nice to me?" I sniff and wrap his shirt around me.

I notice his chest is covered in scars from cuts, bullet wounds, burns, all of which has fur growing over it like trees in a canyon. Despite a thick layer of grayish white fur, I can see a lifetime of war and a soldier who has been built and trained to fight. Everything that chest has been through and seen, and I am stuck sitting here cold and frustrated. In front of Lupine, I should not complain.

"You've been through a lot today." He starts putting back on his vest, which is a series of latches on his left and right side. "And I know how it feels to be covered in blood."

I start wiping down my arms and legs. If there is anyone out there right now whom I can trust to keep me alive, it's him. If I can stay with Lupine, I can survive; Maurice and Bella were right in that sense. Lupine is my only out of this and I want to make sure he stays with me till the end. "Will you be there when I meet Pure?"

His finger slips on a latch from the water. "You want me to be there?" He seems unable to register my question.

Next is my face, which I dry with one hard swipe. "I would feel better if you did."

He pauses for a moment before wiping down his hand on his pant leg. "All right, I'll see what I can do," he says warmly.

I feel a sense of warmth through my entire body. "Thanks."

. . .

After drying myself off with Lupine's shirt, I am given a blanket by the golden retriever. I am told to sit down near the window on a refurbished spring mattress and wait till my clothes get dry outside. I take a look out to the alleyway below and see my clothes hanging outside on a laundry line. It's nice just to sit down and close my eyes for a little bit.

I listen to Yip and Lupine talk to each other in Chinese so I can't really eavesdrop on their conversation. I know most Primes know Chinese because the majority of Primes were taught Chinese by the United States government to aid in intercepting Chinese Army messages and working with freedom fighters within China during World War III.

I manage to shiver and try to keep my mind off of my meeting with Pure or what just happened to me. My eyes wander around Yip's shack and notice something off about the floor. None of the floorboards are nailed down. They are loose, and as Lupine's feet lean on the ground the floorboards lift up, revealing through dim light flat boxes and plastic totes under the floor.

Yip heads to the window and reels in my clothes from outside and hands them over. They are still a little damp, but they should dry out soon. I notice that he also put Lupine's shirt on the reel as well. He hands our clothes back to us.

While putting on my freshly cleaned and folded clothes, I am taken to sit down at a table with two legs broken off and replaced by a cinder brick. Yip is sitting down at the table with a scalpel and a set of vials. He invites me to sit down as Lupine explains that he wants to take a sample to confirm with Yip that I am half Prime by smell. So that's what they were talking about in Chinese.

I ask them if this is really necessary.

Lupine scoots my chair up to the table. "If he doesn't think that you are half Prime then I will take you back home. Do you want that?"

I kind of don't, really. I mean, I would return to normal but never be the same. "No, let's just get this over with." I set my arm down on the table and roll up my sweater.

Yip advises me to take off the sweater. I do, and he carefully hands it over to Lupine. "Okay, kid, I need you to just relax while I take a sample." He dabs some alcohol onto my arm with a cotton swab and then wipes it down with a disinfectant wipe.

Lupine heads behind me and puts his hand on my shoulder. "You will be okay. He's a medic."

He's a medic? Well, he looks like a butcher. "Doesn't look like one."

He cleans off the blade with the wipe. It's a short edge and is polished enough to see the sun reflecting back down onto my arm. "Wasteland's doctors don't get a nice office and diploma to practice medicine."

I guess, and if Lupine trusts him, I guess I have too as well. I ask him to give me a moment to calm down before he bloodlets me. I take a couple of deep breaths and look away from the scalpel. Seeing it would cause me to faint. I feel the edge of the knife cut my forearm. It hurts but not as badly as I thought it would. I can feel the warm blood drip down onto the table.

Yip's head reaches down as he takes a long sniff of my arm. "Oh yeah, there is Prime blood in there, all right." He lifts his head up and grabs a set of bandages and spills some hydroxide onto my cut before wrapping it up. Now that hurts worse than the cut! Holy fuck! I bite down on my teeth and clench my jaw.

Lupine pulls up a chair and takes a seat next to Yip. "Told you." He seems satisfied, as if he's won a bet.

Yip makes sure to wrap the bandage tight. "Kid do you feel...okay? Anything strange ever happened to your body, ever?"

I finally manage to look down at the bandage. The bloodstain isn't longer than my pinky finger, and there isn't that much blood coming up onto the surface of the cloth. Now Yip is telling me that I have Prime blood. Before I could just pass it off as Lupine making a mistake, but now two canine Primes and Kit's scanner are confirming I have something Primal inside of me. I can't keep denying the evidence being put in front of me, so I maybe should start coming to grips that I might be a hybrid.

Yip is looking at me, concerned.

"I mean...I'm sometimes sore, but I just passed it off as a growth spurt."

He finishes up tying up the bandage on the bottom of my forearm. "Hmm... Well, Lupine, you sure found an interesting find." He leans back and rolls over a set of vials. "Do you mind if I run some more experiments on him?"

We both turn to the sound of military boots stomping towards the door. A hinge cracks due to the force of Kit busting the door open. "Over my dead body!"

Lupine immediately gets up and interjects. "Aren't you supposed to be watching the trailer?"

She approaches Lupine in a fit of rage, keeping her haunting eyes on Yip. "It's full and waiting outside!" She points to me and then at the floor in front of her. "Ghent, get over here!"

I get up and immediately head over to her. I don't know who to follow, really, so I decide that if Lupine wants to stop me, he will, but I'd rather be with the actual doctor than this creepy medical enthusiast.

Lupine grabs the hood on my sweater and I stop cold. "How did you find us?"

I see her hand slowly reach to her handgun on her side, where I saw her stash it before. "I just followed the trail of blood and the fucking butchering you and Hoots did of those bandits." So that was Hoots shooting them. "And what the fuck did you bring him to Yip for!"

Yip gets up from the table and starts putting things away into a nearby cabinet and a doctor's bag under the table. "Oh, calm down, foxy, I was just giving Lupine here a second opinion."

She immediately pulls out her gun and points it at his face "Do I have to remind you of my second opinion of you!"

Lupine jumps to Kitsune's arm and lowers her gun down. "He cleaned off Ghent and smelled a sample of his blood, nothing else!"

In the moment of silence I manage to creep toward the door to get out before bullets start flying. Lupine notices my advance and keeps an eye on me to make sure I don't run for it.

Yip steps out from the table and shifts over to a drawer over by his kitchen counter. "Calm your bitch down."

She releases the safety from the gun. "Call me a bitch one more time and you will be picking your jaw bones off the floor."

Lupine sets his hand on Kit's arm and lowers the gun. "Enough."

The mutt starts to whimper and he keeps eyeing one of the drawers over at his kitchen. His hand reaches out to open it. "Yeah, that's right." He smiles and grips the handle. "Listen to your alpha—be a good little bitch."

She jolts her arm up and bats Lupine's hand and she fires a bullet directly into Yip's leg. "You should be able to fix that, right?"

Lupine grabs me and rushes Kitsune, grabbing her gun out of her hand with a vice grip and then rushing us out of the building.

. . .

Lupine is rushing to catch up to Kitsune, who is storming out into the crowd on her own.

47

I jog along Lupine's stride. I think Lupine has more pressing matters than the leash that was around me.

He takes her gun and unloads the clip and throws the gun back to her. "You really didn't need to shoot him."

She catches the gun and loads another magazine. "Yes, I did," she snaps back.

"No, you didn't." He reaches out and turns her around just as she clicks the mag into the grip.

She motions toward Yip's shack with the loaded gun. "That neutered mutt thinks he can shit-talk me after what he's done!" He's neutered? I mean, there were Primes who were castrated or spayed by hunters but I never actually saw one. "I should have stuck my gun up his piss hole..."

Lupine snatches the gun from her hands with one swipe and gets in her face. "Enough!"

Well, obviously Kit and Yip don't see eye to eye on things, or maybe something happened in their past, but I should stay as far away from this if getting shot is the least she can do to him.

She reaches out for her gun and forcefully takes it from Lupine. "Whatever." She backs off from his face and turns back around. "He will be fine. He's filled plenty of smaller *holes*."

"I know you hate him, and you have every right to, but he is trying to change," Lupine proclaims.

She laughs it off. "How do you know that?"

He turns around and comes over to me. He takes his hands and covers my ears. I can only hear the pulse coming from his hands and it's racing. He mouths something to her. I can't hear much except a hum of his deep voice.

She turns to him, rolls her eyes, says something, and continues her stride.

He removes his hands from my ears. I can see that he didn't get the response he quite wanted. "What did you say?"

"It's not important to you."

Umm, hello? I think it is.

"Just keep moving before you get covered in blood and Yip gets blasted again."

I kind of figured that Kit might have been a little on edge this entire trip—with finding out that I might be a hybrid and what happened just now with Yip. Either he is always like this or she is maybe thinking of something else that is on her mind above what is really going on. I don't know what Yip could have possibly done to deserve so much hate from Kitsune. I mean, he seemed decent, if not a little under-equipped and unskilled in his profession. With what I've been through I can only be grateful that I am clean and alive.

. . .

Hoots is sitting on top of the roof of the trailer swinging his legs down and whistling while we approach. "Did you see that shot?!" He seems pretty proud of blowing someone's head off.

Lupine isn't having any of the celebrations. "Yeah, Ghent got a front-row seat."

He just shrugs his shoulders and jumps down beside us. "Sorry, kid, but it was your life or his. Don't worry. I wouldn't have hit you."

I guess I am alive...probably scarred forever but still alive. "I understand."

Hoots gets pushed out of Kit's way as she gets into the trailer, slamming the door behind her. "What the fuck is with Kit?"

Lupine just sighs and pulls out a cigarette. "Nothing."

He laughs and picks the pack out of Lupine's pocket as he walks by. "Well, she's pissed at you for something." He takes out his own plastic lighter and lights one up.

"She's mad at me for taking Ghent with me," he lies.

"No." He points his finger at Lupine and wags it. "I watched you. She is mad because you took her to that child..."

He spins around and grab's Hoot's beak and tightens his grip on it. "Enough." He picks the cigarette out of his mouth and puts it back behind his ear.

I guess I will never know what was so bad about Yip—maybe it's for the best. If these Primes know him that must mean that he was or is a soldier, and God only knows what terrible things he has done. It's none of my concern if it is so evil to my virgin ears.

. . .

Hoots gets back into the driver seat and we start our journey to Kingdom once again. It starts to get dark outside as the light fades from under the heavy blinds on the window. I finished sorting the bullet casings while snacking on the cookies from Bella as well as a decent ham sandwich from the supplies that Maurice gave us. Kitsune also handed me a bottle of water without saying a word to anyone. She remained quiet and to herself the rest of the way there. I can feel the tension in the air between her and Lupine. She is eventually taken up to the driver seat and starts driving while Hoots gets some sleep.

Once Kitsune leaves the middle section of the trailer, Lupine reaches over and taps me on my shoulder. "You can sleep up on this cot above here if you want." He opens up a compartment above the couch and empties out several totes and briefcases and sets them aside. He also gets some blankets and a pillow out from a closet and hands them to me to put up there. "It's not perfect, but it's better than the ground. We will get you up once we get close."

I crawl up into the compartment, which is just long enough for me to lay down with my knees elevated slightly. It's like sleeping in a coffin as I close the hatch just enough to block the light from the fan, but enough to give me air.

Of all the stories I've heard of Primes taking humans and beating them to near death, torturing them, and treating them like shit, I've been treated far better than I'd expect. Minus the incident at Yip's and with the bandits, he has been treating me much better than I could ever imagine. Maybe I have nothing to fear with these Primes, and it's all thanks to Lupine. "Hey, Lupine." I peek my head out from the compartment.

He looks up at me. "Yeah?"

"Thanks for everything today." I smile at him knowing that I am alive, and if he keeps his promise I will stay alive.

He takes a sip from my water bottle I left on the ground. "Get some sleep. You need it for tomorrow." I catch a glimpse of a smile right before the compartment closes almost shut.

That I will.

. . .

I stir in the middle of the night to the sound of Hoots and Lupine talking softly. I peer over the compartment and peer through the air slit in the bottom.

50

Hoots is still nested in the same spot while Lupine's feet are on top of the table. I need to sleep but I want to hear what they're saying.

"I just can't believe you let the crow live, that's all." Hoots is cleaning off the rifle he used to snipe the bandit.

"Ghent was more important," Lupine claims.

"You are betting your shot at Gore's position on a hunch."

"I know what I saw, and besides I am going to get promoted soon anyway."

It's a little bit of a relief to know that I am not just some trophy Lupine is bringing to Pure to get a promotion. If he was going to be promoted anyway, then he was doing his duty more than focusing on getting promoted.

Hoots takes a tiny brush and scrubs the inside of the barrel. "You've kidnapped countless people and treated them like shit. Why treat him any different? He is an American. Keep that in mind."

"I don't care if he is an American, he's an innocent child."

"A child you are handing over to the Zodiac's claws."

"I wouldn't give him over to the Zodiac if I knew they were going to harm him."

Lupine seems pretty sure that they won't. I mean, so far he has shown he knows what he is doing.

"What are they going to do with him then?"

Lupine pauses. "I don't know."

"Guess," Hoots pushes.

"Maybe do some tests on him, ask him some questions." Lupine seems like something is bothering him, other than Hoots' questions, which seem to be skimming cross the thin surface.

I feel my guts turn at the notion of doing lab rat experiments on me. That was about what I expected the PLF would want to do to me, and it sounded awful.

"Dissect him like a frog?" Hoots sounds dubious.

"No, I want him to be given to Fawn." I hear Lupine shift down and I can see him fiddling with something shiny in his hands as the dim light reflects off the fan. "Knowing her, she will keep him alive and safe."

"She's good at what she does. But what makes you think that Fawn will be the one conducting the tests?"

"She won't let anyone else touch him. Brutus and Argo don't have the time to use Ares or Scorpio's resources on something Virgo could do much easier," Lupine confirms.

Hoots then gains my utmost attention. "My guess is that they might try to find who his parents were or where he came from."

My parents? They could find Oasis? I was told by my caretakers at the orphanage that I was brought there from South America after the army found me wandering in the jungle alone. When they asked me where I came from I apparently only told them "Oasis." I've combed everywhere online for this place, scanned it on every satellite image map, and found no documents at the orphanage of my arrival in Detroit.

Lupine switches feet and I can see the object once more. It looks almost like his badge. "That's a real possibility that would fall on our shoulders to find the origin, and shut down the breeding program if it's still running. God knows how many other hybrids might be walking around."

They could help me find Oasis! Ever since I was a kid I've always dreamt of the possibility of finding them, or them showing up at the orphanage to take me back home. It feels like this finally can put closure on this hole in my life I've been keeping filled with dreams and my imagination. Maybe if they are interested in me enough they will find it, and when they find it I will be one step closer to finding my parents. Hell, if one of my parents was a Prime they might even be living in the PLF. I need to convince Pure to find my home, and if I find my home, I find my parents.

Kingdom

My eyes open and blink with the knocks on the compartment door. I find myself sleeping in the fetal position, and my knee has knocked the compartment open more than I left it the night before. For the first time ever I dreamt without sleeping. Maybe it's because I am living a dream, or a nightmare, right now.

Lupine lifts up the compartment door. The blinding light of the fan creaks into my face. "Morning, kid. We are here."

I begin to shuffle out of the compartment. My back is killing me and my legs are cramped together. I need to get out and stretch. "What time is it?"

He moves out of my way to crawl out. "Ten-thirty in the morning."

I normally have to get up at seven for school. Jesus, I must have slept like a baby. I don't know what time I went to bed but it couldn't have been past ten. "Holy shit, I slept late."

"Well, you had a long day." He extends out a hand to help me down then reaches down into a compartment under the seat. He takes out some cereal, a rice cracker type of cereal, and a bowl and sets it down on the table. "Eat up—we also have some granola here." He digs further back into the compartment and takes out a bag of granola.

Food sounds unappealing although I know I should eat. My feet nearly give out as I hit the floor. I stumble back into the couch and then scoot my way over to the table. "How should I approach Pure when I meet him?"

Lupine hands me a bag of granola. "Just act like you would meet your principal."

My principal was Mr. Walter. He was the only person at Raiden whom I actually like. He saw me more as a person instead of another tap from the government's money tree. However, my principal was not a towering beast who took on the United States Army.

Lupine digs out a water bottle to hand me as well. "But first we need to get some more muscle to get you there."

I carefully tap out a handful of granola. "I mean, the way you dealt with those bandits, couldn't you guys get me there?"

He pours some of the cereal himself into his palm. "Those were humans. Now we are dealing with Primes that actually stand a chance against me."

If I could have him put me in his pocket I would. "What should I do to prepare for Pure?" I take the granola and eat some. It's okay. It's better than nothing but worse than the stuff at home. This tastes stale, like it's been back there for years.

"Stay calm and don't panic," he mimics Maurice. "Head up, pay attention, and don't say anything stupid." He zips up her bag and puts it on the table. "Behind all of the muscle and prestige he is a reasonable person. Just keep that in mind."

I can feel the trailer start to make more stops as we slow down at what I assume to be stoplights. We are in civilization, an unfamiliar and hostile civilization for me but something I can work with. We eventually stop, and Hoots comes out of the compartment with a backpack on and several bags of trash. He seems worn out as he heads down the stairs and opens the door to leave.

Lupine grabs the trash left from our breakfast and some other trash in the bathroom and the empty cigarette boxes on the table. I collect all my trash and some other trash around me and put them into Lupine's bin. He puts them all into a black trash bag and throws it outside.

Kitsune gets up from her seat and heads outside. Lupine tells me to get up and walk with him. He grabs my arm and escorts me down into the hallway and orders me to go outside into Kingdom.

I hear a gritty voice that sails up into the trailer like a feather. "Do you know what it means to be on time?"

Lupine releases my arm and tells me to hold back as he steps beyond the hallway's threshold. "What the fuck do you mean on time? I'm early."

"Still not on time, though."

An ear twitches. "Listen, with what I've been dealing with, I really don't want to hear it."

"So, where's this American?"

"He's right here." Lupine grabs my arm and moves me forward a few steps.

Squinting through the sun's blinding light, I see a rundown brick apartment building with similar buildings on either side. The streets are in disrepair, and the drains are clogged with trash and leaves, causing runoff to form puddles of grime. The air is the same as in Detroit, the buildings still remain, but it's a false familiarity. I can't relax here.

I gaze upon a hawk Prime.

He approaches and looks me over. He is similar to Hoots but much taller, and his feathers are dark brown and white-tipped. His beak is polished and shimmers like gold in the sun. His amber eyes zoom in, focusing on every single pore on my body. His wing-arms come through slits in his orange jacket just below his armpit. They extend to his wrist, where five claws encircle my hand.

The hawk slides my sleeve up and taps my pant legs several times with his foot. "You sure that he's half Prime? I mean you've been plenty wrong before." He seems disappointed in my lack of feathers or tail.

"I'm never wrong."

The hawk Prime continues to prod me.

"He—would you stop poking him!" Lupine bats his claw from my arm.

The bird retreats his arm back to his side. "I mean, he looks just like every pasty white-skinned American. You've abducted the wrong person before, you know, or do I have to remind you of a twenty-three-year-old vixen three years ago?"

The idea that Lupine has made a mistake makes my skin crawl.

Lupine looks like he wants to punch him, but he only growls and pulls me away in frustration. At the building's entrance, a double-hinged door stands on its hind legs a massive bear Prime, covered in fur, heavy arms leading up to a bland muscle shirt and short khakis. His head just barely touches the top of the doorway he's guarding. A nose and eyes point to the road and don't break his darkened hazel-eyed stare as I approach. Silver studs draw attention to his rounded ears.

As we near, he ducks into the building and emerges with a layer of dust on his auburn-furred arms. He presents me with dress pants and a dress shirt stacked neatly with a pair of polished dress shoes on top. I head inside the doorway to the building and begin to change into them, discarding my old clothes behind me. While undressing I notice the bear Prime is blocking the view of everyone else with his back to me. The clothes they gave me are a bit oversized, but when I was given oversized clothes from donations at the orphanage I found that I could roll up the shirt, tuck them in the pants, roll up the legs, and tighten the belt to the max notch. Afterwards he picks up and folds my old clothes neatly and carries them back into the van with him.

He glimpses Lupine frustratingly pressing keys on his phone. I slide in front of him to get his attention, but he keeps texting away. "Lupine, I'm ready." He smashes the exclamation mark and looks up at me.

"You look presentable I guess." He orders everyone except Hoots back into the trailer. He tells Hoots to head back to a place called Stronghold and inform someone named Gores what happened.

As I get in, I feel the trailer shift and almost fall backward into the bear, who is squeezing into the hallway, fur brushing the walls. He doesn't attempt further progress; he simply turns around and closes the door behind him. He stands while I sit in between the hawk Prime and Lupine.

According to Lupine, we are heading to the government headquarters. I scan the hawk Prime from the corner of my eye. I notice the badge on his right side. It has the PLF logo with the lion and the eagle, but it reads *Feather Sagittariidae: Sagittarius Gamma*. Even Kitsune has one: *Kitsune Canidae: Sagittarius Delta*. Lastly, Borne's badge reads *Borne Ursidae: Sagittarius Epsilon*.

Feather reaches into his vest pocket for his smartphone. I don't try to snoop, though. "Hey, Lupine," he says as his sharp talons click against his screen.

"What is it now?"

"Just got a text from Tucker. He wants to know how you're doing with the mission. Do you want me to tell him you fucked up and abducted a random innocent kid?"

Kitsune adds, "And took him to see Yip."

I see she still hasn't let him live that down for some reason. I mean he seemed nice, to me at least.

Feather leans his head back. "Man, no wonder Gores doesn't want us to go on kidnapping missions. Should have just left us to arresting Evols and illegals from Wasteland."

I assume the word *Evol* is short for Evolutionaries, whose sole purpose from what I've heard is to annihilate or enslave every human being, put them in collars, and work them to death. They believe the Prime race is the next step of evolution, which differentiates them from the Hunters in the US who seek to kill Primes for sport.

Lupine isn't put off. "Because we can't just keep putting down Evols—that would just make their *daddy* mad."

"Wish we were finally given the green light to just kill him," says Kitsune. "I imagine you'd like nothing more than to put a bullet in our buddy's head—right, Lupine?"

I think I know who she's referring to. "Pantheon? That's the leader of the Evols, right?"

"Yeah, he's a mean kitty. If he got his paws on you, he would eat you for lunch." Feather makes a pouncing gesture.

I want to see how many more questions I can ask. "I heard Pure and Pantheon led the PLF back in the day—is that right?" I need to know if their leaders are Evols.

"Well, look at the big brain on you!" Feather is astonished at my basic knowledge of PLF history. "Yeah, instead of one big pussy running the nation, there were once two."

Time to lay the trap. "You don't like Pantheon then?"

He takes the bait. "Like him?" He starts to laugh. "Kid, I hate that selfish prick. He is just a cat who is still salty about being kicked out of the PLF ten years ago."

I watch everyone else's reaction, and so far none of them bat an eye. Kitsune even nods her head in agreement.

I continue to chat with Feather as we descend deeper into the lion's den. He seems very interested in life outside the PLF. He asks me questions about where I lived, about Detroit, human behavior; he asks so many questions about humans. He asks me if I've ever been to a Prime ghetto.

"Well, not really. I mean, I've seen the walls and the barricades separating them, but they don't really let humans wander around." The city government in Detroit purposely placed Prime ghettos. The goal was to keep the military close to the wealthy to make sure those with power are kept protected against another uprising, so as to not have history repeat itself. The US government passes this to Prime residents as protecting them from humanity, when in reality it's just an excuse to keep a close eye on any Prime resistance groups forming in the ghettos. "Why do you ask?"

Feather picks out a loose feather in his wing flap. "It's just the last time we were in the ghetto. I remember a young girl wolf getting picked up in a limo by a rich human. I couldn't help but wonder what he was intending to do with her. To be safe I pulled out my rifle and shot his driver and the man in the head." He seems nonchalant about it as if he was just doing his job.

I imagine their job is all about violence, killing people, and doing some of the worst things imaginable, but from what Hoots and Lupine did to those bandits it seemed just like another day on the job.

Kit nudges him and he shuts up. "Hey, maybe you can tell him the story of when you sniped Alexander Ortez's daughter—"

Lupine chucks an empty cigarette box at her. "Enough—you're scaring him enough." He nudges me. "We will be there soon, Ghent. Just do what you did before. This time, keep in mind you are going to be the first human ever to be welcomed in this place. No one else knows this, so just act calm and do not stray." He takes out his handgun. "I don't want this to become any messier than it's going to be." In unison, the others bring our pistols and slide and cock in cartridges.

The trailer screeches to a halt. Lupine retrieves his coat and removes an arsenal of items including several handguns, a switchblade, numerous casings of ammo, and my cell phone. The little red light on the side that tells me if anyone has called or left a message is blinking red. Someone has tried to reach out to me since I was kidnapped. It might be my orphanage care mother asking where I am. She is really the only one who calls me. He chucks his jacket at me and tells me to put it on.

"Hide your face." Kit gathers her coat from a side closet. Hoots remains in the driver's seat.

The coat is so massive I can't even dream of putting it on. Instead, I use it as a blanket, covering my body and leaving a small opening for my eyes, peeking out from a flap on the shoulder. "Why the coat?"

"Because it's my stench." He says this without any hint of apology.

The coat is slightly damp from the rain and smells like dog saliva and wet fur. It is two sizes larger than me, and the tails drag on the floor. It is unbearably heavy. The leather-like fabric is reinforced with steel lining, and there is a hefty plate of carbon fiber folded heavily in the chest. I feel a little safer, but mostly just suffocated. It's not like this will really fool anyone, will it? Are there blind assassins out there?

All I can see is the cement pavement turning into a marble floor as the outdoor breeze is replaced with an air conditioner. Borne is behind me, Feather and Kitsune to either side, Lupine in front. They each have their hands on their gun as we cram into an elevator. My heart races and misses beats with each elevator ding. I keep thinking there will be a group of Evols with guns waiting for us. We reach the bottom floor and the doors open.

"Move quickly," Lupine whispers to me under the hood.

My legs shake, but the adrenaline in my blood keeps me upright. My hands grip the cloak tightly. I hear the sounds of other Primes around me, but I can only see Lupine's outline, always alert yet calm despite my shakiness. We are forty steps from the elevator. The marble floor blurs as sweat runs into my eyes. I am barely holding my shit together. Feather whispers to me, "We are making a left turn here." The group shifts, but as I try to move my right leg leftward, it gives way, and I begin to fall. But just before I sprawl out onto the floor, a claw catches my fall. I know I can't thank Feather now, but I owe him one.

We keep walking. Two hundred steps from the elevator now. My worry sets into paranoia, and everything frightens me. I am just about to whisper "stop" so I can catch my breath, but just as I open my mouth Lupine says the words I need to hear.

"We are here."

I hear a door opening and see the outlines of two taller Primes above Kitsune and Feather.

Lupine announces to us, "Lupine Canidae, Sagittarius, with my squad, we are here for our meeting with the Zodiac. Tell him that we have the kid unhurt."

The guard replies in a deep voice, "Show us the American." *No, don't show them. I don't trust them seeing me.*

"That's none of your goddamn business," Lupine spits at the guard. "You don't have the authorization to delve into issues of my squad. Now, let it in."

You go, Lupine, tell that asshole! Wait, what am I saying? The guard grunts and presses some keys on a pad next to him and the double doors open for us.

We enter a dark and quiet room. Finally, Lupine removes the coat and smiles. "Good job."

That's marginally reassuring.

We are in a large atrium. Monolith walls with jutting-out pillars, eleven in total, scale up to a second level where eleven prominent chairs with nameplates and protruding microphones rest. Additional chairs lie behind. In the center of the atrium is a podium with eleven chairs placed behind it on a lower elevation. Each pillar has a standard with a symbol of the Zodiac placed on it—all except one. Gemini is missing. I assume the podium is for me to be questioned. The air is arid and smells recycled, which makes my parched throat even drier.

I march forward with Lupine while the rest of the party takes a seat. Borne takes two seats, so it appears Lupine is going to stand as my advisor for the hearing. "You are going to meet Pure," Lupine says, placing his hand on my shoulder. "Stand up straight." He pushes on my back to straighten me out. "Answer him directly with 'sir,' and the most important thing you will ever need to know is be brave, eye contact, stand straight, do not sass him."

"Yes, sir." My legs shake and my hands sweat. I gulp what I keep thinking is the last swallow of my saliva. I keep thinking of what an achievement it is to have the opportunity to talk with the leader of the Primes, Pure. Stay calm. You are alive and will be as long as you stay calm.

A voice startles me over the intercom. "All rise for leader of the PLF."

All Primes rise from their seats.

He comes from the darkness like a creature born from the abyss of primal nature. I know from the first time I see Pure that this man, this beast, is the leader of a nation of the Primes. He's a towering, dominating lion crafted to be the alpha of all beasts. The face of a lion, the gleam and stride of a leader. A golden mane is his crown, each hair finely combed and cleaned so finely that it reflects the light coming down from above. The tips of his fangs poke through his upper lip, and I can see as he walks up to his seat at the table that his eyes are the iris of a beast, a tamed beast that devoured its master and claimed his seat at not just the PLF, but as the king of all Primes. There are no badges of past victories on his chest, not even a name plate, as if anyone wouldn't know his name. His beige trench coat hangs to his knees. Instead of army gear, he wears fitted suit pants. He doesn't need to accommodate the world; the world provides for him.

"Good afternoon, everyone." His bottomless voice commands everyone in the room to attention. "Should we get this started?"

Zodiac

The room is silent apart from a couple of shifts in chairs and a few throat-clearings. I notice that while the ceiling is dark, faint lines are coming out from the sides of the column-like structure. I imagine they are just air ducts or cosmetics.

After Pure has sat down, a crowd of other Primes comes from the void behind him, each with their own department's seals of the Zodiac displayed on their shoulder. In front of them, posted to the tall black towers that hold each dark wooden desk, is a symbol of the Zodiac. The assemblage includes a lion Prime, less built than Pure, possibly his son; a snow leopard Prime with black lines traversing his face left to right; a bull Prime who has horns reaching high into the air like branches on a tree; a shark Prime who is residing in a room filled with water and a fin splitting his head like a mohawk; a giant lizard Prime whom I believe is a komodo dragon Prime after watching the slither of his tongue; a dove Prime much like Feather, except lacking any extraordinary features, who looks more like a delicate pigeon; a panda Prime, much like Borne except female with a classic black and white pattern; a black bear Prime with several distinct scars on his eyes as if something assaulted his eyes with talons; and a deer Prime that has earrings hanging from her ears and decorative knickknacks from her horns. They all take their seats around the atrium high above us, judging me from every angle. I feel like I am at a business meeting more than being held against my will by Primes, and it's putting me at ease a little. They begin to introduce themselves from left to right.

"Brutus," the other lion, "Capricorn."

"Fang," the leopard, "Libra."

"Horns," the bull, "Taurus."

"Finn," the shark, "Pisces."

"Dagon," the lizard, "Cancer."

"Dove," the dove, "Scorpio."

"Xióngmāo," the panda, "Aquarius."

"Argo," the black bear, "Aries."

"Fawn," the deer, "Virgo."

"Lupine, Sagittarius." Lupine stands more alert and grins with a heavy sense of pride. "Acting advisor to Gores."

The dove taps her mic and addresses Lupine. "Where is Gores Lupine? Did you finally get that promotion?" she teases him.

I hear Lupine crack his knuckles beside me. "He is currently in a confidential meeting, doing something important. You wouldn't understand."

She scoffs and diverts her eyes back to Pure.

Pure clears his throat and motions to himself. "I will be representing both Gemini and Leo." He acknowledges and welcomes them, returning his gaze to me.

If Pure has two departments under him then he must have more power than the others. Makes sense since he is the acting leader of the PLF.

"You must already know my name by now. Please, tell me yours," Pure says. His face remains calm, his eyes unmoving from my gaze. I turn and look at Lupine to try to get Pure to look at him.

I am careful with my words, my main goal being to avoid offending Pure. I know there are no other Primes in the room, but I still feel a laser sight on my head. "Ghent, sir. Ghent Sparrow."

"Ghent Sparrow, well that's an odd name. Where did you live?" This from someone who calls himself Pure.

"An orphanage in downtown Detroit, sir."

"What were your parents?" he inquires.

"I don't know, sir. I never saw their faces." Maybe if I can't get out of this with wits I can with sympathy.

"How old are you, son?" With every question, his large hands get closer to his chin and the more interested he appears to become. Everything is going well so far; just keep it going.

I notice several other members of the Pride taking notes and typing away at a terminal. "Seventeen, sir." At least that's what my birth certificate says, but I was always a little taller than other students at my elementary school.

"Must be hard," his hands are clenched together now, "being so young and all alone."

Gee, thanks for reminding me.

"So can you please describe how you ended up here?"

I honestly don't know why I am here as I am paraded in front of Pure like Lupine's bounty. "I don't remember. I was drugged with a Prime dose and Lupine brought me here." I need to put this on Lupine to explain. Maybe he will finally tell me exactly what happened.

"Well, Lupine, why don't you explain what brings him here?" His nails lightly groom the mane at his chin.

"I saw Ghent in a fight with a human male twice his size. Ghent managed to somehow pin him to the ground. When I approached Ghent I noticed that he was not fully human, had Primal features, and had obviously improved physical strength. So I shot the attacker to remove any witnesses and drugged Ghent to bring him back here," Lupine explains.

Pure's eyes glance to Lupine. "And did you complete the mission you were sent on?"

Lupine shakes his head no. "The mission was not completed per Brutus's request. The crow is still alive."

Pure lifts his hands up and shrugs. "Please make sure that he is dealt with in the coming year."

I feel sorry for the poor fucker that has Lupine going after him.

"Yes, sir." Lupine seems way calmer than he should be. I mean, he technically failed a mission and yet Pure is just letting that go. Pure must be interested enough in me not to care about a failed mission. Wait, why did Lupine bring a dose of versed to knock out the target when Pure says the mission was to kill him?

"Now, with my understanding is that he was abducted because by your word, he had Primal features. Correct?"

Lupine seems put off by Pure doubting him. "Yes, sir. I also smelt Prime blood when we confirmed with a blood test with Kitsune, and you should know that my nose never lies."

Is he boasting to Pure?! The balls on this Prime.

Pure just smiles with a toothy grin at Lupine. "No, I am sure that you have smelt enough blood in your wetwork to tell." He turns back to me and gets up from his seat. "So did you know you were part Prime before Lupine took you?"

"No, sir. I didn't," I state promptly. My hands are soaked in sweat and I think Pure can smell it.

For someone so massive he can move extraordinarily swiftly as he descends a staircase with steps half his foot size. He seems to doubt my Primal origins. "But yet by eyewitness accounts by Lupine, you are Prime. Anything about that day special?"

I feared this moment; if I say I don't remember he will think I am lying. I need to confirm to him that it was the drugs and not me just being unintentionally secretive. "Kit told me the drug Lupine used causes short-term memory loss. I don't know what happened that day except that I got kicked out of my school for attacking someone."

With every step Pure takes, I come to understand just how massive and dominating he is. He is three times my width and three feet taller. His body of toned muscle is impressive, and his golden hair reaches all the way up to his mane, which shimmers in the light. He is everything the US wanted in a soldier physically, a perfect weapon created to fight in the bloodiest war in human history against the Chinese, and then again against his creators. Despite this, I feel like I am talking to my principal. Even compared to Lupine, his presence is dominating. Lupine keeps his nose down and a safe distance from Pure. He stops in front of me and leans with elbows on the podium. I can feel the earth crack under me. "Well, just tell us what you can remember." He smells of strong musk; it is like the sap on maple trees.

I will explain everything I did from that morning to where my memory stops. I got up at my shitty dorm room at the orphanage. I ate some off-brand cereal. I got my things together, went to school by bus, got to Raiden Academy, and went to my first, second, and third period classes. In fourth period in chemistry, I dozed off in class and had a terrible dream, then went to the bathroom to calm down. I came out, then went to fifth period with my history teacher, Mr. Anders. I had a spat with him about something stupid. He is an anti-Prime nut who doesn't know who invented Newton's Law but can call Chinese every slur in the book. I got detention for telling him to fuck off.

Pure grins and chuckles a bit. It's good to see I am at least entertaining him.

"I then went to the principal's office." But there it gets fuzzy. I ran into someone I didn't like. I have a lot of jocks at school who bully me on occasion. "I think someone bullied me, and I might have hurt him. I don't know anything after that."

After I finish, Pure backs up and begins to pace back and forward between the radius of the half-circle formed by the stairwells. "Well, that sure is a strange turn of events for you. Being abducted by a PLF soldier by coincidence. Have you ever attacked someone before this incident?"

I've gotten in my share of little back-and-forth with students, but never attacked anyone. "No, sir."

"Hmmm..." He ponders for a moment before stopping before me at the podium. "Do you have any ambitions or future goals?"

"I did until I was kicked out of my school." Now that I am plucked out of school I am just helplessly floating, waiting for something to come by and snatch me from the air.

"I am sorry to hear that. It must have been hard for you to lose that security." He seems sympathetic, like he could ever relate to what I'm going through. "I want other members of the Zodiac to supply any questions or comments to Ghent." He turns around and addresses the council.

They all just seem to stare at each other, waiting for someone to speak up first. They don't seem quite interested in me as several of them are looking down at their lap. It takes all but a couple of minutes of silence and intermittent coughs, then a sneeze from Dove before she speaks up. "What is the consequence of kidnapping this child in regards to our relations with the United States?"

Argo taps the mic on his desk with a massive stubby finger. "I imagine that they would see it as an international incident if they found out."

Lupine steps up to my mic and scootches me over. "I can assure you that no other humans saw me abduct him. The only witness I came across I shot. I don't think the authorities will believe him when he claims a Prime abducted Ghent."

The dove enters the conversation. "Are you sure about that? From what Gores has told me you are not the most professional at kidnapping people."

I can see his tail droop down and a growl rumbling at the back of his throat. "I assure you that everything went perfectly."

The black bear states, "Besides, no one will think of a missing orphan. It's not like his parents miss him." Christ, man, can you be any blunter?!

Dove peers at the bear. "A citizen is a citizen. Trevor doesn't care who we take..." I assume Trevor is referring to our president, Trevor Graft. It's just weird hearing him being called by his first name.

Dagon interrupts her. "What is he going to do?" He slithers mid-sentence. "Kidnap one of our people?"

Dove slaps her hand down on the table. "No, you tiny-brained reptile. It's called escalation, something you should know about if you actually read a book on foreign policy!"

He slithers his tongue out and sighs. "Hey, I am the *domestic* advisor. Why am I supposed to care about what is going outside our borders?"

While this is all going on, Pure seems to be more preoccupied in watching my movements and eye contact as much as possible. "Enough. There will be no escalations over a simple kidnapping. If no one is to report Lupine kidnapping Ghent, then there is no tie to the PLF. Now are there any more questions?" Unless a local police surveillance camera picked up Lupine carrying me around.

Fawn takes to the mic. "I do, sir." She seems far cheerier than the others, almost excited. "You say that he is a half Prime. Do we know exactly the situation behind his genetic alteration?"

"No." Pure writes something down on his notepad. "I have your assistant Kitsune looking into the matter currently."

Her ear flaps come down. "Oh. Well, I will be sure to meet with her and have her advise me on that then. Thank you, sir."

Fang reaches down and pulls out a small black book from below him. "Sir." He flips to a bookmarked page. "You say this kid is half Prime. Then what kind of laws are we looking at here in regards to interrogation? We are not allowed to question Primes directly without a warrant; however, humans are separated from this law."

Pure rolls his eyes. "We don't have time to debate laws for one single race. If it is applicable we will debate that at a later time."

This whole meeting is boring. I was expecting a dimly lit room and Pure pressuring me with interrogation techniques, borderline torturing me to get answers, but he just stands here relaxed and disinterested in his council. Maybe they are just going to ask me a couple of questions and let me go. From the feeling in the room, I will be leaving here in one piece.

Pure drums his claws on the podium. "Ghent, I want to ask you something, and think about your answer for as long as it takes. Do you have a life ahead of you going back to Detroit?"

Do I have a life ahead of me? Well...if I am kicked out of Raiden, and I would be an adolescent criminal if the police found out that I attacked someone, I would be sent to juvie and lose all sense of credibility that I had. No career path, no money to fall back on, no skills, no family or friends to rely on, a broken life in a world that wouldn't want me.

I clear my throat. "Not really. No, sir."

He nods and closes his eyes a moment with a deep breath. "I see. Well, Ghent, you have two options: We can escort you back to Detroit and let you go back to an unsure future through those doors." He points to the sealed door behind me. "Or I am offering a career and a future, a chance to join the PLF, as our first ever human operative." He takes his other hand and holds it out to me palm open.

He's asking me to do what?! "You...want me in the PLF?" I am just blown back by this as the rest of the Zodiac behind him and Lupine mouth something close to "What the fuck?"

"Yes. I am offering you a chance at a new life, a better life." He seems so sure of himself, as if pride is salivating from his mouth as he stares at me.

At least he is offering me a life instead of a death. I try to regain my composure. "Why me, though? I am just some kid with no training or skills in anything close to being a soldier." He seems so quick to bring me on board despite my clear lack of ability.

Pure nods and looks at me sincerely. "Everyone can learn, though. I mean, Lupine here was some kid that I found on the side of the road in the jungle of South America, and look at the soldier he turned out to be. He is a shining example of the PLF." I see Lupine grin behind me and roll his shoulders back. "The PLF does not judge based on your current skills, but the determination and hard work to become that which we need."

I feel like I am picking the poison that will kill me. I say yes I am thrown into the PLF as a human, basically a death sentence, or I say no and I am taken back to a world that doesn't want me. Pure knows he has me by the balls; he is just toying with his prey. "I am a kid. I just found out that I am half Prime a day ago. I don't think I have what it takes, sir."

I feel a massive weight being put on my shoulder. Pure's hand. "I know you have what it takes. You know why?"

His hand covers my entire shoulder and I can feel his thumb pressed against the back of my neck. If he wanted to right now he could swipe my head clear off.

"Why, sir?"

"Because you are letting me touch you without flinching. You are showing more bravery than any human I've met in a long time." I guess Lupine knew what he was talking about when he told me to keep myself together. I guess in the end he saved my ass twice this week. I can feel Pure's hand lift and pat me heavily on my back. I nearly fall forward into him but I manage to catch my balance on the sides of the podium.

"Keep that head high and I am sure you will find a bright future in the PLF in no time."

As Pure says this Lupine peers up at Pure and opens his mouth slightly as if to speak, but remembers who Pure is and snaps it shut. With time...I could be Lupine, but do I really want to be him?

"Ghent." Pure lifts his hand from my neck. "You okay?"

I snap out of my thoughts and peer around the room and notice my hands starting to shake and legs about to give out. I am still holding myself to the podium, but my hands are slipping. I need some time to think about this. I need to sit down and think. "Can I have a couple minutes to think about it?" I politely ask.

"Yes, we will give you all the time you need." He heads over to the side of the wall and grabs a folding chair and sets it under me gently. He is reading me like a book. That's what scares me the most about him. It's not the size or the fangs; it's the mind behind this beast that took on the US Army.

What are my options? If I say no, I am left to fend for myself back in Detroit with a world against me and my life in ruins.

Besides, the world I was abducted from never accepted me, never provided anything but the bare minimum for me to survive and build some meager existence from. If I go back there now and I turn into a Prime, I would even be further pushed away by society as a freak, as an enemy, as *something* that doesn't belong instead of someone. However, joining the PLF is a challenge I just don't think I am cut out for.

I get up and breathe heavily. "I..." As I begin to accept his offer my mind is constantly pulling me back from the edge before I plunge into the trenches. I don't want to do this; I am not sure I can.

Pure must know I am struggling to find an answer. "Ghent." He bends his knees down to get to my eye level. "I know this is hard for you to decide. It would be hard for anyone in your position." He reaches out and puts his hand on my shoulder lightly. "Just give us a year. If you don't think you are up for it, I will let you go back to your home. Does this sound better to you?"

A year in the PLF. Why would they provide me training and a place to live and spend all of this money on me unless he knows for certain I will stay? Although, again if he is willing to train me as a soldier for no cost to me, and provide me insurance that I will live as he is investing the PLF's time and money into me, it gives me a set of skills I could bring back with me to the United States. Also, a year might give me enough time for what happened before to fall through the cracks. This sounds much more reasonable, but will he let me leave a year from now if I wish to leave? Or maybe I will like it here. This next year could be hell for me, but if I can make it out of this alive I will for sure gain more than I ever could back home. If I am in fact a Prime, and could blend in with this world, this is where I truly belong, in a world among my own kind. Accepting this offer may be the last decision I make as Ghent the student, the human, but if I am to reset my entire life I might as well do it with possibly my own kind supporting me.

I've always supported the freedom of Primes in the United States. The irony of being held captive by the PLF in their territory.

If Pure is willing to change the deal, maybe he's up to offering me something else. If anyone could possibly know something about Oasis, it would be one of the most powerful Primes in the world.

I can say it, I know I can say it; I just hope I don't regret it. "I accept your offer to join the PLF." After grinding my mind into oblivion, I have worn my brain down to the stem. "If you can tell me one thing."

Pure lets go of my shoulder and opens a palm to me and gives a chuckle and a smile. "And what would that be?"

"I want to know everything you know about a place called Oasis."

He seems confused at my request. "Oasis? That camp you were raised in?"

Wait. How does he know I was raised there? I never told him that.

"Well...I don't know much off the top of my head..." He grips the podium, his nails extending and clinging to the wood, and puts his eyes on Brutus. "Brutus, have you ever heard of a place called Oasis?"

Brutus looks down at Pure from picking at his claws with his pen. "No, nothing that I can remember." He didn't think for even a second.

Pure knows something, he has to. Maybe gaining his trust will provide me what he knows about where I was born to find my origins, my family. From there I can truly decide where I belong.

Pure turns his attention to Lupine. "What about you, Lupine? You've been in plenty of jungles. Have you ever heard of Oasis?"

"No, sir, I have not."

I take a deep sigh and shrug my shoulders. "That's okay," I say. "I thought I'd ask."

Pure removes his grip from the table and opens his tablet with a single swipe. "And a fine question it was." He clears his throat, preparing himself and garnering the attention of all in attendance. "As the leader of the PLF, I, Pure, authorize you to join the PLF."

I feel my hair on the back of my neck rise. I don't know if it is my soul trying to run out of the room or my body telling me I survived.

"Now, let's see here, we need to get you in uniform..." He counts on his fingers. "...and registered, a physical, which may end up being slightly skewed. You know what, Kit, get him a human physical. We will also need you to put you in a squad." He shifts his front to Lupine. "You have a slot opened up, don't you?"

Lupine's tail droops down. "No, sir, we don't at the moment..."

"Well, you do now, and it has just been filled." He claps his hands and rubs them. "Lupine, I entrust this kid to you. This will be your ultimate test as to whether you are fit for the promotion you so desperately want."

It feels great to know I will work with Sagittarius, but I know for sure this time my soul is trying to escape.

Lupine's face falls into despair. "Sir, I don't think that…"

"This isn't a request; it's an order. And as an order from the Zodiac, you are to obey." He leans into him. "Please, correct me if I'm wrong."

"No, sir, you aren't," Lupine states through gritted fangs, "but how the hell am I going to make an excuse for walking with a human everywhere around the base?"

It's strange he seems upset at Pure's request for me to join his squad after how nice he treated me and how he supported me through all of this. Maybe he was just bringing me as a trophy to be promoted. That sucks. Of any Prime I've met I think Lupine is by far the most interesting one.

"That will be your first assignment: get this human to look and act like us. The rest is up to you. And please, Lupine, don't screw this up. Well, this is where I take my leave. I will trust you with Lupine, and you will report back here tomorrow for the best part of joining the PLF." His smile reveals a full set of fangs. "Paperwork."

Pure digs into his coat and pulls out a set of papers freshly pressed and printed and hands them to Lupine. Lupine receives them, grip their edges tightly, begrudgingly. "These should get Ghent around the PLF without much hassle." Pure had those papers ready, like he already knew I would say yes. "Thank you, Ghent, for being here. I also thank the Zodiac for their attendance today. Please save any questions for tomorrow, and I hope you all have a wonderful night." He claps his hands together—a shockwave blows back some of my hair—and walks back up the stairs with his head held high like he just won a prize.

Lupine turns his back to me and storms out of the room with his tail down. The rest of the squad follows him.

I look up to the podium Pure just departed and ask myself, "What did I just get myself into?"

Demonstration

I catch back up to Lupine. "Well, I guess you are my commander then." I don't know if it's the adrenaline kicking in from what I just did, or if I honestly am excited to be with Lupine.

"What if I am?" he snarls back.

I don't know why he is so upset; I mean, he gets to work with a half-human, half-Prime. This should be exciting for him. Maybe I can lighten the mood. "I just hope that we get along well. I mean, so far we've gotten along great."

It didn't work. "Till now, I wasn't told by the Zodiac to have you follow me around like a lost kid."

"Why are you so crabby? Before you were all professional but now that you're in charge of me…"

I appear to strike a nerve because Lupine strikes my shoulder and slams me against the nearest wall. "Listen to me and listen to me well! I didn't choose to be your alpha. I didn't choose to lead you around a city filled with people who might want to hurt you because they don't understand you are a Prime."

I try to reason with him. "But you chose to save me back in Detroit."

"I was hoping Pure would give you to Fawn and I would get the credit. Now I am stuck here with you chained to my tail dragging you around. Forgive me if I am not just jumping for joy."

I can't say that he isn't right. He is my alpha now, but I just wish he would put it a little sweeter and not sound so much like a brat. It's true, though, I realize:

I have to follow his rules and orders or else I might be put with someone who might not have so much restraint as Lupine. "Yes, sir."

A weasel Primes in the hallway stare and Lupine finally lets me go.

"What the fuck are you looking at?" growls Lupine, and he flees.

We head for the medical bay where Kitsune will give me a quick physical. Feather puts his talons on my shoulder. "Hey, bud, you all right?"

I made sure that Lupine was out of earshot. "Define *all right*." I wasn't even sure what I was feeling. Scared, excited, nervous. A little hungry maybe?

"Hey, just think about it this way: You just talked to Pure! You have nothing to worry about. I mean, Pure is a big, scary motherfucker, but beyond that he is pretty chill."

He isn't lying. "No kidding. I mean, how did he get so big and menacing?" Most lion Primes are not built like him.

Kitsune interjects, "He was always that way, ever since we knew him anyway."

Feather continues, "I guess they made that first batch with some extra juice."

First batch? "Was Pure one of the first Primes?"

"Yes," Kitsune says, "he and Pantheon were the first Primes ever made and was chosen by most Primes to have the position to lead the Primes after he led the revolt against the United States. While Pantheon sees it more as we are all of his children and should be grateful to him for being a deadbeat dad."

I hate to ask about Pantheon, but I have to learn as much as I can about Prime politics if I want to blend in as much as possible. "I know he is the leader of the Evols, but just what is he to Pure?"

"It's complicated."

I continued to talk with Feather for a while. He tells me how exactly Pure came to power. After World War III, Pure was stationed in Washington, DC, as an ambassador and civil rights representative for the Prime community. In the beginning, Pure advocated for laws and rights for Primes. Despite his connections and efforts, all attempts to grant human rights to Primes resulted in failure, as a hesitant Congress along with a racially divisive ex-President Hunts all determined that Primes would remain segregated from human society. However, with the Prime civil rights movement, and with Pantheon at his side, Pure gathered all the Primes in Washington for a mass protest that would be deemed Roaring Sunday.

Roaring Sunday was the PLF's catalyst. On Sunday, May 11, 2040, Pure, Pantheon, and over three thousand Primes staged a protest in Washington, DC. The Hunters and other hate groups got word of it, and while the protest was happening, they showed up. They beat, caged, burned alive, and killed hundreds of helpless Prime protesters. "We all knew where we were on that day," says Feather quietly before going on. Pantheon became more frantic and urged Pure to start the civil war that would eventually lead to the Prime Revolution and civil war that followed.

Feather explains that the Evols started as an online group of racists and Primes dissatisfied with Prime/human relations. They grew a following after Roaring Sunday and several other incidents and became a significant force online. Pantheon, through his connections, became their mouthpiece to the public as he organized the groups within the PLF to form the Evols, with him at the wheel.

We come to an expansive one-story glass wall that extends around the corner of a quadrant of an intersection. Through the glass, I see Primes in a waiting room and nurses and attendants behind desks. A walled-off sector houses a physical rehabilitation room where physical training equipment is sprawled out. Lupine stops at the sliding door and turns back to us. "I have some errands to run before the register closes in two hours." He points at Kitsune. "He's your problem until I get back." He passes Kitsune the papers and leaves us. Feather and the rest of the crew does likewise.

She folds the paper under her arm and pushes the door open. "Well, what are you waiting for? Let's go."

I can tell she wants to get this over with; she probably wants to head home and sleep after a long day. At the front desk, a cougar Prime types on a computer while chatting with a rabbit Prime beside her. They do not notice me right away, but as Kitsune approaches their eyes immediately jump to me.

"Hello, Kitsune, what can we..." The rabbit, Kaity, inspects me. "...do for you?"

Kitsune hands the documents over to Katherine. "I need room to do a physical. The human is a guest, by order of Pure."

Katherine hesitates. I smile warmly. The less that the Primes are unsteady about me, the better my time here will be. "All right." She looks over the papers and finds the official stamp. She hands back the papers and looks up a room on her chart. "Let's see, we have room 203 open for you."

"Could you send a couple of things as well? I need some equipment." I don't think a physical is the only thing Kitsune has in mind for me.

"What do you need?"

Kitsune reads off a list of medical equipment, but I recognize none of them. I look around to see if any other Primes are looking at me, but none seem to notice me. Maybe they think that a human would never be roaming these halls.

"And I would also require a blood draw kit and machine."

Shit, I know what those are. I feel like the whole experimentation thing might not be too far off.

"Come." She takes off toward a door on the left side marked 200-240. She opens it up for me, and we travel down a long hallway. We pass doctor rooms on the right, various testing rooms, and hospital beds that split this room in two. White-aproned Primes work but again don't notice me. I remember what Lupine told me, that Primes have a heightened sense of smell and that they can smell me a mile away. I must still smell like Lupine's musk from his coat; I guess that wasn't such a stupid idea after all.

We head into office room 203. Kitsune knocks to make sure office room 203 is unoccupied and then unlocks it. Inside is a single doctor's office with an examination table, two chairs, and a desk with a computer. There is also a sink equipped with several glasses of various medical instrumentations

"All right, sit there," she instructs me and points to the end of the examination table.

I push myself onto the end of the table and let my legs hang down, the table being only slightly too tall for a human. "Okay." She grabs a page on the packet. "Have you had any of the following lately? Itchy fur...um..." She makes several checks on her clipboard. "No...you don't have that.... Tail not applicable. Do you have any health issues?"

"Not that I'm aware of. The last physical I had I was healthy." That was five years ago, though. I wonder what she wants me to say.

"Your doctor's an idiot for not recognizing you're half Prime, so I'm making sure."

"Well, that's what you get for discount government doctors."

She ignores my comment. "Any medications?"

"Lorazepam."

"For?"

"Anxiety." The combination of school and living alone is the main cause of that.

"Do you have a family history of any medical issues?"

"No family history in general."

"Any mental health issues?"

"Stress around any kind of fire."

"So you're pyrophobic."

"You can say that, yeah."

"You will fit right in." She remarks. "I'm going to check your heartbeat. Take off your shirt." She puts away the folder and opens the drawer to get a stethoscope. Next she wraps a blood pressure measuring device around my arm, takes my pressure, and then administers various other tests including my hearing, sight, and breath capacity. Lastly, she checks my coordination by placing a ball in my hand and telling me to move it back and forth without looking at it.

During the coordination test I focus on her. "So, when did you become a medic?" I want to learn more about her. If she is the only one who can save my life from a bullet wound, I don't want any bad blood between us.

"During the war, I wasn't fit to be out in the field, so they put me in the medical corps." I'm surprised she answered me given how quiet she was previously. She only really talks when you specifically ask her something.

"You're lucky you didn't have to fight out in the field. I guess fighting isn't your strong suit…"

She reaches at my neck and pinches hard on my shoulder, making my entire arm go numb, and holds me down one-handed. Her other hand reaches to my neck on the other side and pokes at a single spot on my neck. "Don't think I can't fight you single-handed."

Okay, maybe she is just as much of a fighter as Lupine. "Sorry."

With a sigh, she calms herself. "You civilians are just too stupid to realize what we go through. You guys see the torn ruins of a city, but only after they've sent the janitors in to clean up." That's true. All the books I've read were only photos of what happened *after* the fighting.

"It must be hard, seeing all of that." I hope my sympathy doesn't come across as hollow.

"After you see a man crawling at your feet, both his legs blown off…" She slows down her sentence. "…and his back burned so bad you can see his ribs…after that everything else seems like a boo-boo."

Jesus. "Was that in China?"

"Yeah." I decide not to ask any more about a topic she obviously doesn't want to talk about. She finishes her examination and stows her notes in a tan folder. She opens the door and pulls in a complicated device on a cart that from what I remember was used to take my blood sample way back when I was a kid to find out what type I was. I was screaming the entire time. Luckily the nurse was nice enough to give me a cool bandaid and a sucker afterward.

"All right now. The final step: I need a blood sample from you."

I swallow a bit of bile that comes up at the notion of a needle. I need to make an excuse. "Didn't you already take a couple before?"

"Yes, but I took those to find out what you are." She rolls over a device that has four index finger long and wide vials loaded into the side, as well as a needle with a thin plastic tube going into the machine. "Now I need to find out if anything is wrong with *what* you are. Now stick out your arm."

Shit, that didn't work. I've always had a fear of needles; just the notion that a small bit of metal is being pushed into my body and taking things from it makes me queasy and uncomfortable. "Um, remember when I said that I had a fear of fire?" I laugh nervously. "Turns out I also have a fear of needles."

She deadpans me. "I don't really care. It won't hurt that much. Just think back to, I don't know, something that makes you happy."

I would if I could, and just as I start to find something, I feel a butterfly needle being pushed into my arm, followed by a drawing sensation from beneath my skin. My arm tenses and my vision blurs for a split-second as I try not to jerk my arm, but the tremors in my arm give way and I involuntarily jerk my arm with the needle still inside. I can feel the needle quickly shoot out and a spray of blood out right onto Kitsune's face and collar. I can guarantee the drugs have worn off as it feels like my muscle is seizing from the pain and my fist white-knuckles my knee. I immediately look at Kitsune as a steady stream of blood flows out of my arm. Kit just stares at me with wide eyes, the needle in one hand and her other hand shaking with an open palm.

I decide to take my shirt and press it against the exit point on my arm. "I'm sorry, Kit!" I nearly faint as I hold my arm.

My calls to her seem to snap her out of her daze and she drops the needle and gets up, runs toward the door, and sticks her head out into the hall. "Nurse! I need you to help! A needle slipped while taking a blood sample!"

Why doesn't she do it?

Kitsune exits the room and immediately a dove Prime rushes in and is shocked that I am a human for one, but once she gets over it she immediately heads to my arm and issues pressure onto the hole. Where is Kit going? I look over at the dove Prime, whom I can see is named Soar.

She asks me if I am all right and I tell her I feel dizzy. She tells me to keep the pressure as she gets a bandage ready. She opens a cabinet and pulls out a cloth bandage and wraps my arm above the hole to issue a tunicate. Once the bleeding has stopped she unwraps another bandage to cover the hole.

All the while I am thinking about what happened. Kitsune is a trained battlefield medic; she's seen her fair share of blood and gore. Was it because I got some on her face? I mean, she knows I don't have any blood pathogens, but maybe it's just to be safe? That looked too...she really didn't see what was happening for that half minute. I've seen veterans having PTSD episodes, and she sure looked like she was having some sort of episode.

Once my injury is cleaned up and the area swabbed down with cleaning alcohol, Soar leaves to get a new T-shirt. It's a simple plain white T-shirt, and it's a little too big for my size, but it will work, I guess. I tell her thanks for helping and ask her where Kit went.

"She headed toward the bathroom. I will go check on her to make sure she's okay."

As soon as Soar gets up and opens the door, Kitsune slowly edges her way past her and sits back down in her chair. There are still drips of water coming down from the whiskers to the side of her face and damp fur can be seen around her eyes. "Soar, you can leave. I got this." She is shaken up badly as she is still trembling when she reaches her notepad on the desk and starts to write slowly down on it.

"You sure, Kit?" Soar kindly asks.

"Yes. I am okay."

You sure as hell don't look like it.

Kitsune finishes up with her examination—a quick smack with a knee hammer, an eye and ear check, and some more documenting—before she sends me back to the lobby. I don't feel like asking her what happened. She doesn't seem too keen on talking to me, or anyone, at this time. She only tells me to wait out in the lobby for a centaur named Stall. "He will be hard to miss," she states before heading back the way she ran down before.

I take my leave and walk back the way I came in. Not much has changed since I went into the doctor's office, except all the Primes in the waiting room have left.

It's the first time I've been alone since I was kidnapped. Just a nice couple minutes alone feels like heaven right now. Even though making a run for it passes my mind, I know that someone is watching me—and even if I were to run, where would I go? There is no point in running if I have no plan or way to get back. Besides, I am given an opportunity to do something, something stupid and dangerous to my health, but something to do. An opportunity of a lifetime that no one else in the world has a chance to live.

I look around for Stall but do not see any centaurs. I locate a chair where I can't easily be seen through the glass walls and use a magazine to hide my face. It is a Prime version of *Time* magazine called *Natural* with current news articles and editorials on contemporary Prime culture. The cover story is about Pantheon. His face is interwoven with DNA strands.

Pantheon is a panther Prime with the same facial features as Pure, except that Pantheon's fur is jet black. His eyes are a deep green that concaves into a teal before funneling into a dark iris. In the photo, Pantheon wears a leader-like expression, but unlike Pure, this expression includes a sort of cockiness and pride. It's almost like he knows that whatever is written about him is right and he is proud of it. It's something to read, and the more I find out about the PLF the better. The article reads:

Evolution or Revolution?

Evolutionary leader and former political figurehead before the Primal Revolution, Pantheon has announced a new program to enact the Pure Blood Initiative, a program targeted against neighboring human communities in the PLF. In a statement given by him in a recent interview: "We can't let terrorists live and breed so close to our borders without surveillance. To preserve Prime harmony in the PLF, human integration must be quashed. This also protects the Primes at home from eventual terrorist activity."

The anti-evolutionary leader Shallow has rebutted the statement made by Pantheon: "We will not listen to radical racist statements made by the Evols or his cult followers. We will remain neutral toward the US government and the human population living in India, East Asia, and budding communities on the outskirts of Wasteland. However, we are monitoring activity in the areas, and we are preventing any sort of communication with the US government."

With the current tensions between the US and the PLF at a record low, Primes are now finally starting to feel a sense of calm as recent polls show Primes feel the safest they've felt since The Liberation. In a recent statement made by Pure at last week's press conference, "Human beings, if proven to be honorable citizens and true to their word, should be given an opportunity to live in the PLF. All it takes is time and everyone doing their part to ensure harmony can be created."

The rest of the article is statements from various Primes I don't know, and most of them deny any involvement with Pantheon or the Evols. After rereading the material, I have to admit that I could replace words like Pantheon and Evolutionaries with Hunters, and the article wouldn't be any less accurate. If there are communities of Chinese around the PLF then that might be an interesting place to go to if I get let go or have an opportunity to get out. I flip through to see if there is anything else of interest, and I come across a vibrant and laminated ad for a hotel in Singapore.

Travel to Singapore! Highlights include fine dining... It continues with various descriptions of high society in Singapore and the opening of the new top-rise club, The Silver Monkey, opening its doors this year to the public!

Besides the overtaking of the government and land by PLF forces, it's strange how Singapore remains untouched from the war. Its buildings, landscape, and people really did not change.

I hear the door open behind me and look up to see a centaur clop into the ward. He has a giant saddle-like drape made of leather and cloth spread over his horse side and an army jacket on his human half. His badge is displayed properly in front of him below like a license plate: *Stall Equidae: Gamma Leo*. A belt connects the two sections. The difference between him and other Primes is that his human part is completely human while his horse side is ultimately horse, science successfully recreating the Greek myth. His mane acts as a mohawk that stretches from his head down to his tailbone and then fuses with his dark coat. "I imagine you're Ghent." He speaks in a hoarse tone. "Follow me and stay close."

"Okay." I consider asking if I can ride him but imagine that he would take great offense to that.

We walk down the halls back to the road where we arrived. Still no Primes around. Not since the meeting with Pure. The galleries are vacant of any activity, and all the doors that were once open are now closed. A PLF soldier dressed in full riot gear and an M16 pressed against his chest protects the parking garage. I can't see what the Prime is behind the helmet, but he has a tail. Stall gestures for him to make way and proceeds to open the door. The breeze chills me after the last couple of hours in a warm and confined office complex. The sound of the wind echoes in the garage. PLF soldiers with automatic rifles guard each floor. They stare straight ahead without acknowledging me. Stall takes me all the way down the ramp to the street-level exit.

Beyond the poll gate, a black minivan is surrounded by Primes dressed in suits. They are waiting for me. Despite heavy security, I still don't feel safe. The fact that Pure needed to send this many bodyguards and military cement my worry that there are Primes out there to hurt me, or maybe it's a show of force to demotivate any possible attacks on me. Either way I still need to be aware, and at the side of those who are ordered to protect me.

"Head down to the van with me. We are heading to an undisclosed building to hold you there till tomorrow." Stall hops into the back of the van and lies down between benches, one of which I sit on. I would love to know more about Stall, but I can imagine the amount of shit that he has had to endure to live in this form, and I don't want to sound like I am reinforcing what others might have denoted.

We sit in silence for a while. He is unwilling to look at me, and I can't help but peek at him, trying to understand how his daily life works.

"You are wondering about my horse half, aren't you?" he suddenly asks me.

It seems my patience is rewarded. "I just never saw a Prime like you before, that's all."

"I am a rare breed, that's for sure."

82

I notice his Zodiac sign is Leo. "Say, you're part of the Leo sign." I point at his badge. "What does that mean?"

"Leo is the executive branch of the Zodiac. We also serve as Pure's personal bodyguards as well as the protection service for all council members and government figures."

So that's why he picked me up instead of one of my squadmates. I guess that his job would be better in protecting me if their job is protecting someone, while Sagittarius seems more like a job in doing just the opposite.

I ask Stall questions, and he answers me. I start with learning more about each division as I probably need to learn the divisions of the military since I will be a part of it.

"Well, you have Aquarius, our environmental protection agency, led by Xiongmao. Pisces, our navy run by Finn. Aries is our national guard led by Argo, soon to be led by Gores. Taurus, our economy division run by Horns. Cancer, our domestic policy branch, led by Dagon. Virgo, the medical department led by Fawn. Kitsune is a gamma there as well."

Wait, he knows Kit? "How do you know Kit?"

He pauses his explanation and opens his phone up and types into a web page browser. "She is one of the best doctors in the PLF. A little hot-headed, but can patch you up faster than a grandma can a teddy bear." He shows me an article on his phone. (There are enough unread message notifications on the top to cover the entire bar.) It's written by Fawn, and Kit is standing next to her in her medical gown with a professional gaze at the camera. "Fawn and Kitsune: Breakthroughs in Modern Medicine for Primal Anatomy." He says, "You honestly should be lucky to have her as a doctor."

At least I can be lucky a little bit here and there right now. "Sorry if I interrupted you before; just wanted to ask."

"All right, where was I? Oh yeah, Libra is our justice department, led by Leo. Scorpio our foreign affairs led by Dove. Capricorn our strategy department led by Brutus. Sagittarius, led by Gores now, but Lupine is shooting for his position. Lastly, you have a weird one. Gemini was the executive branch led by Pantheon and Pure; however, when they split up they moved the Gemini department to Leo. Gemini is now filler, really, it's for miscellaneous matters. No one really leads that department anymore. Leo is led obviously by Pure and is the executive council branch."

"Didn't know I was going to have to take a history lesson a thousand miles from my school," I joke to slide into a more serious matter. "So you know Kit and Lupine?"

He further explains that he was part of Sagittarius until being promoted to the secret service after he saved a mission from failure. He got a medal and a job offer from Pure himself.

"Why did you take it?"

"I needed to get away from Sagittarius. I didn't like the work or some of the people involved." Who could he be talking about? Lupine immediately came to mind.

"Was it Lupine?"

He smiles a little bit. "Why would you think it would be him?"

"Well, you know...he isn't the..."

"Most lenient? No, it wasn't Lupine, but, interestingly, he sprung to mind."

"Then who was it?"

The smile disappears. "His *buddy*."

The van halts in front of a different run-down building. Instead of bricks, its structure combines steel beams and plaster laden with holes and broken windows. The street is blocked off by police barricades and is empty of any cars or Primes. Down the road, I only see the wall of police cars glinting the light from their black car hoods. The smell of garbage and open sewers permeates the air.

Stall brings me up to the cobble steps toward a sizable rotted door, as thick as my arm, which creaks like a screaming baby as Stall opens it. Inside, the rustic decor appears untouched since the '20s. The stairs in the center nearly fall out below the weight of Stall and make me press lightly on each step as I climb. They smell of antique wood and dust. The lights in the hallway flicker, revealing alternate sections of wallpaper, half leaves dancing in the wind, the other half leaves dead on the ground.

We arrive on the second floor. Stall stops at the door with a number two, a missing integer, and a three. He opens it. Sun shines through two full windows onto a single couch and an old TV. I enter, wondering if we are alone or not. The kitchen boasts a countertop, stove, fridge, and dishwasher in a row. On a table supported by a brick, an upside-down glass wobbles. Along a dim hallway, I see the corner of the bathroom. The ceiling has several pipes and beams crosshatched, one of which is shaking and humming leading into the toilet.

It reminds me of my dorm back in Detroit. "What is this place?"

Stall stays outside of the room, and I notice there isn't enough room for him to maneuver inside. "This used to be a drug den; we kicked out the bad element here and made it into a holding pen. You will be staying here for tonight and maybe tomorrow night. We usually use this place to interrogate officials, but we turned it into a nice apartment for you to stay in while you are in Kingdom. It has all the essentials, and there are some prepared meals in the fridge if you get hungry." If this is nice, I hate to see his definition of evil. Realizing I haven't eaten anything since the trailer I look in the fridge, where I find a couple of sandwiches, fruit, and two full cases of beer behind a couple of near-empty spirit bottles. "You can have some of that beer in there."

I don't necessarily feel like getting drunk for the first time while being a captive of the Primes, so I make an excuse. "I'm underage."

"Well, you're in luck—there is no drinking age. And from what you just went through to get here, you could use one." He isn't wrong. I guess beer wouldn't hurt. I'll have something to eat too.

Most kids my age share their first beer with their father or mother. I am sharing it with a PLF centaur soldier.

"TV works if you want to watch some Prime stations. They might be a little different from what you're used to at home, though." He clicks through some of them to show me, but I don't recognize anything. I see moments of sitcoms, a soap opera, which could be interesting, but I ask him to stop at a news station called PNN. I sink about three inches and feel like I am being eaten by the cushions.

"Hey, do you want to maybe want to hang out here for a while and share a..." I turn around to him but he has already left with echoes of clops down the hall and down the stairs. I guess he is just as busy as Lupine.

Oh well. I take a beer out of the fridge. Luckily, it's a twist-off. It is bitter and unappetizing, but it is calming, and after a couple more sips, the bitterness recedes. I finally can lay down, turn on the TV, and relax for once. I never have had such a long day in my life. After everything I went through, I deserve a little rest and relaxation. In fact, I think no one on the planet has had a stranger day than me. I look back out the window and think of just how far I've come from this morning, and how far I now have left to go. I've chosen this path to be a soldier, to get more information on what I really am, where I came from, and who I truly am and want to be.

A news flash appears on the TV. Several groups of protesters gather holding signs reading "Death to humankind" or "Skin their hides." The news station has muted the audio, but I can still hear the frightening swell of their voices. The Evols look like regular Primes. No brandings or markings. The Evols seem to be rioting outside of the PLF headquarters, where I just was. Now I understand the garage parking lot security and why they took me out the back. But why are they rioting now, though? Do they do this often or is something else going on?

I grab the remote to turn off the TV, but just before I hit the power button, a news story comes up on the screen.

"Evolutionary leader Pantheon is speaking about riots from a livestream over Fang from an undisclosed location. Let's cut to the live feed."

It switches to Pantheon, dressed in a white tailored suit, preaching to a crowd of press and supporters. "The protests that occurred today were not of anger or hate but were of worry. Worry that our current PLF leaders have failed to protect the cities we've rebuilt. The family and friends we've made here, once protected by the PLF, are now being threatened by Pure's irrational decision to let a human join the PLF military. There is no further proof that the PLF has lost its way when I was alerted that an armed PLF soldier fired recklessly at innocent Prime civilians. This only shows the slow degradation of the PLF and that its leadership is unable to control its soldiers. I want this Prime brought to justice and the human sent back to the US immediately. Humans do not belong here. Never have; never will."

I don't care what Pantheon thinks. I do not fear a single Prime, as big and menacing as he might be. Those Primes outside on the street protesting me joining the PLF, the possibly thousands that are afraid of a human walking among them, those Primes are the ones that I fear the most. All I can do is hope that Pure can unite his people for his cause, that Leo and Sagittarius can protect me, and lastly that I can survive night after night in the body of a city with its white blood cells hunting me down.

I immediately turn off the television, but as I head to bed, I keep hearing his voice jolting me awake, which keeps me fearing my skin for the first time in my life.

Pledge

A honking horn sounds. I reach for my alarm but only grab an empty space on the short tan drawer next to me. That's not right. Wait...I'm not at home. I raise my body and sit at the bedside. The walls, the air, and the jacket hanging in the empty closet in the cramped apartment bedroom still hang there. I am a PLF soldier now... I talked to Pure. Now I feel like I have a hangover, but I guess it comes with being kidnapped and joining a country full of a race you don't understand.

I put my gear on and head to the fridge. The broken clock ticks toward eight. My hand goes to my jacket pocket, searching for my phone, and then I remember Lupine still has it. Shit, the only way I have of contacting anyone is gone, and probably the only way of figuring out what happened two days ago...or was it yesterday? I don't know anymore.

I hear a knock on the door. It takes me a second to navigate my way back to the living room, which is bleeding in the morning sun from the window through the drawn shades.

I open it, and Lupine rushes past me and into the room without even saying hello. He is still dressed in the same clothes he wore yesterday. "Did you eat breakfast yet?" he says urgently.

"No...I just got up...," I say, still groggy from a restless sleep.

"Get some cereal from the pantry, and eat it quickly. We are on a tight schedule today, and we've got a lot of shit to do."

I open cabinets till I find a bowl and pour milk into a bowl of generic brand

Honey Coated Oat Pieces. "What's the plan for today?"

"Your initiation into the PLF, filling out paperwork, taking the oath, finding a place safe place to house you, a shit ton of work to do so hurry up."

I guess I should hurry up and eat quickly if we are going to be rushing today. He looks like he hasn't slept in a while and might be a little more irritable today. Also this cereal is stale. I look at the box and see it expired a year ago.

"And after that fucking hairball last night told the whole fucking town that you're here, I had to beef up security for you." That's right, Pantheon *did* tell everyone a human was in the PLF army, but at least he didn't show everyone what I look like or where I am. "Didn't help that he somehow found out you were here last night and got a picture of you leaving."

While Lupine waits for me to finish, he reaches into the fridge and pulls out a beer. "Mister pretty kitty last night," he growls. "If I were Pure I would pull that stub of a tail through his mouth and...ugh."

"Isn't it a little early to start drinking?" I ask concerned, he will be driving me there and he already looks sleep deprived.

"Why do you care? And hurry up. We have to leave in five minutes."

I take my last bite. "Are you okay to drive? I mean you look a little tired."

He downs the entire bottle. "I am fine." He bleaches powerfully. "Also Feather is driving us there. Now let's go—Feather's waiting."

I put away my dishes in the sink, sweep my hair down, and get my socks and shoes on as quickly as I can. Lupine is on his cell phone again, hastily typing away. His claws click with every press. It's probably scratched as hell.

The sun is bright at the street level. The barricade down the street remains and is now flooded with more police and squad cars than before. The PLF has maintained the same colors as the US cop cars; however, they redesigned the logo and the name of the vehicles. *PLF* is written in bold with the definition etched beneath it.

We walk toward a mail truck parked in front of the curb. "Never knew the mailmen were armed to the teeth," I joke, getting Lupine's attention.

"Very funny," he sarcastically remarks. "It's our disguise vehicle for today." He gestures to its rear. "Get in the back with me."

During the ride, Lupine texts on his phone, not paying any attention to me, or maybe he is putting all his emphasis on me, and that's what he's texting about. I don't dare ask him. He seems like he is in overdrive and doesn't want to waste any of his time on my questions. The drive takes the same amount of time as the previous night; we must be going back to the capitol building.

. . .

A couple of seconds after the car comes to a halt, I hear three consecutive bangs on the door. "Come on out!" It's Feather yelling from outside.

We leave the van, stepping out to the back alley, which is blocked off on either side by squad cars and armed guards. These were the same guards accompanying Stall last night. I tried to find Stall among them, but I couldn't spot him. Feather and Lupine flash their badges, and we are let inside. The doorman doesn't spare me even a glance. Maybe they are ordered not to look at me. Maybe once I start looking like a Prime they will start to notice me.

As we proceed along the corridor into the administrative district, I recall the offices and the layout of the place enough to know where I am, including where to go to see Kit and where Pure and I met. However, instead of taking the hallway to see Pure again, we keep straight, toward the medical unit. We pass the gift shop and cafeteria district and so too the full glass windows of the medical community. We walk until we hit new territory.

An impressive fountain engulfs a four-way intersection. In the middle of the basin is a massive statue depicting a strand of DNA. Instead of one giant ladder of DNA, there are arms clenching arms, hands embracing hands, and claws gripping claws, of many different types of Primes. All form a genetic ladder that reaches up the hallway to the ceiling. Underneath the statue lays a tiny plaque commemorating the icon: *We are many by familia, but one by Kingdom.* There is one thing that stands out to me most about the figure. In the crux of the strand where the two meet, there is what looks like a lion's arm embracing a cat's arm. I make a mental map of this area just in case I need to travel here alone. Lupine yells at me to rejoin them, and we continue to the West Tail of the capitol building.

Feather stops near Atrium Number Four and tells us he has to take care of a few things. He takes his leave, heading toward another intersection. I wave goodbye.

We head into a similar atrium where the same five large-screen displays hover above a small desk. However, unlike last time, a turtle Prime is sitting behind it, sorting through a high stack of folders and papers placed on his chair. Pure is standing besides a giant's chair beside the table, and across from him in an ordinary chair sits Brutus. They are all dressed formally and focused on the papers. They do not notice our arrival until the guard outside slams the door shut. The airlock secures itself with a massive sucking sound.

Pure stands and strolls toward me dressed in the same suit as before, except I can smell a fresh press and it smells perfectly clean. "Good morning, Ghent. You seem well. How was your first night in Kingdom?"

I know how bad it could have gone. "Weird for sure, sir. I didn't sleep very well and—"

He clears his throat. "Well, it's good to hear that we are treating you all right," he interrupts politely. "Now let's get started with the paperwork." He pinches a chair and pulls it out for me to sit in. Lupine takes a seat on the outside of the atrium, away from the table. Lupine pulls out his phone and starts reading something on the screen. "First," says Pure, "I need you to take a pledge." He motions over to a side door where a young fox Prime male holds a flag wrapped and neatly pressed in the shape of a triangle. The PLF flag is the same size and shape of the US flag, except there is a white triangle pointing down the center with a red outline behind a black backdrop. In the center of this triangle is a black rectangle parallel with the triangle pointing downwards. On top of the bundle is what looks like a makeup kit. When the fox Prime comes to the table and sets down the bundle in front of Pure, without saying a word or looking at me or Pure, he opens the case up to reveal a black ink sponge and a washcloth from his side pocket. He hands me both of them and then walks back to his position.

Pure unfolds the cloth and lays out the flag onto the table. He presses down and irons out the wrinkles in the flag and then straightens it out to match the sides of the table perfectly. He takes the ink pad and tests it out with his thumb. "When a soldier is initiated into the PLF they place their print upon their own flag as a symbol of your inclusion into the PLF." He puts the case in front of me under the rectangle. "So, hold up your non-dominant hand."

I raise my hand, and Pure also raises his, perpendicular to mine. It is scarred, and tiny pieces of his leathery palm are missing. "Now take your dominant hand and press down on the ink pad." I do exactly as he tells me. The ink feels wet like paint. "Now place your hand onto the square to mark your imprint." I press down on the silky canvas. I feel like the ink isn't the only thing seeping from my palms as I press down onto the flag. "Now keep it there while I recite the oath."

I take my last breath in as a US citizen.

He inhales my final breath. "I Ghent Sparrow..." I begin to repeat every word he says. "...a human civilian ex-pat of the United States, do solemnly swear to serve the Prime Liberation Force. I am sworn to uphold all Prime laws, defend against injustice, and repel foreign or domestic attacks on Primes."

The ink begins to dry on my hand as it sticks to the flag. I feel like every word I say makes me take one step further away from my country.

"I am to obey my alpha designated to me by the Zodiac." I quickly glance at Lupine, who is sitting down and frowning at his phone as he scrolls down. "And follow their orders without question even in defiance to my personal beliefs or species."

Somehow, I feel like I've made a huge mistake.

"I will rise to any occasion and succeed in any mission, even if it costs me my life."

This might just kill me.

"So help me."

I look up at Pure, who nods at me to repeat the final sentence. I need to say it.

"So help me."

He puts his right hand down and instructs me to lift my hand off the flag slowly. I peel back my skin off the flag and see my handprint on the flag put squarely inside the center of the square. He neatly folds the flag back up exactly the size and shape it was given to him in. Then he doesn't even need to call over the fox Prime again to retrieve the flag.

Pure then takes the stack of papers on the chair and moves it over to the table. "We are sure of making history today here. Remember that, Ghent." He drums his fingers on the stack. "You are history, the first human to be in the PLF."

And maybe its last.

Brutus approaches from the side and raises his hand. "Sir, I have a concern for many members of the Zodiac."

Pure peers at Brutus. "I'll allow it."

"They doubt the fidelity of this whole thing. They don't wish to accept this kid as a Prime based on a couple of test results that could be easily manipulated."

"All right." He shifts in his seat. "I figured one of them would bring this up. That is why I brought a special someone with me." He pushes one of a set of buttons beneath the desk.

After a minute or two, Kitsune appears in her doctor's coat.

"Kitsune, can you please update me on your findings?"

Was she researching the samples I gave? I don't know if it's still the adrenaline wearing off or the fact I am being examined like a rat that makes me squirm.

She reaches down into her lab coat and pulls out a notepad filled with doctoral scribbles and medical jargon, then flips to a page in the middle. She takes a deep breath. "Well..." She thinks for a couple seconds. "...after taking Ghent's blood from last night, I decided to do some experiments. I looked at his blood cells and found that under stress, the cells' DNA can shift into a...well..." She seems to be struggling to search for a word. "More Primal genetic code."

"I did some further tests with this and was able to turn his blood cells into Primal blood types. So theoretically, if all of his cells can turn into Primal blood types, then it is possible for his body to adjust."

I squirm just thinking about every cell in my body changing simultaneously and turning me into a different species.

"After I turned them into a P-Blood type, I let them be for a couple of hours without stress, and when I came back to them, ninety-nine percent of the cells had reverted back to their original state." Well, at least I know I could potentially shift back if they changed me.

"All right." Pure claps his hands, reassured. "Now unless there are further questions, I will inform Ghent how to fill out these forms." Brutus's look shifts from second-guessing to a level of admiration of the strange creature I am.

Pure leads me through several stages of paperwork and immigration forms. The process takes over two hours to complete given the complications with my past and my race. During this time Lupine pulls his chair alongside Kit as they talk about people I don't know. They chat while the turtle Prime, Pure, and I fill out the forms. My signature and date devolve into scribbles after the twentieth line.

On each page and before each signature, Pure describes every single aspect of what each page states. On occasion, the turtle Prime clarifies where Pure slips up. Nothing seems to be missed, nothing left uncovered, and I just go along with him, even though I know how much I shouldn't be willing to sign my life away. With Pure next to me, he has a sense of control and calm, a sense of welcome. He is someone I could ask for help. It's true that I am helping them, so it is only polite that he does, but I also realize he doesn't have to act so cordially.

In all my life, I never had such importance put on me. I am sitting inches from the leader of the Prime Liberation Force, the man who defeated the US government battle after battle, and the man who single-handedly saved the US during World War III. What would have happened yesterday if I said no yesterday to his offer? I would be a nobody, but with each of these signatures, I am closer to being someone who can actually contribute to a group, be a part of the closest thing I've had to friends ever in my life. Travel to places I would have never dreamed about, to finally find out who I am. Yes, *that* would make anything worth it.

Pure brandishes the final piece of paper from the last folder. "Boy, that was one hell of a session. I guess if being the leader of the PLF doesn't suit me I would make a great bureaucrat," he jokes heartedly. "Anyway, thank you for joining us today, Shella." The turtle Prime bows her head and with her cane walks away. I've never seen an old Prime before. I wonder how old she might be. I know Primes age quicker than humans in the beginning of their life, which made them appealing to manufacture as soldiers, maybe she kept aging at that rate and never slowed down.

Pure motions to Brutus. "All right, Brutus, it's your turn to speak on behalf of the PLF."

"Thank you, sir. All right, Ghent, this document in front of you is the most important single piece of paper you may ever sign in your lifetime. This document states legally that you are a citizen of the PLF, and you have all the rights and are legally bound to our laws. This also states that you are to serve in the PLF until your service is completed and that Lupine, who will also sign, will be your alpha and be in charge of you, and finally I will be overseeing Lupine to make sure that he is following protocol."

Pure consults Brutus. "That's asking a lot. I'm sure Gores will also keep a close eye on our best," he peeks over to Lupine, "and yet more devious, operative." He picks up the pen and hands it to me.

This is the point of no return. If I sign this, I will become a soldier of the PLF. I do want to spend time with the PLF. I want to feel safe around Lupine and everyone, but I can't let go of the worry and doubt that Pantheon instilled into my mind last night about those who don't want me here.

The pen is nudged by Brutus a little closer to me. "Do you have any other questions before you sign?"

I take a moment of deep reflection. All the details of the operation are on hold till I become a Prime. I have to go on faith. I am assured safety by the PLF. I will forgo everything that I ever worked for. I will delete myself from the world I know and enter into a new world where no one knows me, no one knows of my past, what I did, whom I know. A new life is ahead of me, a new beginning to a story that may have turbulence and suffering, but a reward that is well worth that effort.

I slowly pick up the pen. I put the pen onto the paper. The ink soaks into the paper. I quickly scribble my name on the page and drop the pen. As the pen hits the desk, I feel the weight of an entire world fall upon me.

Pure is resting his hand on my shoulder. "Congratulations on joining the PLF!" He smacks me on the back and I nearly fall forward and hear my spine readjust. "I am very proud of you, Ghent; I hope that we will form a very close relationship."

Well, Pure, I just hope that you can keep your promises and you know what you're doing.

He stretches his maw open and roars loudly. "Man, doing this sure takes a lot out of you," he yawns, "and I imagine that the rest of you are beat as well. We will conclude this session here. Tomorrow you will be starting your training under Lupine, so Ghent, please enjoy your time here and keep that head held high." He picks up the papers and his tablet and heads up the backstairs.

We all get up out of our seats and pick up our belongings as soon as Pure is out of sight. At the exit, Brutus stops me. "It was a pleasure to meet you, Ghent. I hope that you and Lupine get along."

You and me both.

He studies Lupine, who reaches for the handle. "It seems like Ghent will make a great addition to your team." He seems like he genuinely means this, and I'm curious what he thinks I can offer.

Lupine opens the door for him, and we take our leave, but before that, I look back into the atrium and wonder if I have everything with me, or if maybe I left something behind. Here we are, Lupine and me, soldier and commander.

Feather is awaiting our return outside of the atrium door leaning against the wall on his phone.

"I thought you had something to do?" I ask him, surprised to see him.

He looks up and then shoves his phone away. "I did them. I got those done, had a nice lunch, spoke with a couple of friends, and walked all the way back here. You guys are the ones that took forever."

Speaking of which, how much time passed while we were there? "What time is it?"

He looks back at his phone. "Twelve-thirty." We were there for four and a half hours! My stomach grumbles, I guess my body took a backseat to my mind during that whole ordeal.

We start to travel to the parking lot, Lupine with my papers under his arm, and hands on his phone texting away. He turns the corner to arrive at the elaborate fountain in the center when a Prime runs straight into Lupine, knocking the files onto the floor. I immediately take a step back, and Feather grabs his gun, readying it to fire.

"Hey!" Amongst all the paper is a cat Prime, about half Lupine's size, athletic build, flat chested, effeminate and coated in autumn fur. He is wearing a simple white t-shirt and cargo pants. Dog tags are pierced into his pointed ears, and several bracelets adorn his wrists, and another rings the end of his tail.

Lupine looks down at all the papers on the floor. "Feline, what are you doing?"

He seems oblivious, grinning as if he meant to run into him.

Feather puts his gun away and scolds him. "This isn't the time, Feline, we are on..."

He doesn't care. "Have you heard of the human that is...?" He notices me scared shitless. As soon as he sees my face his defined irises widened like he was ready to pounce on a mouse, he opens his mouth almost to pause for a moment as if to say something and pauses before leaping at me. "Right behind you!" He sidesteps Lupine and skips up to me. "It's so nice to meet you! My name is..."

"If you don't shut up," Lupine approaches him from behind, "and get back to your dorm in the next ten seconds..."

"What's your name?" He completely blows off Lupine's order.

It is nice though to see a happy, excited face after being surrounded by crabby people and tense situations. "I'm Ghent. And I take it that you are Feline."

"Five," says Lupine. "Four."

Feline tries to fit as much as he could in five seconds. "It's nice to meet you! Say we should get to know each other later; I've always wanted to talk..."

"Zero."

Lupine attempts to grab Feline in a headlock, Lupine manages to get his arms around him but right before Lupine's arms can touch his neck, he slips out of Lupine's grasp as if his neck muscles narrow and he slides out of Lupine's zone of control before Lupine even has a chance to go for another hold.

He spins around, farts a raspberry to Lupine and waves to me. "I will see you later Ghent! Nice to meet you!"

Damn, he is one agile cat.

Lupine growls and looks like he is about to bark at him, but restrains himself with a grunt and bends down to pick up the papers on the floor. While collecting them he pauses over a stamped document with the headline 'Living Situation'. He scans the document quickly and grabs the page with his hands and crumples it up and shoves it in his pocket with a grumble.

Feather comes up from behind him and pinches the paper from his pocket. "Why did you crumple this. It's an official PLF document." He uncrumples it and scans it over. Once he finishes with the final period he caws a bit with laughter and nudges me on the shoulder. "Well shit I guess you are going to be living next to Pure with the big shots in Highpoint kid."

Next to Pure? I might be his neighbor, that's a real head scratcher. "He is trying to keep me safe, I guess." I scratch my head and notice that I haven't showered in a while and my hair is all greasy.

Lupine swipes the page from Feather's hand. "Or he's intentionally trying to piss me off."

Well, if he is trying to do that he's succeeded.

Feather shrugs "Anyway, it's better than living with Primes in a boot camp like we did."

Thank God that Pure knows better than to keep me in his lion pit where he knows he can watch me and make sure I am not harmed. "Was it bad living in the barracks?"

Feather finishes with his phone. "It was fine I guess, lots of grown men Primes all in fighting with each other to be the alpha, but Lupine and I had no problem with that. Lupine, you remember living in the barracks?"

"Remember what? The constant sharing your shit? The constant noise of your bunkmate jerking off at one in the morning?"

"That was *a one-time* Lupine; I can't count how many times I had to..."

Out of a hallway leading out just before the gate, Feline reappears before Lupine and almost runs into him again. "You talking about that time in the barracks where Lupine and Kit-"

Lupine puts his hands around his mouth and leans into his face. "Get the hell out of here you runt!"

From behind Feline, I feel a slight tremor beneath my feet, and a shadow approaching behind him.

"Slipped out of your hands again?" From the hallway, a gorilla Prime, black as coal and a voice of iron jumps out. He is taller than Lupine and as human-like as Stall. His face convenes the human gene in most Primes, but his body is akin to Borne's, built, massive, and dominating. *Gores Hominidae: Sagittarius Alpha* is positioned level to his pocket protector army jacket. This is the man who orders Lupine around, well he is sure scary as fuck enough to do it. He looks cross-armed at Lupine whose tail immediately falls to the floor.

"You also told me that disobedience isn't obtained, it's taught." Lupine says.

"Through example, and so far, how have you been setting an example for Ghent?"

"I am an amazing role model," Lupine claims wholeheartedly, "you should know that."

I decide to introduce myself to him. I feel like he should know I don't mean any harm if he knows my name and sees the uniform. Maybe this is an excellent chance to examine how Primes introduce each other. "Hello, Gores sir, it's nice to meet you."

When I offer my hand, he grabs my arm with his massive hands and pulls me inward, twisting my arm behind my back and holding me in a vice-like grip.

"Didn't you learn from your mother not to trust strangers?" He lectures to me as I gaze at his badge displayed on his chest fastened with a gold pin. I knew then that this must be Lupine's commander. Just by feeling the squeeze he is putting on my arm I can already tell that he is ten times stronger than Lupine.

I attempt to break free from his grasp but he continues to hold onto me. He picks up my arm and looks at it, then transfers his gaze to scan the rest of me, as if examining me like a rack of meat. I hated it when people mentioned my parents. There was no graceful way of telling people I was an orphan. "No mother to tell me how to behave, sir."

"Well, consider this a lesson free of charge." He lets my arm go and spins me back into Lupine; I bump against his chest as he pushes me back between us. "Well you best be getting him ready Lupine, you have a lot of work ahead of you."

Lupine gazes at me and groans. "Why weren't you at the meeting this morning?"

"Pure instructed me to mobilize some of our units to quell some unrest among Evols, our favorite pussy cat is riling them up with that announcement made yesterday."

I assume they are talking about Pantheon.

"Did we at least track down where he is hiding out?"

He shrugs his massive arms. "Thought we did, but when we sent a SWAT squad down there all we found was an empty storage unit."

"Did you check the gutters? I'm sure he's lost somewhere in the sewers."

"I just need some nip to get him out." I figure they must be talking indirectly about Pantheon to avoid any eavesdroppers.

"I heard Brutus has some if you need it, or else you could go kick around his kittens for a bit till he shows up."

"Maybe I will, maybe stop by Tails to get something to eat."

"Sounds good, I might join you as soon as I drop this pup off."

Gores moves along with Feline back into the hallway; we just came through. Feline turns around and walks backward, eyeing me. I wonder what is up with him. He seems like a ray of happiness among a harsh swamp. He may be a little ditzy, but he made Feather and I smile, and that is exactly what I needed right now.

. . .

98

Feather says the road to Highpoint will take thirty minutes, but by the way, he is driving; we will be there in twenty. Lupine is typing away at his phone like a testimonial recorder.

I swing my legs so they dangle from the bench. "What you texting about?"

He keeps his focus. "I am texting officials to keep you safe and all your documents in order."

I did notice that all of this moving around Kingdom and the base seemed flawless; I guess Lupine was acting behind the scenes to set up meetings and order people around to make this work, all from his cell phone. "Well... I just want to thank you for making this possible."

He suddenly stops texting. "I am just doing my job, and I take pride in doing it well." He continues tapping away at his screen.

It sucks not hearing more from Lupine, but at least he is acknowledging me and paying attention to me. Also I did just meet him yesterday, and I can tell he is not quite a people person, maybe if I find something that he likes, or we find something relatable to talk about.

The car suddenly comes to a halt as Lupine perks up his ears as I hear some commotion outside of the van. A sliding door opens up in the front of the truck, and I see Feather reach back and motion Lupine forward. It is only large enough to poke his head through. Through the open door, I hear shouting and chanting. I walk up to the door and listen in from the side.

"How the fuck did they find out?" Lupine says.

"Pantheon told them to come here." Feather says.

I tug gently on Lupine's tail. "What's happening?" He jerks backward and shoves me to the side with his foot.

Feather pulls out his phone. "He sent a message over Fang," he starts to read from his phone, "The Zodiac has chosen to surrender its security and allow a human to join the PLF. This foolish and irrational choice by Pure will lead to the collapse of the PLF from within, creating weaknesses in our army, which will surely lead to our defeat against the US army."

"God damnit, I thought Brutus dealt with him." Lupine leaves the door and opens his phone up as well to read the post.

"He did, Brutus replied. 'The new recruit will not harm our security, there is no security threat nor is there any reason to fear. The Zodiac has the utmost support of Pure and faith in Primes to welcome our new recruit, and will not let radical Primes carry out such accusations without repercussion."

"If I were him, I would just tell Pantheon that if he doesn't hold his tongue, I will cut it off." Lupine claims.

I head over to Feather and look over at his phone. "What's Fang?"

Feather clicks it off as soon as I peak over. "It's the biggest social media platform in the PLF." He turns his attention to Lupine. "He is obviously using this to attract new people to be Evols." Feather elaborates.

I feel like I should contribute, even though I don't know anything about Prime politics. "Why wouldn't Pure announce me joining the PLF instead of having Pantheon do it?"

"No idea. Maybe Pantheon beat him to the punch on it." Feather answers as best as he can.

That doesn't make sense though that Pantheon found out about me before Pure had an option to tell the PLF that I was joining. There had to be someone within the PLF that leaked the information.

Lupine stands on top of the bench and reaches for a latch on the top of the van. "I know that, but he wasn't planning on one thing."

I head up to the slot with Feather. "And that is?"

"What I'm willing to do to do my job; Feather, take the wheel and move to the gate on my signal." He gets his gun out and climbs to the top of the van. Now I know Lupine is an experienced soldier and a protector of the people, well at least I think he is.

Feather pokes his beak through the slot and looks up. "What the fuck are you doing!"

Lupine climbs out of the van and gets on top of the hood, and he motions Feather forward. I peek over Feather's shoulder and see a crowd of Primes gathering in front of the gate with 'Highpoint' displayed in silver fencing. The car approaches the gate, and the congregation begins to block the way. Is Feather going to ram the protesters? I mean I trust Lupine and Feather to get me there but I worry that they are going to get some people seriously hurt. I look around to find something to brace myself against. Feather notices me and tells me to buckle my seatbelt and keep my back from the wall of the truck.

He cups his hands together to shout at the crowd with all of his might. "Move the fuck out of our way now! Under official PLF order!"

I start to hear banging and the truck starts to sway left and right. I am just trying to hold onto my seat. Please let the walls hold. From up top, I hear the cocking of a handgun and a round fired. Immediately the banging and shaking stops and the shouting of anger turns into shouts of panic.

"The next round will be at anyone who gets in my way!" Lupine screams at the top of his lungs to the crowd.

I can't hear the muffled shouts or what is going on outside but I feel safer they are no longer touching the van.

I notice Feather through the windshield which has sustained some blunt damage that cracked the glass, we pass into a barricade as several riot police remove wooden logs to make way for the van. They replace the barrier as they cage us in between the rioters and the army.

"You stupid mutt, you know how many sensors just went off at that gunshot! The whole fucking city police is going to swarm here now!" I hear a Prime climb up onto the top of the van. He is shouting just as loudly at Lupine.

Lupine shouts back at the Prime. "Well then maybe you can do your job and disperse these fuckers!"

"The police can't arrest all of these people they haven't done anything wrong! You are the one who shot a gun off in a crowd of riled civilians!"

"What did you want us to do? Take the kid out and parade him in front of everyone!"

"You should have contacted us via the radio and called for assistance like you are told to do!"

"Don't get your tail caught in a knot. I will hear about it later, but right now I want to dump this kid off at this address. Where is it exactly?"

"I will make sure you hear from the Police Commissioner for this. It's down the road two blocks and then turns a right at the third block; it's the apartments at the end!"

Lupine starts to climb back up onto the van. "See you can do your job as a GPS, now do your job as a soldier of Leo and get rid of these fucking ferals!"

The van stops at our destination and Feather swings open the door. I jump down to the road and look around at Highpoint. Highpoint appears to be a series of streets laid out in the formation of the sun with a large roundabout connecting them all together. In the center of the roundabout lays a park with vibrant oak trees, a polished and expansive playground complete with a wooden fortress, and several sets of slides and swing sets. The streets are freshly paved, and not a single piece of trash can be seen: even the gutters are swept clear of any debris. The buildings that line both sides are high-end condos and full houses delicately built and modernized with solar panels, glass balconies, and a perfectly trimmed front lawn with an ornate fountain in the center of the roundabout driveway. These Hollywood-style mansions give off a glow of radiance and status that I've only seen in magazines and movies, a light that creates a sense of power over someone like me who could never see myself *not* living inches from another person's apartment. The van parks out in front of a condo complex with multiple condos that form a three-sided box with the front open up to a parking lot.

"This is where I'll live?" I am agape at how cool this is!

"Apparently...a really nice place too, just a few blocks from Pure's mansion." Feather points toward a hill, atop which sits a mansion.

"You mean that giant house up the hill?"

"Yeah, it's where he and his family live." I didn't know that Pure had a family. I wonder what kind of life that is for his kids to have Pure as a father, or for his wife to have Pure as a husband.

Feather notices Lupine is pouting as he checks the address over and over, verifying, again and again, to be absolutely sure that he is confident that his life is being unfair to him. "Don't tell me you're jealous, Lupine."

"Me, jealous?" He is clearly cynical. "No...it's just after you were given a sweat lodge of sweaty animals to live in for your first few years in the PLF...seeing this makes me just feel like my work is surely appreciated."

"Well, at least he won't have to live with you, Lupine." He tries to look positively on his obviously negative situation.

"Pure isn't that much of an asshole to do that," he agrees.

We walk up to the address, 201 8th Ray Drive, and climb a set of stairs to a balcony of four different doors connecting to four separate condos. From the corner of the balcony, I see a security camera blinking a green light. Almost tempted to wave high to the security guard watching this. The bottom of the raised condo is supported by beams that must prevent damage from earthquakes and flooding. There is a key on the third door with a tag reading *Sparrow*. An alarm de-activates as I key the lock and swing open the door.

I step into spacious living quarters. Wooden floors with a thick red and black pattern rug hold up bookcases full of books and elegant dressers, while a large TV hangs on the wall above a leather couch. A glass wall with half-open drapes welcomes light into the room and allows the bird resting on the balcony to enter through the screen. Light lamps are arranged, each with their own sense of modern art; abstract shapes create my own future in front of me.

A full stainless steel and marble kitchen greets us, with fresh groceries on the island. An assortment of apples, oranges, pears, bananas, and even a cantaloupe await, along with vegetables, cans of different soups, some ground beef, and an assortment of cooking spices, oils, and everything else I would need to feed an army. A clean stove aligns the right wall, while the left holds the oak dining table and chairs.

In one of those chairs sits a shark Prime—Finn, from the Zodiac.

Lupine is surprised by Finn's arrival, while I am at awe by this Prime in person. "Finn, sir, what are you doing here?"

What I saw of him on the monitor was only the start of this creation; his gills on the side of his neck are covered by an apparatus strapped on the back, which filters water through tubes. The device lights up with every cycle and is split into two parts with each part resting on either side of his back fin. His legs, which are a split tailfin leading to thin feet, give his skin a sleek and slippery feel. His hands and arms are human in proportion but with webbed hands and sharp fins protruding from his upper arms. He is inhaling through tubes inserted into his shark-like nose and looking at us with his human-like eyes. He opens his mouth to speak, and I see a full rack of tiny sharp teeth, all connecting and aligning with each other correctly. Under his gills I can see a badge with his name polished to a golden shine, *Finn Lamnidae: PLF Pisces Alpha: Zodiac.*

"Pure would have been here, but he is busy dealing with Pantheon and the public, and Brutus is busy dealing with Evol riots around the city. So he told me to meet you here. About that gunshot..." His voice does not match his physique as it sounds squeaky as if a dog toy was stuck in his throat. At the end of his sentence, another cycle of water rushes through his machine.

Lupine's tail droops down like a dog that got caught in the trash. "It was within policy. Besides, I didn't shoot anyone—it was a warning shot."

"The public didn't know that. What if someone had a gun and fired at you, at Ghent?" Finn appears to be getting upset with Lupine. I mean, he is right. What if someone did have a gun and Lupine was shot.

"Look, Pure wanted him *safely* at Highpoint and I got him here. Mission accomplished."

Finn just sighs and gets off the chair and walks awkwardly to the couch. "Lupine, I expect a full report in Brutus's or Gore's box tomorrow, or I will have to put your sorry ass on a podium and you can explain to the PLF why you shot at an angered mob." He points at Lupine and turns his attention to me. "Now where is our little Ghent?"

I am admiring the bookshelf; there is a collection of Prime history books and several old classics written by humans. "Here, sir." I don't feel safe shaking his... fins...after what Gores did to my arm back in the barracks. "I have to say this is pretty nice for you guys to give me such great accommodations."

"You will also be allowed to use Pure's private training rooms and recreational facilities on the compound. Lupine, you are also allowed access as long as your entry has something to do with Ghent. So no uncovered day shifts to the spa to hit on bitches, okay?"

Feather turns away from Finn and heads down a hallway on the right. I feel like Pure also put me here so I can get used to life in the PLF and to make me as comfortable as possible.

"So I guess I'm a prisoner of luxury then."

Finn gets up from his seat. "You agreed to this. Just remember this is for your own good. You heard the crowd outside. All those Primes want you out of the PLF, either alive or dead."

"I am fully aware of this." I've been told it so many times that it's starting to feel diminished by the possibility that they are trying to scare me to stay at Highpoint.

He approaches me near the door. "Glad you know that."

Lupine seems a little bitter about this whole situation. "It's wonderful that *he* is well protected and comfortable."

"What, do you want him to be put with you? Because if you secretly wish for that, I'd forget about it, because Pure won't allow it with your record."

"I knew my failures would pay off eventually," Lupine mumbles to himself while looking out the window.

"All right, I will leave you three to your devices. Ghent, if you need anything, just dial star two on the phone here, star nine for an emergency, and star six for Lupine. Any questions?"

"No, sir. Thank you for letting me stay here."

"No problem. Good night and I will see you around."

Finn heads to the door to leave. I notice as he grasps the door handle to open it that the knob slips under his slick skin. He wraps his hands in his undershirt to get a better grip. I go for the door and open it for him. He is surprised by this and thanks me once more before making his leave.

I close the door and take a deep breath of the clean air inside. "I can't believe I am going to stay here."

Feather reappears. "No shit—this place is amazing."

"At least I get to leave my house whenever I want," Lupine remarks.

"Didn't you hear Finn? It's dangerous out there." I collapse on the couch. I sink in it comfortably and rest my head against a plush pillow. "I mean even the couch is more comfortable than my bed back home." I close my eyes for the first time all day and feel like I'm able to relax my body at least.

"Don't get used to it, you spoiled runt. Tomorrow morning we will start training, and by the time I'm done with you, the ground outside will be as comfortable as that couch."

I just want him to leave; I've had enough of his orders and complaints today. "Don't you have some paperwork to cover your ass with?"

He growls at me and clenches his teeth before sulking to the door. "Six o'clock sharp tomorrow. Be up and ready."

Feather follows. "Say, Lupine, do you need some help writing your public apology? I can help you with that."

Right before Lupine slams the door: "Another word and I break that beak."

Finally, silence. The whole condo is mine, and I am entirely alone. For the first time in my life, I am living comfortably. I've gotten this far, I just need to learn to become as strong as a Prime, learn their culture, and adapt to life in the PLF. That is my next goal, and now that I feel like I have a decent grasp on my situation, I can finally relax. I may not know what is going to happen tomorrow, next week, next month. I just have to go with the flow now and listen to Lupine and Pure's orders. The more I am obedient to Pure, the sooner I can find out what he is hiding, and find out where I came from, and more importantly, who my parents are. Who knows, maybe I will like it here, enjoy Prime life, and maybe become someone here. I spread out on the couch and flick on the TV.

"Breaking News" is sprawled on the screen with the icon of PON, Prime Official News.

A cat Prime reporter appears on the screen. She is right outside Highpoint. The crowd is gone, replaced with cop cars and armed military scouting the area. "The protests in front of Highpoint are over, and the groups have been dispersed by PLF officials through the use of tear gas. Witnesses claim protesters have attempted to scale the gates, push past security, and there were rumors of vehicles being brought with the intention to run through the gate's entrance. With none dead and a couple having minor injuries, the PLF has yet to release a statement regarding the human that has joined the PLF. We have phoned multiple sources, and all have been hung up on."

I felt bad that someone had gotten injured, but maybe it serves them right for making such a stink about me. I am just a human kid—well, I was a human kid, I guess. I switch to a different station, PNN, where Pure stands behind a podium looking as proud and collected as ever while gripping the sides of his podium with his claws.

"The PLF will not stand for this level of violence against a harmless human willing to join our armed forces."

Physically harmless yes, but to the PLF's image I've done more harm in one day than the United States could ever do.

Limits

"**I** will huff, and I will puff this fucking door down unless you open it in the next thirty seconds!"

I open my eyes to a countdown timer running in my mind: 30, 29, 28... I reluctantly jump out of the most comfortable cloud I could ever sleep on to grab my pants and throw on a white T-shirt in the closet while running to the door. "I'm coming!"

Lupine is just about to knock again as he almost hits me in the head as I open the door for him. He rudely strides in with a plastic topped tray with his cigarette box on top under his arm.

"You're not ready?"

Damn, I've already disappointed him, and we haven't even started training yet. "It's 5:30. You said to be ready by 6:00—sorry if I was *late*." Of course, I probably wouldn't have gotten ready by then anyway since my alarm wasn't set. I couldn't figure out how to set the alarm last night, so I hoped that my brain knew better. Not the way I wanted to start training with Lupine, disappointing him.

"The first rule about training with me..." He rudely enters the condo. "...be early for everything. You haven't eaten anything in a while, so I got you some food from the cafeteria." He slides a tray with a plastic top over it onto the table. "Eat it within ten minutes, shower for ten, and it will take us ten minutes to get there and inside the training grounds." Someone is strangely punctual considering I can't imagine he got the best sleep of his life last night. He seems a bit more up and at 'em than he was last night when he left.

I thank him for the food then take fine china out of the drawer for scrambled eggs, bacon, and a piece of toast. It looks a lot better than everyday cafeteria food—he must have gotten it from Pure's cafeteria, meaning he stopped and ate there before coming here. "So, what are you going to teach me today?"

"Depends on what you know, but I can tell you by the time you are as good as me you will be able to kill a man with that fork." He points at the fork in my hand. "To start, I want you to remind me how I said you were going to feel after today." I look at him strangely. "You heard me. I want you to repeat the exact same words I used."

Umm, I don't remember. He said a lot before he left yesterday and I was exhausted. "Something about that couch being as comfortable as the ground?"

"No." He pulls out his cell phone and opens up a notepad. "By the way, that's twenty pushups when we get there."

"Just because I don't remember what you said yesterday?"

"Just remember everything I say, and you will never have to do a pushup in your life."

I wash down my last bite with some tap water and head into the bathroom suite to clean up. As I rinse off in the expansive shower and the water drips from my head, I take a look at my hands pooling water, and I think to myself, *What exactly am I?* As I swipe soap over my arms, legs, and chest, I try to understand just what inside my body lets me transform. There are no mysterious markings, no symbols to press, chants to say. My body carries no instructions, and I bear no memories regarding my Primal side. I don't have a spot for a tail, slits in my arms for wings, or ears where my hair is. All I have is that scar on my neck, and even then it doesn't look like anything but a few lines going down from my neck to my shoulder blades. This body is particular; this body is unique but useless until I find the key to unlock its potential.

I finish drying off, shrug my uniform on, and brush my hair down before opening the door to a chilling wind through the main window in the living room. Lupine is smoking while gazing out onto the view below.

"How do I look, sir?"

"Weird, but it will work." He throws his cigarette outside and closes the screen.

Says the talking wolfman.

. . .

We get out of the car in an empty parking lot. The sun has just risen from behind the dome where the training facility is located. No guards are patrolling any part of Highpoint, and there are no cars other than ours, so we walk in silence toward the entrance.

The doors into the facility are automatic sliding doors adorned with polished stainless steel. We follow a path that creates T intersections when it hits the empty desk. Ceiling fans with lights hang from the glass ceiling, and artist recreations of various PLF battles adorn the walls. Below them rest ornate lounge chairs and couches and stained-glass coffee tables so spit-shined clean that I can see every dust particle that meanders to rest upon them. Either we are the first people to use this place today after it was cleaned or we are the first people to have ever used it.

We head to the left toward the training grounds. Each room we pass has various exercise purposes: one has a swimming pool, one has a bunch of athletic testing machines, one is full of treadmills, one is full of medicine balls, and one is a spa. Too bad that one is closed.

Having grown up a dirt-poor orphan with a miserable allowance of ten dollars a week, seeing these buildings, the room I am staying in, and all the service provided to me, it's all a whirlwind of a life that was forever beyond my reach, but now is right in front of my eyes. It's not just my body that might be changing; it's my eyes, as they have finally seen a rose-tinted world of the upper class that I finally see as the world giving me a chance.

We reach the end where double doors let us into a small entrance hall that has two locker rooms to each side for the two sexes. Beyond the locker, doors open to an enormous gymnasium where a half-dozen exercise machines line the walls as do racks with hundreds of weights, exercise mats, dumbbells, weight rods—everything we could ever need to exercise any part of the body.

In the center is a slightly raised circular platform with a line of white paint dividing its circumference. The rest of the floor is made out of waxed wood and painted with various boxes that designate areas for specific exercise routines. The exercise plans are neatly put on the wall in a basket, and as we walk toward the center circle, I realize just how large some of these machines that are used by Primes actually are. There are some that even Borne could not apply, and some that just say "Reserved for Pure" on them, which are beyond any exerciser's imagination.

"Wow!" I spin around to look at everything this room has to offer. "Does anyone else use this?"

Lupine drops his coat over a balancing beam nearby. "This is Pure's personal training facility and he doesn't need to train at six in the morning."

No wonder why he is built as he is. Even after the war, I think it is just built into him to exercise consistently to keep his physique. I mean if you sacrifice that much for something it would be a waste to let it go.

"All right, take off your jacket and place it on the stack of mats along with anything you don't want to be broken." Lupine takes off his jacket to reveal a pure white wifebeater, his dog tags stuffed in the collar. His arms are a thick combination of muscles and fur that blend together to form a gray and black creation made from years of training and strength building. His chest is a plate of furred armor. When he removes his shoes his feet are elongated by the bridge and his toes are not actually longer than mine, but his heel is placed several inches above the base of his foot, and a bone connecting his ankle to his shin is slightly longer. "Also, take a mat while you are at it and pull it to the center."

I find a blue training mat and pull it over. It doesn't weigh that much, and the polished floors make it slide effortlessly across the room. "All right, we will start out with those pushups you owe me."

I look up at him, a little dumbfounded. I mean, I don't remember how to do a pushup, and I don't know if I can even do one. I might as well fake it. I feel like he will get less mad if I try to do it instead of me just saying I can't. I put the mat down and fake doing a pushup with my back curved and my hands facing outwards.

"Oh, don't tell me you can't even do a simple pushup." He is saddened by my pathetic form, but I imagine he could have added more pushups if I told him I couldn't do them.

"I didn't have PE at my school." I totally did, but I skipped it a lot and went to do homework in the library instead. All the jocks would always poke fun at me by pointing out how weak I was, so I always had a chronic health condition to make up, which I looked up in the library.

"Well, I guess we will need to put ten more on there to practice."

He squats down, pushes down on my back with his foot to put me in the proper position, and releases me. "There, that's how you do them."

I barely manage to get the fifteen done before my arms give way, and my palms become numb. I try for a sixteenth, but my arms give way and I flop to the floor.

Lupine only sighs and puts his hands on his face. "Well, it's a start, I guess. I'll just add fifteen to your tab. Now get up."

"Want me to shake my arms out and finish them?" I feel like I should at least get my pushup debt out of the way, and I want to show him I am willing to work hard, despite my error this morning getting up.

"We will let your arms rest for now—no use overworking them. Now I want you to punch me in the face as hard as you can," he bluntly requests.

This seems like a setup. "Really? Hard as I can?" I mean, I hate him for making me do so many pushups but not that much. I also have an idea about what he can do to me, and I feel like if I stick my hand into that bear trap.

"Are you going to enjoy it?" he taunts.

"I don't want to hurt you," I joke.

"Sure." He stands still with his hands clenched behind his back like he knows I can't hit him. "Kick my ass, kid."

I move around him, and he tracks my movement: my feet, my hands, every part of my body is being monitored. I try to find an opening where he isn't watching my right hand, but I keep feeling like he knows that my right is going to swing, so I will try with my left. If I can hit Lupine on my first punch, I should earn some sort of respect from him, something that after my sorry excuse for a pushup I desperately need. I decide that just as his feet turn, I should swing. I find the moment, take a step forward, clench my fist, and aim for his nose. He ducks and grabs his left arm and folds his left arm under my arm like a snake around a tree branch. The amount of pressure he puts on my arm is almost enough to crack it. I fall to my knees, trying to get him to let go, but he only holds me by the arm and straightens out my arm with his.

"Thumb out—don't want it to break on contact." He waits for me to respond, but I don't. He meets my eyes. "Again." He lets go and keeps following my movements.

I take my thumb out just like he says and attempt to punch with the right. Again he coils around my arm and straightens it out. "Straighter at me."

I take a straight punch at his chest. This time, he blocks it with his hand and pulls me forward to straighten my arm. "Still not straight enough. That's what happens to you when you don't punch forward. Again."

I think I am disappointing him. If he shows me how to punch maybe I can mimic him. "Could you show me how to punch, so I know what I'm doing?"

"I see you learn by visual aids." He seems to accept my suggestion.

I cautiously approach him. "I guess I do..."

Within a blink, I feel a fist enter my stomach, knocking me back a foot and leaving my ass on the mat and my stomach back where I stood. The floor turns into a giant blur of tan and I feel my breakfast come back up my throat before I force it back down again.

"That's how you punch someone." He seems to have enjoyed that more than he should as he rubs his fist with his other hand and cracks a knuckle.

"Did you really have to hit so hard!" I feel like he is just about to kill me.

"I barely hit you." He laughs.

"Can you hit me a little lighter next time? I don't want to be bruised up at the start."

"Sorry, but you don't order me around here, kid. I am the one giving the orders. If you don't want to be hit, then dodge or block my attacks." He retakes his stance.

I need to move in a way that he can't predict. He seems to focus on my hands. If I can distract his eyes for one second and make them focus on something else, I can get him. Wait, he will try to grab my arm again like he did before, and he can only do so if my arm is far away from him, so he has room to grab it from the side or under. If I can get close to him and punch straight into him, I might have a chance to close the gap and use my feet as a distraction.

I rest my thumbs on the side of my palm, curled in a fist, and start out by moving the same distance as before, but before I swing my right arm, I take a quick step forward and use the momentum to make my arm go straight like I am pushing something forward. As soon as I move, he attempts to grab my arm but misses just enough for me to get my fist to make contact with his chest. I feel a surge within me. I can't believe it! I hit Lupine! Once my fist contacts his chest, I feel a surging pain in my arm like I just punched a wall. He is a robust, unmovable force, and my fist is a child running into a wall at full strength.

He takes a jump back as I lose balance and fall onto the mat. "That was better—not what I wanted, but an improvement. Do ten of those pushups and then head over to the punching bag."

Was that a grudging respect I heard in his voice? I feel pleased with myself. Well, I mean he probably would have followed my movements a lot more closely if I was an actual enemy, but I got a pass from him! I'm actually getting closer to achieving something.

Lupine pulls out a punching bag and its stand. I look at him in disbelief. "Why didn't you just pull the bag out before?

"You learn by visual aids, don't you? See, remembering what people say isn't hard."

"Understood, sir." I shake out my arms and head over to him.

He instructs me to practice punching while he watches. He regularly corrects my positioning, my feet, my shoulders, my hands. With every punch, with every single correction, I feel like I am getting closer, but I know somewhere deep inside my blistering hands and throbbing fingers that I have a long way to go.

"My arms feel like balloons." I sit down after...fifty...no, I think it was seventy. Eighty?

"Then you still have feeling left in them. Finish off those pushups and then take a break."

I try my best to finish them but right now my arms feel like there is nothing there, and when I try to hold weight with my arms I collapse. "I feel exhausted, I can barely move my arms, and I can't punch anymore." I tried, but it's just not working out.

"All right then, let's practice kicking."

"I have a feeling I won't be walking home."

"Don't worry." He grins with his sadistic smile. "By the end of this, you won't have any feeling at all."

I sluggishly drag my arms over to the punching bag. Lupine begins to teach me how to kick, and he demonstrates how to properly kick someone—well, at least it isn't me he is kicking.

"Oh, *now* you use the bag," I comment.

He swings the bag into my face. "I am only using the bag because if I kicked you, you would be sent to the ICU with ruptured organs and a broken ribcage."

That's reassuring. Does it mean we won't spar? I feel like I am going to be visiting Kit a lot more than I promised her.

"You are making him look like weakling, Lupine."

I turn around to see Kit walking up to us with a bag strapped over her shoulder. She isn't wearing her uniform or a doctor's coat; she is dressed in a casual red and black plaid button-up and a pair of black jeans.

"Kit, how the hell did you get in here?" Lupine holds the bag straight, so it doesn't hit him in the face.

"I'm part of your squad. I have the same access that you do."

That still doesn't explain why she is here. Unless she trains just like Lupine does, I don't see a reason her for being here. I kind of don't want her to see me fail to do simple pushups. "You coming to train here too?" I inquire.

"No, I'm here to make sure your mentor doesn't kill you."

He turns his attention to me. "Start kicking like I did, Ghent," orders Lupine. I begin to attempt to kick how he did before, and it's going well.

"And he's probably feeling more alive than ever."

"You aren't using your regimen on him, are you?" Kitsune asks, concerned.

"What else would I use?"

"He will be a puddle by the end of every day if you run him like Gores did on you." It's good to know someone is looking out for my well-being. "His body..."

"Well, if his body wants to survive it's going to need to turn into a Prime, and that's what Pure told me to do," he clarifies.

"Whatever. Just make sure that if he falls unconscious or starts puking blood I will be around." She takes out a thermos and hands it to me. I rush to it and start chugging. A sports drink but nothing designating it as one. Oh well, it tastes good whatever it is. Tastes like strawberries.

"Here's a drink for you to rehydrate, and here is a sweat rag. Don't exert yourself, and if you feel like you are going to faint, tell Lupine, and if he gives you shit, tell me."

"Thanks, Kit." I smile back.

"Don't tell me you're spoiling him too." He seems a bit jealous.

"It's your job to break him down. It's mine to put the pieces back together."

Kicking training continues for half an hour. I'm glad she stays. Kit keeps an eye on me while she does some work on her tablet on top of the mat where Lupine sat. I feel like every single tick of the clock is a kick, and every minute is a kick to my head. I can barely see through the sweat, and the blisters that are sure to form on my legs are itching like mad. However, nothing compares to the fact that when I fall to the ground, and for the first time in my life, I cannot stand. "I'm done. Can you drag me wherever you need me next?"

Lupine is doing leg presses on a nearby machine, and my question interrupts his text messaging. "While you are lying down there, do those ten pushups you owe me."

I'm tapped. "I can't... I can't move a single muscle."

He pauses for a second and smiles at me. "Good. Now let's go take a shower then go over some basic gun training."

I don't know if there is a God out there, but thank you. "Good, 'cause I smell." I clamber up to my knees and then my legs; I feel like they are both asleep. I walk like my feet are made of metal over to the wall, which I lean on as I shuffle to the locker rooms. Kit sees us wrap up and lets us know she will be in a small clinic built into the building.

Out of earshot of Lupine, Kit whispers to me, "If he puts a bullet in you let me know and I will take it out and put it into him."

We enter the locker room, which is similar to those at the barracks but has much clearer floors. The lockers there are more substantial and fewer. There is an area off to the left that is locked behind a coded door and has several signs stating to not enter. I imagine that's Pure's private room. I follow Lupine to a set of empty lockers, where he ditches his gear, takes a towel, and walks off to the showers still clothed.

He leaves me alone, so I am not afraid to take my clothes off while he is away. I hear him turn on the water a few shower rooms down and avoid that one at all cost. Just seeing him like that would not only be awkward, but I imagine he does want some privacy. I think he doesn't want me to see anything, and I do not blame him one bit. I prep myself against the shower wall with my arms and let the water rain over me, a small flood. I use the time to stretch my body and do nothing but relax. It just feels good *not* to be continually impacting something with my legs or arms; just that is indeed bliss. I turn the water cold to lessen the swelling.

I take a towel from a nearby rack and put it over my waist, making sure to look out for Lupine, who might be lurking around any corner. I head back to the locker and find him with his towel on, thankfully. He is sorting through his stuff, looking for something. As I approach him and try to keep my eyes off him and focused on my locker, I can't help noticing his back.

I know from reading about slave camps that Primes were whipped continuously, burned, branded, and beaten, mainly by criminals working at illegal drug plantations, but I had never seen them up close before. Interlaced with the fur, his back is lashed in a tic-tac-toe formation, a set of lashes from top to bottom, then a collection along the sides, and within each lashing remnant there are burns that travel up his body in three indistinct lines, and these lines are shaped like a sound wave reaching up to his neck and traveling down to his tailbone. His neck has a circular ring around it from the base of the neck, a scar that stands out among the rest, a discoloration most likely from a collar that burned his skin. The last thing I notice is his tailbone; where his tail extends outwards is sliced and slightly bent to the left, like someone smashed his bone with a hammer and left it to re-form. A lifetime of scars, a mural of pain, and an incredible story waiting to be told resides on his back, and he doesn't seem to care if I see it.

"What are you looking at?"

I snap out of my scanning of his back to notice that he is entirely naked, and I am looking at his waist. He has scars wrapped around his inner thighs all the way to his groin. He looks at me with a distrustful face.

I quickly turn around, slamming my shin on the bench, in-between us. "Oh, I'm sorry." I turn my face away from him. "I just noticed your back."

He turns back around. "Oh, that."

There are so many questions I have for him. Where did he get them? Was he created by the US military or an illegal lab? What did he do before the PLF? I think this is best to be left alone for now. I don't think he trusts me enough to ask about his past if it's riddled in scars.

He peers over his shoulder as if he is waiting for me to speak.

I get dressed in a second uniform pair that Lupine points out, one for non-physical sessions. He points to a hamper to put my dirty clothes in and tells me they will be put back into my locker in the morning, cleaned. I guess that's nice. I don't have to do my laundry, and I don't expect to go anywhere else so all my other clothes might as well be only for when I am at the flat.

The cold shower sure seemed to help my legs. I seem to be able to walk normally for now. He takes me back toward the building's entrance. As expected, several other Primes have started to file in. Lupine pulls me toward him and instructs me to stay to his left side. Most of the Primes in the building notice me, but for some reason, don't linger to observe me or don't seem fazed by a human being so close to Pure.

I hug close to Lupine as we pass through each hallway, turn each corner, and climb down each staircase all the way down to the basement on level three of the complex. The building morphs from a pure gym to a bunker with layered concrete walls, locked doors, and rooms with no windows. Lights barely lit dangle from exposed wire stapled across the ceiling, and I hear echoes of footsteps in front of us and from behind falling in sync. I ask Lupine what this part of the facility is for.

"It holds everything that Pure and the Zodiac would need in case we were bombed."

This is the fallout shelter for Highpoint. I imagine one of these hallways leads directly to Pure's house so he would have access to this bunker any time he would need to escape. These might have been dug out during the Prime uprising where the US ruthlessly bombed the area around here after it was captured by the PLF. Or possibly this whole area was a military base before the PLF reclaimed it as Highpoint and built Pure's mansion on the foundations of a base.

We make it only a couple of feet from the staircase leading to this level of the basement before Lupine turns and opens up a thick steel door into an expansive armory. Every single gun is neatly hung from a slot on the wall: assault rifles, shotguns, handguns, scoped rifles, heavy assault weapons, rockets, grenades; anything that would be needed to defend Pure at all cost is spit-shined cleaned. The oak frame to each of these sections of firearms is rested on steel roll-out cabinets embedded into the cement wall. None of them have magazines loaded into them. In the center of the rectangular hallway stretching at least half a football field long is a gunsmithing work station, equipped with a bullet manufactory, stacks of empty casings, pounds of gunpowder stored in plastic jars, and more roll-out drawers, each with a picture and name of a specific gun on the front of them.

117

We are alone in this gun nut's wet dream. As soon as Lupine steps into the room he turns back to me. "You stay here." He points at the entrance to the workshop.

Aww, I wanted to go inside and look around. I mean, I am not usually interested in guns, but when would I ever get a chance to handle some of these guns? "I swear I won't touch anything." I don't think he believes me.

"No." He heads down to the handguns and starts to pick up several.

"Do you think I know how to load these guns or fire them?" I've never handled a firearm in my life.

He sighs and puts a standard handgun into his waistband. "That is what I am trying to teach you. Once you are taught how to handle these, I might let you in, but for now I don't want you to come in here and fuck around with these, okay? These are incredibly dangerous, and I don't want to have to take your ass to Kit explaining why you were shot."

I peek my head in. "She would take the bullet from my ass and shoot you with it."

For the first time ever I hear a chuckle from him before the cocking of a shotgun.

After a couple more minutes of watching the dust gather on the cement floor, Lupine emerges with several large bags and pockets clinging with small boxes of ammo and two handguns stuffed into his pants. "All right, we are going to head down to the firing range. There I will demonstrate to you just what these firearms can do." He shuffles a large bag over his shoulder via a strap, and we continue back up the stairs to the level above.

We travel back to the gym hallways, except these doors and rooms are not labeled as the ones on the first floor. Instead, they are only given a number. From behind each of the doors, I hear the sound of guns firing, along with faint conversation and the clicking of rounds hitting the floor. I am taken all the way down to the far end of the hallway. The sounds die down as we reach the end of the hall. Lupine turns and flips a green card over to a bright red; I imagine this is to mark it's occupied.

I am starting to get excited. We enter a firing range. Sheets of target dummies, all human, are stacked next to me. A disposal bin for casings and ammo rests across from them. A long shelf provides a place to set guns and to place people's hats and phones. Bright lines of lights hover overhead, providing adequate lighting for aiming and firing. Wide indentations on the right side provide a space for the shooter to shoot, while also giving room to maneuver around without bumping into the bottom of the inserts. Even some of the long rifles and shotguns could be laid down horizontally, and there would still be room.

The firing range is a long, empty hallway that is equipped with hanging cover belts on the ceiling. The length of this firing range must be at least a football field long, with a side range that goes at least another area longer. I imagine that's for the snipers to practice long-range shots. I didn't care about exercising, but I was really interested in seeing what I could do with a gun.

Lupine sets down each one of the guns on the shelf and reaches into the insert and takes a pair of headphones from a side locker where there are a variety of sizes and shapes of headsets. He hands a normal pair to me. "These have mics attached to the side, so we will be able to talk clearly even when I am firing."

Cool. I put it over my ears and realize these are sound-canceling. I can't even hear Lupine take the rounds out and insert them into magazines. I get close enough to watch him slip the shells into the magazine of a handgun. His thumb and finger movements are almost effortless as he slips each bullet into each slot. He even manages to do it one-handed as he reaches into one of the longer bags and pulls out another box of ammo.

After he loads a couple of magazines for each gun—an assault rifle, a shotgun, two handguns, and a long rifle—he takes a pair of headphones and puts them around his neck instead of on his ears. "Now these handguns here are standard issue in the PLF. This one..." He pulls out the gun that he had when he shot the bandits. "...is called a Badger. It's small but fires quickly." He loads a clip into the chamber and then turns into the stall and fires down the hallway without really aiming at anything. I feel the same thump that I felt when I was mere inches away from the gunshot.

I see the headphones rattle when he fires. "Um, aren't you supposed to be wearing the headset over your ears?"

He sets the safety on the side. "I am used to these sounds. They don't bother me as much as they would you."

I'm surprised he isn't deaf if he shoots these without ear protection that much. "What, you going deaf or something?"

He places the Badger on the table and grabs the other handgun. "I wish I was."

He picks up the second handgun. "This one is a more close-combat handgun as it packs more of a punch but has more of a kick. This one is a Cobra." He loads a clip into the gun and fires it down the hallway. With this one, I definitely felt the shockwave radiate as it rippled the gunsmoke in the air.

He puts away the Cobra right next to the Badger and pulls out one of the smaller assault rifles. It has a shorter barrel than the long gun and the clip size is much lower. "This is our standard issued assault rifle, the Tiger. It fires at a single fire or a burst depending on the mode it is set at." He shows me a switch on the side of the gun. "Down for burst, up for single."

As I get up close to the gun I notice several grooves in the handle of the weapon where Lupine's hand goes in. I see several buttons placed around the grip. "Is that one the safety?" I point to the one next to his palm.

He moves his palm away and displays the grip. "No, that is the button you press to eject the grip. You see all Primes have different sized hands, much like humans, except the variety is far larger in scope. So we make all our guns with replaceable grips that fit all kinds of Prime."

That is actually really cool. "Hey, when will I get to handle one?"

He tightens his grip on the rifle and clicks the safety. "When you've learned basic gun safety."

"That's simple, don't shoot something you don't want dead." I simplify.

Lupine loads a clip and instead of pointing it down the range, he aims the barrel directly at me! I lunge down under the shelf. He relaxes his stance, and a smile cracks from his stone-cut face. "Like you never point a loaded gun at anyone you don't intend to kill."

I shakenly get out from under, trying not to hit my head on the bottom of the shelf. "You could have just told me that!"

He motions me to continue with my words like he is expecting a response with a visual cue. Oh, wait... "Because I learn from visual aids," I begrudgingly state.

He points the rifle down the range and fires between every word. "He can be taught."

After several more demonstrations of the rifles and weapons, he has me practice loading magazines. He leans against the shelf and watches me approvingly as I seem to get pushing in the bullets into the slot reasonably quickly. When I finish a handgun magazine, he empties it down the range and then tells me to reload it. After about the third time sitting in dead silence, I seem to have it down. I am not nearly as fast as Lupine, but I sure as hell can load a magazine better than I can do a pushup. Maybe I am better at guns than physical labor, I wouldn't mind being the gun guy in the group.

On the fourth magazine, I nearly slip my thumb and crush my nail when I hear Lupine talk.

"Did you actually want to join the PLF?"

Why is he asking me this out of the blue? Is he looking at something on his phone? "Well..." I bend down and pick up the bullet from the floor. "There was nothing left for me after you kidnapped me, so I think deep down I wanted to give it a shot for a year to see where this takes me."

By the time I get one single bullet in, he already has gone through half a mag.

"Did you really have nothing back there? I mean you seem pretty book smart; you could have gone to college, lived a normal life as a human being."

No, I never wanted to be a pen pusher in some office; I strived to be something more, something unusual. As I sit here with Prime loading bullets into magazines in the bunker of the leader of the PLF, I wonder if this is what I really wanted all this time, a life of the unknown. Is it better life than a fabricated experience?

"Ghent?" He snaps me out of a trace and points down at my mag.

I accidentally loaded a bullet backward. "Oh, sorry—I just was thinking of... stuff." I reset the entire mag and start over. I look over to Lupine and notice he is done with his mag and is starting to load another one. I decide this is the closest thing I will get to bonding with Lupine. "Did you want to join the PLF?"

His finger slips on the bullet and it falls to the floor. He bends over and picks up the casing.

"Well, I guess we are done for the day," Lupine says while he walks to the entrance.

I limp along with him. "So, now, what do I do?" Please say go home. Please say go back.

"Head home, relax, watch TV, read a book. I don't know what you like to do."

Thank fucking Christ—maybe now I can actually sit down and relax. Wait a minute, how do I get back to my house? "You are going to drive me home?"

"One last time. After today I want you to make your way here on foot. It's safe as long as you stay within the gated community. Security also has been increased in the mornings and after we leave."

Really? He expects me to walk my way back after training? "What are you off to do?" I ask, curious about what he does in his spare time.

He stuffs his phone into his pocket and takes out his keys. "Go back to my office. Make sure my ass is covered before legal work comes up and sticks its dick in me."

I get into the seat and put my seat back. "Did you get into trouble for what you did?"

"Well, I've done stupider shit in my life and I am still here, so I guess they are going to make me make a public apology or some sentimental shit."

"Apologize to the protesters who wanted to hurt me?"

He slowly pulls out of his spot and starts to drive me home. "Fucked up, isn't it?"

Gores really must cover a lot of Lupine's mistakes; he seems to be protective of Lupine. "So, did Gores train you in the PLF?"

"Yeah, I graduated from the training corps with high praise from him about five years ago."

My wrist still hurts from when he twisted it when I met him. "He seems a bit rough. I imagine he was a joy to train with."

"You think *you* have it bad," he affirms. "Try doing what you just did four times a day starting out, and then moving to six times by week four."

Jesus Christ, he did that every week?! "That's insane!"

"Hey, it worked for me. His motto he always screamed at me was 'If I can't talk the weakness out of you, I guess I will have to beat it out of you.'

Despite how hard he trains me, at least he isn't driving me as his mentor did. I mean, he knows my limits now and has decided that he won't put me through what he did. Still, if I want to be a part of the PLF my body has to be ready for anything. Lupine's first goal is to make me tough enough to endure what I have to endure, then he can truly begin training me to be a soldier.

Tooth and Nail

It has been three months since I started training with Lupine. As each day passes the punches and kicks are getting harder and faster, and without any sort of biological advantage, I am left having my body bruised and strained every night. It was only two days ago that Kit had to treat my arm for a sprain and Lupine only told me to sleep it off and be ready the next day. *That was a soft kick,* he said. Fucking bullshit! Lupine smashed down on my leg with his yeti feet with enough force to crush a human skull. I limp out of the shower room still dripping in sweat, and an ice pack taped to my left shin. I know I should have gotten up a little quicker, so he didn't trap me under his foot, but he still knows that his punches and kicks still hurt like a cement block impacts.

While I can't say that I like his method—it is dangerous and potentially deadly—it's working. I can feel myself getting stronger and faster with each passing day. I keep a mental note of how my body is changing as I train with Lupine. Sure, I'm curious to see what two weeks of training with Lupine can do to me, or maybe it's just a way to give me proof that it is in fact working. Either way, I have noticed some things: I can walk to the gymnasium without being worn out when I get there, and I have considerable increases in muscle tone throughout my body, along with several bruises and blisters.

It has been only a week since he let me handle a gun, and to be honest I was hesitant to hold it around Lupine. I didn't want to accidentally hurt him or myself. Even when it was empty, I felt like it was loaded and primed to shoot. I guess watching him shoot every gun and explaining the functionality of each of them wore out the glamor. My first shot from a Badger nearly took out a light on the side of the shooting range. Lupine pinched in between his eyes and sighed, but really I was just shocked how much recoil there was, and the sounds scared me. The one gun that I refused to fire is the shotgun. The Bull is a shotgun designed to shoot through plaster walls, and the kick from it nearly broke my arm bracing the stock. I told Lupine I refused to shoot it and he was actually understanding of me. He told me that there are some guns he won't fire himself.

"For example," he informs me as he picks out a gun from the storeroom while I stand just outside the door, "I fucking hate this gun." He pulls down a tommy gun-looking drum attached to a short barrel. "This monster is called the Python. It's an automatic shotgun that can fire its entire drum of one hundred rounds in two minutes." He takes off the drum and inspects the inside of it. "When Gores handed me this gun and told me to fire, it nearly killed me. The recoil made me drop the gun and a shot nearly took out my dick. The one time I've ever heard that ape even close to laugh was when I was close to castrating myself."

He likes to refer back to what he went through with Gores every time I push back about his training tactics. I've heard the words "you've had it easy" more times than I can count around him, even when I am going through water training with Lupine, when he ties up my legs with rope and throws me a knife, and picks me up and tosses me into the water. I panicked and failed to get untied the first time; I had to signal to him to save me.

"These ropes were chains when I did it."

I know he's trying to make it seem not as bad as he had it, but it just comes off that he is gloating about how badass he is.

The only good thing about getting hurt with Lupine is having Kit come over to him and chew him out for getting me injured. She is the only Prime I know who can go toe to toe with him and yell at him for how reckless he has been with my safety. For example, we are going through hand-to-hand combat and he demonstrates how to fight against someone with a knife. Of course, *normal* instructors would use a fake plastic knife to simulate a knife, but no, he takes out his real army multi-tool knife with its teethed back and hole in the center.

"You will try harder if the blade is real."

As Kit cleaned the cut I got across my cheek and my left shoulder, she was ranting about how stupid he was for doing something like that. "I swear to fucking god if I knew this is what I would be doing with my qualifications and my merits, I wouldn't have been a fucking medic." She quickly splashed some isopropyl alcohol onto my wound. "Stitching my own god damn teammates just because my commander is a fucking stubborn moron."

After I got stitched up she got a signed document from Gores telling Lupine to stop the physical training aspect until Kit cleared me. Even after being told by Gores to cut it off, Lupine still insisted that I continue doing pushups as to "not get soft."

That week Lupine took me to a meeting room and went through some of the acronyms, hand signals, laws of warfare, and more education aspects of the PLF. When I say teach he mainly handed me some of his old PLF textbooks and manuals and told me to go read them at home. He rushed through most of the classroom training sessions, even letting me go early because he couldn't stand being in a classroom for hours on end. At least it gave me something to read and study while I was back home. The TV stations got boring and what crime drama, spy, and history books, all written by Prime authors, were there I read through.

The only time he ever seems to be remotely fully involved with my training while in the classroom is when he shows me clips and videos on the projector of Prime history and the PLF's viewpoint on events. I was seeing a whole new way of looking at the world. For example, from what I was taught in The States, Primes chased down and hunted down humans fleeing the west coast during the uprising. The Exodus was broadcast on live video feed from those whose houses were torched and families chased out with military vehicles and gunfire to get them to move. However, as Lupine showed me, *most* PLF members provided the cities they were sent to occupy three days' notice to evacuate and leave the area before the siege began. When I asked what happened to those who didn't evacuate, Lupine told me that they were captured as prisoners of war and dumped at the border once the ceasefire was called. I didn't know that, but I can see footage of Primes handing out flyers to humans.

"They had plenty of warning before we arrived. Humans in the area were provided pamphlets and audio warning from our squads before we advanced, but some humans thought they could fight us back and were defiant. We were told only to fire back if we were shot at, which I bet the US forgot to mention."

I always felt like we were never getting the full story in The States when it came to the news stations and other media, but the PLF has the same reasons to distort the facts and the media. In the end it just leaves me not enlightened, just more confused, as now I know both my countries are lying to everyone. I am in the rare position that few Primes in the PLF or humans in the US have: I am able to know what both sides are saying, and maybe with this find out what really went on during these moments harnessed by both sides to rile up their own political fervor.

I ask him to pause the video when he is fast-forwarding through some videos of human video streams compared to PLF's armed forces video feed. It's on a screenshot of a lion Prime in full PLF armor with the seal for the Evols, a strand of DNA bathed in sunlight, patched on his arm. "Isn't that the Evol patch on a PLF soldier?"

He takes a deep breath and continues the video. "Yes, this is before Pantheon was kicked out of the PLF, where his army's patch was the Evol patch they use today." He pauses at another patch, which is the patch of the PLF today. "Pantheon's army and Pure's were kept separate, and for the vast majority of Primes who were in Pantheon's group they were the troublemakers. Human media thought they were all Primes."

He closes out the video and opens a file named Evolutionary Atrocities. He opens up the folder and picks a date, May 11, 2042, the anniversary of Roaring Sunday. "This was the Evols *celebrating* the anniversary of Roaring Sunday." He plays the video and we are taken to a Prime taking a video with his phone of an inner city with ruins of freshly bombed-out apartments, shops, and a nearby park. Gunfire covers whatever the Prime is saying as he pans his phone around squads of Evols rounding up humans, pulling them out of the buildings, and throwing them into the street. Those humans who resisted the Primes were immediately restrained, then sent over to a burning pile of...something...and thrown upon it.

Lupine pauses the video. "You okay with me continuing, or do you get the picture?"

"No..." I swallow some bile coming up as I see Evols in the background with knives in their hands and approaching women and children separated to the right of the burning pile. "...I don't."

He closes out the video and reopens the other video we had open. "Once Pure was made aware of what was going on with Pantheon's army, he kicked them out of the PLF and started an internal investigation for war crimes in the PLF. Once it was traced back to Pantheon's orders, some people assume that it was the spark that got Pantheon kicked out of the PLF. His army was all tried and court-marshaled for their crimes. After they were removed from the PLF, they formed the Evolutionaries, with Pantheon as their alpha. What I showed you isn't nearly close to the worst things Pantheon's army did." He pauses and scratches his shoulder where his patch would be. "The things that they did would make any hardened war veteran squirm. That is why we at the PLF strive to weed out Evols and take down Pantheon. Especially our Zodiac works directly in destroying Evol hideouts, taking out terrorists working with the Evols, and keeping an ear on Pantheon's activities. Most activity we encounter is in Wasteland, where the Evols have fled to recruit and to prey upon humans. Evols are trying to claim land 'for the PLF' by kidnapping, killing, and destroying human outposts like the one in Bismarck."

He takes off his badge from his coat on his chair and points to it. "We follow strict protocols when dealing with moral infiltration. When we have a mission, we are sworn to obey the PLF's moral codes." He begins counting with his fingers. "No killing civilians, a soldier is to die as a soldier, negotiation and peace over violence, and the most important one of them all, do nothing to your enemy that you would not want them to do to you."

"Wait, if Pantheon had an army before they were dissolved, why didn't Pantheon start a coup to take back control of the PLF? He had an army, right?"

He shrugs. "Don't really know. Everyone has their own theories, as most of the internal communication between Pantheon and Pure remained classified. Some say that Pantheon knew he couldn't beat Pure's army; some say that Pure negotiated with Pantheon to forgive his war crimes in exchange for peace amongst the PLF. It's all up in the air regarding what really was the thing that kept Pantheon and Pure at peace during that time. I honestly believe it was Pantheon understanding that if he were to fight Pure during the war it would only cause the PLF and Primes to weaken, giving the US an opportunity to retake the west coast, which Pantheon would rather die than see."

Before I left that day Lupine unpacked an army duffle bag he had brought with him and handed me a stack of books tied together with twine. "Here is your study material for the next couple of days."

Intelligence gathering, geographic locations, negotiating...well, Lupine did tell me that I didn't need that one. But everything I read while at home laying on the couch with the windows open and a nice breeze coming in while having a glass of tea really makes me feel like an adult. I have a job, be it insanely deadly and harsh, a house to myself, and everything I could ever want supplied to me, and I am only seventeen years old... I think. It feels more like I am in...heh, my prime.

But I haven't gotten to know Lupine any better. Showers are still awkward at the gym, since I noticed his scars. He hasn't spoken to me much after that and never brings up anything. I don't know if my discovery turned him off to any further discussion on the PLF or Prime life in general, but it sure seems like he doesn't want to discuss any part of his life outside of that facility. He doesn't bring up family, even though I know most Primes don't have families as they were created. The world around him seems to focus on what he has to do for the day and that is it. He is always there when I open the door to see him working out or setting up for our training exercise. He is always clean, drinks only water, and is one hundred percent unwilling to accept that I am in pain a vast majority of my time with him.

Life at Highpoint feels like living as the most pampered prisoner ever. Food is delivered right outside my door. Sometimes it's full meals; other times it's a bag of groceries. I've had time to practice cooking with the limited time I do have in between beatings by Lupine and laying down on the couch and trying to get feeling back in my arms and legs. Kit has instructed me to eat as healthy as possible to make sure my body is getting enough protein and vegetables to ensure my body is functioning at one hundred percent. She gave me a cookbook to use as a guide. I used to cook for myself back in Detroit but it was mainly boxed food, frozen meals, or rice and noodle dishes that an eight-year-old could make. I used to not like cutting things with knives before, but ever since I started wielding them with my training I am less scared of cutting quickly.

The news, on the other hand, is an endless treasure trove of information for me. Learning the current issues and the stance of the different groups of Primes, and learning about Prime life from a single twenty-four-hour news station is an asset to me. If I am to assimilate into Prime culture and live here, I need to keep up on current topics, trends, and the overall sense of how Primes live their normal lives. I think everyone I talk to, including Lupine, will open up if I understand them more, and can talk to them about things that any normal Prime would.

I head down to the entrance and plop myself on the couch for a while to recompose myself and to secure the ice pack to my leg. I pull up my sweatpants to slide up the bag and tie the bandage tighter so that it doesn't slide up and down my leg while I walk home. While tightening the knot, I snap the dressing and cause the pack to fall onto the floor. "Shit," I whisper under my breath.

Kit is still here. I guess I have to go back to her and get a new strap or bandage. The pack goes into my gym bag, and I press on my leg to lift myself up. I feel my whole leg start to burn. If there is someone that I am thankful for around here, it is Kit. There is no one else whom I would rather have here. She knows the best remedy to any of my wolf-inflicted afflictions. She usually hangs out in the medical lab built into the medical emergency room just down the hall to the facility. I should get her something to thank her for everything she's done, and also maybe get something for her as an apology for getting her sprayed in my blood back at the capitol building.

The problem is I don't know what to get her; she doesn't seem to be interested in anything that females are usually into. From what I saw on TV they like most of the things human girls do, but I don't think Kit would like jewelry or chocolate. She doesn't seem like the sentimental type. Maybe I should get some new medical supplies. Her scalpel that she spins around in her fingers like a pen and uses to cut bandages seems a little old and worn down, and perhaps a new one would tell her that I appreciate her help. The problem is I can't get outside the facility to get her a new one.

I am about to enter the hallway back down to Kit's office when I hear the automatic doors open. I turn around cautiously since no one usually comes around at this hour. I see Feather, Borne, and a once extinct animal, a pangolin Prime who is half my height hunched forward with an armored shell structure encasing his back along with an army duffle backpack that goes over his hunched shoulders. He stands on bipedal legs but hunches over as if he is going to fall onto his hands.

The tail is a long, flat tail like a beaver but connected entirely to his back. The tail is nearly his length and drags just a couple of inches off the ground. He appears to be wearing the equivalent of baby's first cargo shorts, and his shirt is the size of Borne's thigh pant leg, which is a button-up light plaid shirt over a white T-shirt. His eyes immediately track to me behind a pair of glasses placed on an elongated nose and three whiskers on each side. By just taking a guess, I imagine that this is Tucker, the last member of Sagittarius that I know about. He is the Prime that Bella and Maurice were talking about regarding fixing their broken pump.

"There is that freak of nature that I've heard about!" He waddles over to me and opens up his armored body for a hug. He seems as open as Feline but has the gruffness of a college bro. He hops up and hugs my waist for just a moment. I awkwardly hover my hands just above his shirt, and I can feel his coarse skin just below the cloth. Borne just cocks his head and stands at attention at the door while Feather follows.

"I imagine you are Tucker."

"Holy shit." His hands are three claws and a thumb, a long straight nail supported by a dry skin curl around my waist. "Did I hear that? He got my name down without knowing who I was!" He seems friendly and harmless; however, I still know that he is in Sagittarius, meaning he can even kill me if he wanted to. "Has that mutt been talking about me behind my back again?"

Finally, someone who can lighten up my mood! For so long, I have been stuck talking with a cement wall in Lupine. Any sort of positive emotion feels great right now. It's hard to know you're poisoned until the antidote starts feeling good. "You could say that."

We separate ourselves, and he points toward Feather.

I don't think Lupine might have reminded him about Maurice's deal with Lupine. I want to make sure that couple gets what they are owed. "Also, you need to go fix Bella and Maurice's fucking pump—message from them."

His eyes widen and then he grins smugly. "Already did that last week. Took Arrow our van out for a road trip to help them out. They were asking how you were and I told them you were safe."

It's good to hear that they got their pump fixed and that they remember me.

Feather usually shows up much later or earlier than this to go to the shooting range and test out Pure's guns. He has given me some pointers on shooting when Lupine wasn't available.

Wonder why they are here today. "Why are you guys here? Heading to train?" I ask

"Hell no." Tucker comes up from behind me and pushes me toward the door. "We are here to rescue you from Lupine and show you a good time."

I suddenly fear the punishment I would get if Lupine found out. He's trained me to grow anxious in his presence, by the mere sound of his voice.

I search for a response. "Sorry, guys, but I can't leave the base. I mean I hate to say no—I really want to escape this place—but I have to obey orders."

"Oh, come on," he keeps pushing me. "That mutt will never know you are gone."

I really want to tell Lupine that, just to see how quickly he would hunt Tucker down for using "that mutt" in front of me. "Besides, it's not like you will be in danger. You are a PLF soldier, and you got the best half of Sagittarius guarding you."

Lupine never really knows what I am doing outside of this building; at least he never asks what I do. Would he really care if I left for a couple of hours? Wait, maybe I could use this opportunity to get a thank-you gift for Kit. "What are we going to do?"

Tucker gestures outside. "Just a tour around town—go to a couple of our favorite spots to hang out."

Something I might need to know for later. "Can we make a stop and help me get a gift for Kit?"

"Sounds like someone likes Kit," Tucker taunts from behind.

"I just want to thank her for helping me with Lupine, and that's it." I don't think he believes me, but I don't expect someone with his personality *not* to give me shit either.

"It's all right. You can like someone and not necessarily want to get into their pants." Infinite wisdom from such a small man, rather a pangolin. "Anyway, I know a place we can stop to get something made for her that she will like."

That would be worth it. To have one made for her would make it much more memorable. Personalized.

"I know a guy that owes me a solid, so it would be free of charge."

I agree to the terms, and we head outside. I just make sure to take one last look back to see if Lupine isn't watching me from the shadows.

131

Borne opens the door of a Toyota six-seater white van to let Feather into the driver's seat. "Why don't we let Ghent ride shotgun?"

I am honored to be given a chance to see how Primes drive. For too long I've been denied being able to look at Kingdom through a window instead of inside the back of a truck. I flash back to my first ride in the van with Lupine. A feeling of regularity, comfort, and normal sitting next to a Prime driving down the PLF has set in. I know I am safe and can take in the sights around me. I guess before I got kidnapped I never truly felt comfortable among Primes; there was always that sense of uneasiness that was hammered into me with the media and the environment of segregation in the United States. That has all since faded and now I feel comfortable enough to drive shotgun with a PLF soldier.

I immediately jump into the passenger seat and turn around to see Tucker right behind me. The entire van shifts to accommodate Borne's weight; he takes two places behind Feather. The dashboard of the car is filled with cigarette burns, and a few loose shell casings are rolling back below my feet. Ash and gray fur strands are shifted into the leather, and the radio is plugged into a phone placed in Feather's cup holder, while mine holds an empty pack. I would have to guess this is where Lupine sits, given all the smoking he does, and the fur stuffed under me that smells like dog dander. This car seems to be a road trip van that the squad uses to transport themselves around: claw marks and scuffs line the inside of the door, and the seatbelt connection is loose at best. I wouldn't be surprised to find a loaded handgun inside the glove compartment.

"Hold on." Feather reaches over the glove compartment. Indeed, inside is a Badger with an awkward grip where the magazine is slanted back instead of straight down from the chamber, a pair of shades that he takes out and puts on.

Tucker pokes his head in between us. "So, where we going to take the fella?"

Feather revs the engine. "Well, I was thinking of taking him to the Tooth and Nail."

That sounds like either a fight club or a bar, and I really hope it's the latter.

With the window rolled up and a soft gleam on my face, I keep low just so my eyes can peek over the window to see outside. I don't want people knowing I am in the car.

The window then starts to roll down as Feather holds down the button. "It's okay, Ghent you are safe. Just relax and get used to being seen by Primes and take in the city."

Tucker leans over my seat. "That's the plan after all for today—just relax, bud," he comforts.

I guess as long as I am with them it wouldn't hurt. After being in Highpoint for as long as I have, even the new smell of the city—car exhaust, restaurants cooking open barbeque pits, and the wind blowing in some sprinkles of sewage—is comforting. I get comfortable and lift my head to see the big picture of a city in motion. From the front seat, I can see the freshly paved roads of asphalt and the fresh paint shimmering in the sun. It is oddly beautiful. A series of high-end apartment complexes line the street we head down, Primes of all sizes, of all animals, track around the sidewalks and get into their vehicles. Each climb and cram into cars and trucks, depending on the limitations of their size and shape.

The cars they drive are in different sizes, much like our own back home, but they are slightly higher, shorter, and broader in every location. It is especially apparent when looking at the driver seat. Despite the variety of cars and drivers, the roads are well kept, drivers are orderly, and everything seems to be functioning smoothly. The driver's plate for each car shows the PLF flag in the corner, a series of three numbers and then three letters. Each has different logos displayed in the background, but most of them show an over-exaggeration of how beautiful Kingdom is with its meadow encroaching on a modern city with a glowing citadel at its center.

The fashion around here seems similar to the US; however, the array and variety of different sizes, accommodations, and innovations amaze me. Shirts for Primes with spines, needles, tails, horns, wings...every appendage is accounted for. I can't imagine what clothing stores must be like here. Do they accommodate for one specific group, or do they cater to all types? I feel strangely at ease. I have traveled so far away from my home, yet sense familiarity here.

It has been quite a while since the PLF took over this city, but its American heritage can still be felt while just driving down the street. Some of the original buildings from the US are still standing with modern add-ons. It is an old city with the original skeleton but with surgical repairs to make it function. Restaurants serve American food, including beef and pork, even as I see some cattle types walking around. How is that possible?! Antique stores sell knickknacks to older Primes, of which there are very few. A newspaper stand outside sells papers, bars dot the street corners, and there is even a cleverly named strip joint called Instinct placed neatly between a gas station.

By the time we reach the inner city, there hasn't been one single cop, a single police officer patrol, nothing. The closest thing is a bouncer outside of a high-end nightclub, and he isn't even armed, not even with a nightstick. A lack of any sort of security or protection makes me think: Is it really that safe around here? Are there not terrorists inside the PLF? Well, I guess that in a way, *I* am the terrorist, a human being inside a race of people who despise my race. I think I should be asking myself: Do I feel safe around here surrounded by Primes? I guess in the end we don't really feel like we are discriminated against till we are thrown into a world foreign to our own, and then we see just how different and terrifying we are to the outside world.

Within the inner city the skyscrapers, which are either half-finished or under repair, reach up to the heavens and create a maze of alleyways and one-way streets. I see several Primes working on renovating a storefront on the bottom floor, gutting the entire thing to install a fitness center. Physical labor for Primes must not be that difficult. I mean, they have a rhino, a gorilla, and a bear Prime working on lifting five cement blocks by themselves. I can't imagine how long it would take an average human to move a single one of them, let alone five.

Feather stops for a yellow light, so we are placed smack dab in front of an intersection as Primes cross in front of me. I get a close look at average Primes, and I am still astonished by the range and variety of types passing by. The number of different animals seems endless! The only kinds of Primes I haven't seen are bug Primes, but I guess that's for the best because I couldn't imagine a spider person or a beetle. I don't like beetles. I do see several duplications and a pack of wolves. Would I call them a pack or a group? I mean they are animals but—oh, never mind, I will just call them a group. What does it matter how I think of them? They walk by me before I got a closer look. They must have been teenagers, but it's hard to tell with Primes because their height doesn't give it away, and most physical features that humans most associate with puberty are nonexistent. Just before the light turns green, I see a hound Prime right next to me walking his dog. Just when I think I've seen everything, here is a half human-dog walking a dog. They both seem happy.

All in all, the city seems to be just finishing its rebuilding during the cease-fire. As we take the corner down a road for a block and swerve into a spot right outside of a bar called the Tooth and Nail, I have to ask myself if everyone in this town can live so inclusively yet be completely different, and if there isn't a sense of racism within the Prime society that I haven't yet experienced yet lies beneath the surface. With all of the different "races" of humans, we have found ways to segregate, discriminate, and stereotype people. So how, in a society filled with such diversity, isn't there a massive problem with racism?

Feather puts the car in park and undoes his seatbelt along with everyone else. I am looking at the building with a sense of excitement mixed with dread rushing through my veins. The building outside displays itself as a classic brick and mortar look along with a PLF flag displayed promptly outside. A sign states there was an Armistice Day brunch last week. The neon sign holding up the name is turned off, but the red tint around the glass has pooled rainwater on the bottoms of each letter. Bird shit outlines the sides.

Tucker reaches over and taps me on the shoulder. "Here we are."

"Tooth and Nail, huh?" I open the door and step outside onto a sewer grate, which surprisingly doesn't smell of sewer.

He pushes the door closed with both hands and hops onto the sidewalk. "Yep, it's our special spot. When we get done with paperwork or working out, we head here, slam a couple of drinks, and bitch about other Primes."

"So it's like every bar in the US." I'd never been inside a bar, but I didn't have to tell them that.

Feather locks the car. "A place where every Prime knows your name."

Borne heads up to the door and opens the door for us.

"Careful." Tucker moves in front of me and motions to the door with his thumb. "The door is too heavy for a little runt like you."

I take a look at the inside of the door and see that it is a steel door that is almost as thick as I am, with varying tints of metal and strange tiny symbols etched into the door frame and the door itself. The door also is not a flat surface; it has ridges and spots protruding to form mini cliffs within the door. This isn't ordinary steel. "What is it made out of?" If it is heavy enough to not let me in, why have it be the entrance for the bar?

"Melted down guns," Borne answers. He scoots inside of an entry room where fliers and posters are nailed to a notice board.

Feather opens the inside glass door. "Every single soldier we know from the bar that dies in the war, we smelt down his gun and add it to the bar."

A way to remember the fallen. I manage to make out several years and a couple of first names on the door. Borne finishes sliding into the room just as Feather and Tucker move out into the bar. My eyes adjust to the dimness of the bar as I step inside.

The bar itself isn't more substantial than the flats at Highpoint. Its main fully loaded bar lines the right wall, and several TVs hang above an oak-crafted and maroon varnish bar counter. The booze is contained in glass cabinets that slide open via two expansive windows in the center. A sink and bartender's tools are gathered on a counter in front of the window, and a small conveyor belt carries dirty glasses outside. The TVs are not on, but instead, Primes are sitting on high bar stools talking to each other. From the hardwood floors mopped spotless to the booths on the left-hand side slightly elevated by a small set of stairs, everything shouts Chinese made, yet the owners have included plaques and pictures of PLF soldiers on the wall, including several medals and guns encased in glass hanging by a wire.

Near the back of the bar is a hallway for the restrooms, and away into the kitchen a group of Primes is sitting in one of the five booths in the back and what I presume to be a couple is placed in the booth right next to the door. There are two Primes at the bar waiting for drinks from the bartender. The barkeep has the composition of a wolf, yet has facial aspects of a hound. He is formidable in appearance underneath a tucked-in polo shirt and an apron hanging below his waist. He wipes down a glass with a rag, the same color as his fur, a dark gray that is straight and hangs down from him. He looks up from the counter to see who is coming in.

"Feather." He speaks in a Chinese accent. "Borne." He nods toward Borne. "You." He points at Tucker with the glass and glares at him suspiciously. Lastly, he motions at me, but just after he opens his mouth, his eyes widen, and he nearly drops his glass. "And a human?"

The entire bar goes silent, and they all look at me. Most of them are surprised by my entrance, while others are cautiously sizing me up. I guess I wanted attention today, so I should expect things like this.

Feather immediately tries to kill the tension in the room. "Don't worry, guys, he's cool." He walks over and motions us to sit on the edge of the bar nearest to the door. The group at the bar picks up their drinks and moves down to the other side.

The bartender puts down his glass and heads back to the hallway and opens the door for the kitchen. "Hey, Nail, come look at this!" he shouts.

I hear an echo back in the same accent. "What?!"

"A fucking meatbag!"

Is that supposed to be a slur for me? I don't know enough to care if it is.

"What!"

"A human!" He stomps his foot.

"No, I heard you. What the fuck is a human doing here!"

Moments later from the back emerges the bartender with Nail, who either is his twin or a clone. They share the exact same build, fur color, everything; the only difference that I can find is that Nail is missing one of his front fangs and that he has a slightly raspier voice. "What the shit did you bring into my bar?" He puts his hands on the bar in front of Tucker.

The other Prime sits behind him, leaning on the bar.

Tucker hops onto the stool and spins toward Nail. "He's part of the PLF—don't get your tail in a knot."

"PLF, eh?" Nail smiles and laughs at the notion.

"I don't believe it. Is this some stupid prank you are pulling on us, you little prick?" The other takes another look at me.

I sit on the stool next to Feather in between Borne and keep my eyes on his hands. I notice that a couple of his fingers are missing: the middle finger, the ring finger on his left, and the pointer and his pinky on his right.

Tucker presents me to Tooth. "No, just ask Borne and Feather here; he's a Prime."

So, Tooth is the one missing the nails, and Nails is the one missing the tooth. The person who named these Primes is an asshole.

All at the same time, I tell him that I agree with Tucker. Feather says, "He's special," and Borne just nods his head.

"Well, I'd be damned." Tooth moves some condiments and cork coasters out of the way. "Well, you are a Prime, right? Then come over here and prove it."

Prove it?

Feather slides in between Tooth and me. "I really don't think that you need to..."

"Shaddap, you oversized chicken; you know the policy. If you are strong enough to open the door, you are strong enough to sit with me and wrassle." He slams his elbow on the table. I can see his built figure from his arms. He is obviously stronger than I am, and he has the physical advantage of being a Prime. He knows I can't win this, so why is he challenging me? "Get over here and wrassle, Prime boy." He challenges me with a grin.

The other Primes in the room begin to gather around my squad. They all exchange looks and whispers. Some even take out their wallets and place bets, most likely for me to lose. "All right, everyone, let's all watch this 'PLF material' get his arm snapped like a twig. Bet now, 'cause you are not going to ever see this shit ever again, I can tell you." He is quite enjoying himself.

I feel a push from behind. Tucker is shoving me forward into the countertop right in front of Tooth. What do I get from doing this? I mean, I can earn the respect of everyone in the bar if I win, but I can't win an unwinnable battle. However, if I don't go along with it, I am placing myself in a worse position by not following bar protocol, which could get me banned from entering. In the end, I am better off doing it and failing than not doing it at all. I just hope I don't lose an arm.

Rolling up my sleeve, I put my elbow on the table. My arms are twigs compared to his branch, and his hand could grasp around my hand and crush it like a walnut if he wanted. I feel powerless.

"All right, you two," Nail coaches us both, "I want a clean wrassle. No shit, no shit talk, and no bullshit." He merges our hands together and puts his hand on top. "When I release my hand, we start." He glances at both of us. "Ready?"

I've never arm-wrestled anyone before, but if I am to be a part of this bar I need to prove how far I am willing to go. I hesitantly nod. I keep my eyes on his eyes. Just push down to the right and try to win quickly, or should I try to be cute and push to the left first and then to the right to throw him off?

"Ready. Set. Wrassle!"

Immediately I feel him inch his hand toward the right. He's trying to be cute, so I push my hand down quickly to grab him while he fakes me out. I get halfway down there before he reverses course and quickly pushes with full force the other direction. I can barely hang on after he gets my hand inches from the counter. I hold steady trying to outlast him.... Oh, who am I kidding? I can't survive him! I feel him start to slip. I swing to the right, and he immediately slams down to the left and pulverizes my hand onto the counter.

Nail throws a hand up to Tooth's side. "Tooth is the winner!"

Tucker pats me on the back. "You did good, kid. For going against the Kingdom's champion at arm wrestling." Tucker points up to the ceiling where there is a headboard with several plaques and trophies written to Tooth. Most of them read *Kingdom Arm Wrestling: 1st Place.*

So I didn't have a chance to win. This was just a test to see if I would do it.

Most spectators are content with the show, and some seem a little more relaxed having me inside the bar.

Feather laughs at how shit I did and puts his claw on my back and pats me. "You did fine, kid—at least he didn't take your arm off."

Tooth puts the condiments and coasters back in front of us, and fist-bumps my arm. "Well, hummy, you sure lasted a lot longer than some Primes around here, so I give you that. Maybe after a couple of weeks, you can come back when your little arm stops hurting and try again." Tooth seems like he enjoys me being there. Maybe the true prize is just the admiration of the group.

A couple of glasses are dropped off by Nail, and he scoops some ice into them. "Say, kid, you want some ice for that hand?"

I put my arm in my lap. It's a little sore, and whenever I sprained my hand or smacked it hard against Lupine, Kit would get some ice on it. Sure, I would like some ice.

He holds off on putting ice in my glass. "Then order a drink and hold it in that hand—I ain't running a charity."

"Okay, give me..." My mind goes blank. What do men usually drink? "I don't know." Maybe Feather can give me some advice. I would ask Tucker, but he doesn't seem like someone to ask for information. "What do you drink around here, Feather?"

Tucker injects himself and points out a bottle on the bar reading *Full Moon Gin.* "Hey, how about you get a G 'n' T?" I look at a dazed Feather, who just asks for the usual, and Borne taps three claws on the table like they are talking in code.

I feel like I insulted Feather somehow. "Sure, I will get one of those."

Nail takes out two glasses, one large and one small. "Tall or short?"

I don't want to drink that much, especially around them. I wonder if they have a smaller than short because for a Prime a short seems like a large. "Short."

I see that Nail gets the drink ready with the speed of a master while Tooth grabs a beer called Coons, which is a dark beer with the face of a raccoon on the bottle, and puts it in front of Tucker. For Borne, he gets a vodka martini in a glass the size of Borne's paw, and for Feather, he only grabs a soda dispenser and puts in some dark cola-flavored liquid. In their motions and the two moving around, I get them mixed up. "So, Tooth, where did you serve in the war?" I get the attention of one of them.

"No, he's Tooth, I'm Nail," Nail corrects.

Tooth takes my drink from Nail and puts it in front of me. "We are brothers."

"Identical in every way."

"Minus dick size—I got a few inches on him." He points down to his crotch.

"Oh, do you want to show him?"

"Nah, I don't want to humiliate you in front of customers."

Tooth explains that they started this bar right after the war as a VFW for the area. Since the bar is right next to the stronghold, they get soldiers from the citadel and all over to come in and have a couple of drinks and talk about their war stories. They were both first stationed in China when the US tried to *democratize* the country after World War III. They explain their job was to help enforce peace in Shanghai by doing daily routes through the city with army machine guns strapped to their car. After the civil war with the Primes broke off and China was absorbed by the PLF, they left China and joined the PLF back in a newly found Kingdom to rebuild the city, and with their service they got to build the Tooth and Nail to escape the military life and settled down to help out those veterans in need.

"And that's where we are now," Tooth finishes.

As the need for soldiers declined, I imagine a lot of them left to start a civilian life. After all, a lot of them had just fought in two brutal wars. "I imagine a lot left because they saw and did things they are not proud of." Maybe I can get him to confirm if what Lupine told me was true about the war crimes.

He looks at the wall of pictures of veterans. "Unfortunately yes, everyone that comes through these doors saw things they would not rather talk about, until they are drunk enough to start breaking down and bawling at us. That's when you bring them in the back, let them cry it out and sober up, then give them a pat on the back and see them the next day." These two really seem like great guys, finding any way they can to give back to those who served. Despite all the horrors that war creates, I can imagine that some of them have amazing stories of heroism that echo through these halls.

"You should hear some of the stories from these guys," Tucker tells me.

Who am I to get involved in other people's demons? "No thanks, I don't want to get involved with other people's lives. I mean these guys are war veterans, and who am I to ask them?"

Feather's phone vibrates on the table. "They will always be willing to tell you stories. It's a way to remember their friends and fallen brothers, and it's common to hear Primes talk about the stupid shit they did with their friends."

Tucker holds up his drink. "Like that one time Borne and I snuck out of our hotel room in Singapore and got smashed bar hopping and Borne ended up chucking a human out of a two-story window."

Borne bumps my shoulder and points to Tucker's back. He then taps on the back of Tucker's shell with the back of his hand and I see Tucker reflexively tuck into a ball that sits perfectly on the stool like a display of art. His clothes even compensate for the tuck and stretch without ripping.

He squirms inside of his shell and tries to grab Borne's arm. "You *know* I hate that! Help me unroll, damn it."

We all get a good laugh while I just sit and wonder how Tucker's body works if he can crawl inside of himself and curl up into a ball. Borne pulls back his backpack and lets Tucker spread out his waist and legs to open back up.

I decide to finally take a sip of my drink. The ice has already melted, and the liquid is dribbling over the side of the glass. Since the drinking age back home is twenty-one, I've never experienced spirits. I was never invited to parties in Detroit and couldn't afford anything like this. When I put my lips to it, my mouth burns as if I am breathing in gasoline. I should finish it regardless of whether I like it. It would be rude to waste it. "Holy shit, that tastes like pine cones."

Nail raises an eyebrow at me downing it like that. "Of course it does. It's gin. What did you expect it to taste like?"

The drink immediately hits me like a burning semi. I shouldn't have done that.

"I've never had gin before. I am only seventeen." I think.

He empties the ice from the glass into the sink and rinses it out. "Oh, that's right, your pussy government doesn't let you drink until you've grown some hair on your sack."

Tucker leans over and picks out a lime from behind the counter. "You're only seventeen?" He squeezes the lime slice into his beer. "Damn, kid, you are pretty young to be in the military!"

"Getting them in younger and younger these days, a human to boot," Nail points out.

I don't know much about the PLF's stance on integrating humans into society. I might as well ask, even though it might seem a bit out of touch in regards to where I am now. "Are there other humans in the PLF?" I ask Nail.

The glass gets put on the shelf behind him neatly in line with the others. "We do. They are just scattered around in small towns on the border of Wasteland."

"Small towns" is the same phrase we use in the US to describe the camps of Prime refugees and ghettos.

I think back to the article I read back at the medical bay. "I mean Pure is trying to integrate them into society."

"Pfft." Nail leans back and looks over the rest of the patrons of the bar. "*Integrate* is not the word I would be using around here kid. Last time we heard the word *integrating* was out of Hunts the Cunt." Man, I haven't heard that nickname in quite a while.

Feather leans over Tucker. "Pure thinks that the best way to start inhabiting humans back into the PLF is by using chinks."

I guess Feather still has some grudges against Chinese then. "Why them?"

Nail sets down a glass of water and fills it for me. "Because they've learned to know their place."

The Chinese people in the United States have endured a similar hellscape to the Primes post-World War III. Entire families of immigrants that escaped communist China, and even those who have been here for generations, were all suddenly public enemy number one. They were spied on by not just the US government, but by their neighbors. Colossal restricted areas in major Chinatowns were created to "keep the Chinese populace safe during an increase in hate crimes against Asians," as it was worded. Every Asian nationality was assumed to be Chinese. It didn't matter what you were; if you looked Chinese you were deemed to be a communist boot licker. Even after the communist party fell in China with the help of the Primes, the virus latched onto the Chinese race and persists even to this day. It was a shame that the virus also manifested onto Primes, who then seemed to take out all their anger on the Chinese population in China that Pure inherited from Ex-President Hunts after the war as a sort of war trophy.

I feel like I should change the subject. It's apparent that Primes are still split on the whole China issue, as well as human beings in general, so maybe race isn't the best thing to mention in a bar of war vets. I think it's best to keep it to domestic issues and questions.

Tooth and Nail leave to service some other patrons in the bar who are continually trying to get their attention, only noticing because the conversation stalls out long enough to hear them tapping on the table.

I feel like I should get to know these guys a little better. Maybe I can start by talking about Kingdom. "So what is it like living in Kingdom?"

Tucker empties his glass and turns it upside down on a coaster. "We don't technically live here; we just like to visit often."

"We are on the road a lot," Feather mentions. "That trailer that you first came in on is more of our home than our actual houses."

I can't imagine living in that trailer.

"It's not very discreet, especially when you tint all the windows black and cover them with metal. How did you guys even get past the checkpoints in that thing?" I inquire.

"We don't use checkpoints," says Feather. "When we take you back to the US, you will see firsthand how we sneak in and how we get out. It's actually not difficult despite what your government tells you. As long as we don't interact with normal humans, everything usually goes smoothly."

He should mention that to Lupine, apparently. "I guess Lupine doesn't uphold that rule."

Feather shrugs his shoulders. "Well, he makes his exceptions, but we all make exceptions to the rules. When your squad is tasked with espionage, any rule is open to some criticism."

When anything can happen, there can't really be rules. Lupine never expected to save me back there. "I guess."

Tucker leans over to look at me. "Now let me ask you, what's it like living in the United States right now?"

"For Primes, they are still discriminated against and kept in ghettos." There are a couple of ghettos in Detroit. Humans are discouraged from entering Prime ghettos, and Primes are encouraged to stay in their neighborhoods as a means to keep them safe from humans by the government. President Graft has made it clear to us that he sees Primes being a part of society, but the steps taken are slow, unfelt, and usually backwards. "Humans still just find them..." I struggle to think of the word to use. "...unnerving."

Tucker nods. "Yeah, when we go into the US, we are looked at and carefully watched, but we are no longer constantly mocked or heckled on the street. Might just be because we are all just tired of being actively racist at each other and have left the government to passively do it for us."

I couldn't see Lupine getting shit thrown at him. I feel like he would snap in two any Hunter without a second thought. "Maybe they just got used to you being there." I throw out there. "After all, when change happens people rarely take it well. It's only when they learn to live with the change that they accept it as normal."

Before people saw Primes as the enemy because all they saw were soldiers. Primes with guns, Primes in soldier uniforms, Primes killing others. Humans never saw Primes in church, sitting at bars, in school, enjoying life. All the news showed was them wreaking death and destruction. US citizens never saw what Primes truly were behind the uniform they were created into.

"I don't care what they think of us," Feather explains. "We were treated like shit after World War III, and we will be treated like shit if we go back now."

That response doesn't seem like something Feather would normally say. "Why do you say that?"

"We are not human. We were not born into this world; we were grown into it. Would you trust your neighbors if you found out they were all ex-military?

Would they snap from the pressure and attack you?" He makes Primes sound like dogs, kind and loyal until they turn on you and attack. I don't understand why he so negatively regards humanity, my race.

"Primes and humans can live together once people no longer see Primes as weapons or inhuman." I don't want to argue with him but I can't help it that he is oversimplifying this subject.

He smiles and holds his head up high as if he claims victory over me. "You just know I am right and can't make up a..."

Tucker kicks Feather under his stool. "Hey, stop it with that political shit. I hear enough of it at the stronghold—I don't need to hear it from you." Thank you, Tucker.

I apologize to Tucker, who feels like the type of person to avoid conflict. Instead of fighting, he wants to converse without conflict. So far he hasn't offended anyone, said anything offensive, and just wants peace among his friends. "Sorry, it's just that I've grown up with fucking idiots at my school who don't understand the world outside of their echo chamber, and I usually have to explain to them what's going on with the news."

"You can see a lot of the world from a classroom," Feather murmurs sarcastically under his breath.

"Anyway..." Tucker changes the subject. "How is your training with Lupine going?"

"It's been going well. I can't say it isn't working, but I just wish that he would go a little easier on me."

Borne finally speaks. "Kit told me he is using his training regimen on him."

"Is he trying to kill him?" Tucker slams his hand on the table. "I've seen what Gores put him through and that shit is crazy!"

I guess I should be grateful that the student is teaching me instead of the true master. "It's not the same. It's toned down slightly to accommodate for my lack of Primal..." What word should I use? "Genes." As long as Lupine doesn't hear me bitching I will be fine. This might be my only chance for a while, if ever.

Borne takes a final sip of his beer. "Well, it looks like it's working. You look much stronger than you did when we first saw you."

He's not wrong there. "Yeah, I feel actually a lot better than I did in The States."

145

I seem to be less tired, more alert, and look built too. Maybe all I needed in my life was a good healthy habit. I mean, a couple months ago I never would have thought I would look like this.

Tucker pokes my arm. "I mean, you still aren't strong enough to beat Tooth or Nail, but you can always come back and try your luck again."

The grizzly taps his beer with his extended claws. "So you can't bet against him and make some more quick cash?" he lectures.

I finish the last of my drink assuming we will all be leaving soon. "I understand." Being poor for my life, I understand just how far people will go for a quick dollar. I've never been tempted to steal from someone or con them, but I would have never had the funds to go to a bar like this, or own a house like I have now. I feel better than I ever, I have a home, I have a job. I can't shake the feeling that the PLF has given me more than just a sense of purpose. It's given me people to hang out with and talk to.

Everyone slams down their drink and packs up their stuff. Tucker gets up first and puts down a couple of bills from his backpack, which look like American currency except the front is Pure's face, and on the backside PLF soldiers hold up the flag in front of a war-torn city while others around it pick up stones and rebuild. In total, our bill was thirty-two with tips. "Well, if you're ready, let's get that present for Kit. Borne, can you text Shooter that we are going to be stopping by in a couple of minutes? Tell him to heat up that forge he's got. His number is..." He looks at his phone.

Borne already pulls his out and dials in a number. "He isn't going to like this." Why wouldn't he like this? What does that mean?

"I don't care—just tell him we are on the way," Tucker declares.

I finish the rest of my drink in one go. "Who is Shooter?" I then immediately regret that.

Feather scoots by Borne, who starts with *ni hao* and speaks Chinese into the phone. I hear a gruff voice coming from the other end and a couple of laughs. "He's our munitions expert, the guy who makes all of our guns and weapons."

Tucker opens the door for us. "He used to work in a gun workshop in China before he fled to join the PLF."

Speaking of China. "Have you guys been there?"

146

Feather confirms. "Sure, lots of times."

"Is there anywhere I can learn Chinese?" I mean I couldn't learn it in The States, and it seems like everyone else knows it. It will probably be an incredibly useful skill.

Tucker jumps up to smack me on the shoulder. "Sure! Borne can teach you all the Chinese you want. He is fluent."

Well, maybe English isn't his main language. That's why he might not talk a lot. "That would be awesome!"

The bear takes a deep breath and mutters something in Chinese.

Tiger's Smile

We get back into the car and begin our drive down to Stronghold. On the way there I ask Tucker what brought him to the PLF. I want to figure out just where they came from. Then I can evaluate their skills and know just how long they've been with Sagittarius. So far, he seems open enough to discuss it, and I would like to know what kind of life this pangolin lives.

He tells me that he was manufactured during the first wave of Primes. He got sent out not to China but out to Japan to reclaim Tokyo for the Japanese. "Millions of Japanese were held hostage by the Chinese government. If the US stepped one foot into Japan, they would kill them all by gassing them." Tucker's team was charged with killing all Chinese forces in Japan. It took over seven months of fighting, but they eventually kicked out all the Chinese from Japan and found the Chinese general in charge and captured him, he was later convicted of war crimes and executed. Tucker's squad were given medals of honor and praise for their participation in the war. That operation is what gave him the opportunity to join Sagittarius after the war and later to be part of the formation of the PLF. "That's where I also met Shooter and brought him to the PLF."

I am impressed that, for as small as Tucker is, he did so much and managed to survive the war.

Out of my window, I see a ground-level church sign reading *Faust Elementary School* spelled in replaceable letters. We stop at a school stop sign, and the schoolyard is in full view of the road. A grade of Primal children is all at play. A jungle gym set is sprawled out over a vast field.

I try to count how many different species I see before me, but lose myself in the variety of them all. Stags, badgers, cats, wolves, alligators...no, that one is a crocodile. They all are joyfully playing in the midday sun, unified in a youthful adventure, all set out to free themselves of the rules. I see adults trying to corral the children and keeping eyes on them from above. They are the first generation of Primes untainted by the horrors of war. I wonder what they would think of me and what they would do if they saw a human being. What are they being taught about us? Are they being brainwashed into thinking we are the enemy, or are they learning that humans and Primes can live together someday? A future of hope, or no future at all.

Tucker nudges me from the side and asks what I am looking at with such fascination. I tell him the school out there, and he only smiles and asks if I remember my days at elementary school. I guess he didn't want to talk about himself the entire car ride.

"Not really." The only thing that I remember vividly of my elementary school was Parents' Day, and everyone asking where my mom and dad were. At that moment, I realized how alone I was. I saw all these mothers and fathers raising their children, holding them, talking to them, comforting them, and the only thing that ever came close to a sense of comfort was the hope that they just lost me and were out there searching for me. Am I supposed to believe that they are still alive? I mean just look at what happened to Lupine, and what has happened to all the orphans back at the orphanage: Do they all hope that their parents will walk through those doors and everything will be okay? I look out one last time to those children and try to find myself in that crowd, but the car speeds away before I am given a chance.

"Hey. Feather, speaking of which, how is your kid?" Tucker asks.

He props his head on the window with this arm while driving with the other. "Good. He is just finishing up with his placement tests." Feather seems disinterested.

Maybe I can ask him about what history they are learning. "What kind of history classes do they teach?"

Feather turns on the air conditioning to full blast as the cool air blows his feathers on his neck. "Mostly history of the PLF."

"Must be pretty short courses," I joke.

"They don't touch on the United States until they are older." He lightly touches on my answer.

I think he knows what I am getting at. "Do the schools put us as the bad guys then?"

"They let the kids decide on that. They just present the *facts* of what happened."

So they let them decide, but it doesn't mean they can't bend the facts to make humans sound barbaric.

I feel like I should shy away from politics around Feather. He seems not the debatable type. "What does your kid want to do, Feather?"

He rubs his temple with his hand and stares straight ahead without answering. I look at Tucker for an answer; he mimes him holding a gun and peeking through a scope. I feel like I shouldn't step on Feather's personal matters since he doesn't seem proud of his son for wanting to be like his father, but who am I to say whether his son should follow in his father's footsteps? Even still, I can see where Feather is coming from.

We arrive at a foundry that seems to produce smog and black smoke in equal parts. Everything from the sidewalk outside to the fence surrounding the facility is covered in a light layer of soot. I take a step out along with everyone else and head up to the gates. We flash our badges and get escorted into the foundry. Inside I can only hear the sound of metal grinding against grindstones, the clanging of massive cauldrons of molten steel, and gongs of hammers smashing down upon sheets of iron.

I probably should stay close to Borne just in case something were to fall from the rafters above. No one else around here is wearing safety helmets or wearing much protection. They must either be confident that they will do everything correctly or they are just averse to safety.

Towers of lava end with taps at the bottom, where workers empty the liquid into molds and roll them off. Each worker is covered head to toe in flame-proof gowns, and each of them breathes through a hazmat mask. I hold my breath while we walk down the center of the foundry toward the back. Above me, I see several Primes walking parallel to us on scaffolds made of steel and rust. The sun can only reflect back on the dust particles in the air, so space darkens as we approach the center. Dim lamps over our heads and portable light fixtures powered by generators on the sides give some light.

"Shooter! Where are you?!" Tucker puts his hand to his mouth to amplify the sound. I still barely hear him, and I am standing next to him.

One of the nearby workers waves at Tucker. "He's in the workshop in the back!"

He gives him a thumbs-up. "Thanks!"

In the back of the foundry rests several doors that lead into a smaller, quieter workshop where the clanging of heavy metal is replaced with precise taps from hammers to etch, form and fix gun parts. Primes sit in chairs at individual stations hunched over with tiny hammers and jeweler glasses on making guns and bullets. I wonder if these Primes are part of the military. Even with the entirety of China under PLF rule to export cheap labor, the PLF still employs Primes to make their weapons. Just goes to show how much the PLF doesn't trust Chinese craftsmanship. The workers all seem pretty happy working. They all look well fed and lively amongst themselves.

In the center is a large table the size of three of the work stations, where there is only one Prime at work, a hefty panda Prime with a workman apron strapped around his waist and a filthy T-shirt under it. He is the spitting image of a blue-collar man...panda. He has a cigar in his mouth, and he continually rekindles it with a torch next to him. His bifocals are focused upon a small bullet casing as he is filing it with not a black powdered but a black viscous liquid.

"Yo, Shooter!" Tucker still maintains his foundry voice.

He holds up a finger and retains his concentration. "One second!" He has a thick gruff Chinese accent. He finishes off the bullet by tightening a cap on top of the head. "What is it?" The first thing he notices when he looks up is me. "What is *he* doing here?!" He reaches for an unsharpened blade and points it at me.

Tucker immediately gets in between Shooter and me. He holds up his hands and tries to calm him down. "Whoa, Shoots, he's all right!"

The other Primes remain concentrated on their work, unshaken by the commotion. I hold myself close to Tucker, but since I can't stand behind him, I move over to Borne.

"Bullshit!" He moves to a small swinging door on the side of the station.

Feather approaches Shooter slowly. "Just put the blade down!" He is in between the station and Tucker before he stops.

"You should know better than to bring him here!" He still holds the blade in his hands.

"I will explain once we get out of here! Let's go outside for a smoke!" Feather leads us outside through a door marked by an exit sign.

I maintain my distance from Shooter as well as stay next to Feather and Borne. The fact that Shooter is acting hostile to me means that he either has a grudge against me, which since I have never met him before only means that he just hates me for being human. He doesn't know anything about me and yet he immediately pulls a blade on me without a second thought. I wanted to say something but I guess it's better for Feather to de-escalate things before I decide to open my mouth. The way he saw me and freaked out almost can make me think he's an Evol, but then again I doubt Feather or Tucker would bring me to an Evol.

We are dumped into an alley between the gate and the building where shipments come in and trash is taken out and put in giant dumpsters labeled *Metal*, *Recyclables*, *Waste*, and *Other*.

Shooter takes out a cigarette and lights it with an etched steel lighter that reflects blue in the lone ray of sun. "Explain."

Feather does the same. "He is—"

"Not you." He points at me with a gnarled finger. "Him."

Borne reaches back and nudges me forward toward Shooter. "Don't worry, he won't bite," he tells me quietly.

Yeah, he won't bite *you*. I slowly approach him but keep the distance that Lupine can't reach with his knife when we train. "My name is Ghent and I am a human and I am part of the PLF." I want to make sure he knows who I am and that I am respected by Pure enough to join the PLF. If he supports Pure he will understand. If he doesn't support Pure...well, then I will find out.

After hearing me out, he flicks the butt into a dumpster. "You look like every hairless, skin-wrapped sack of wasted meat I've ever met. What makes me believe you?" He doesn't seem to believe my story at all.

"Pure initiated me himself into the army, and Kitsune tested me..." I try to explain as best as I can while judging just how far I need to stay away, both physically and mentally, from him.

"If Pure decided to let a scrawny, inferior human join then I am moving back

152

to China," he comments.

I take a step toward him. I shouldn't be afraid of him, despite his size and his tough attitude, and I should not be fearful of Primes who happen to be biased toward humans. I know why they hate humans. I've seen the horrible way we treat Primes in the States, but I am not that. I am much more than just a stereotypical American and I need him to see it. "Look, I get it. You hate me just because I am not a Prime. Fine, you can hate my skin but don't hate me." I approach closer to him with my head high.

He is unwavering in his defiant stance. "You have some serious balls telling me this."

"I've been going through hell every day training with Lupine. You don't scare me, and you shouldn't be afraid of me." I sound brave but my heart is racing and my palms are getting sweaty, twitching back with a flight instinct.

He folds his arms and approaches me. "You really think that you scare me?"

I get up to his arms' length to me. "You are the one who grabbed a knife when you saw me," I point out.

He keeps his eyes on me but tilts his head back, almost amused. "Out of anger, not fear."

I am standing right in front of the eight-foot tank. "I understand why you are angry at my kind—I don't blame you. However, I am not like them. If you are really a member of the PLF then you should respect me as a member of the PLF, not as a human."

His amusement fades and a pensive scowl molds into his face. "What did you come here for anyway?"

I doubt he will help me but I need to try. I can't read this guy enough to know what's going through his head. "I am asking you to make Kitsune something."

"Why come to me then? There is nothing she needs that I haven't already made her," he deflects.

"I want it to be special, though." Something that she will use a lot. She is a surgeon from what I remember the day I was kidnapped. "A scalpel, made for her."

He gives a single chuckle. "What are you trying to get out of this?"

"Look, I just want her to know I am thankful for everything she's done for me. She's helped me a lot the last couple of months with Lupine." Maybe if I make it look more like he's doing a favor for her, he will be more likely to agree. "This isn't for me; it's for her."

His lips curl and he kicks some scrap metal near him toward the wall. He looks toward Borne and starts speaking in Chinese to him. Borne talks back, and from what I can gather they are discussing something relating to me and Kitsune and our names come up for a fraction of a second with how fast they are speaking. After some back and forth he grumbles, spits on the ground next to me, and waves us into his workshop. "What did you have in mind?" He seems a little more open to me. Maybe it's because he imagines me as Kit, but at least now I have a chance to get to know him better.

I detail out what I think would be perfect for Kit. He scraps my idea and creates something he knows would be perfect for her. He orders us to grab a couple of chairs and wait in front of him. He moves all the weapons from around me and leaves me isolated in a corner while he sits and talks with Borne in Chinese. I attempt to make conversation with him, but he ignores my advances and continues to work.

While he works, I can see the mastery he has in his art. Each hammer swing, each movement on the whet wheel, all are delicate yet forceful, beautiful yet harsh. The steel melds with his mind and becomes a creation of his own will. Tools accommodate for his large hands. He collects the required materials and gathers them around him.

He starts by smelting down a brick of steel in a cauldron and empties it into a mold; he then carves the handle while it heats up, and pours. Once the metal is heated up, and into the mold, he takes the mold and wears it down to the shape of a scalpel. On a wet wheel, he makes the edges of the blade and folds the blade several times, heating it up and quenching it over and over. After about an hour, the final product is polished and engraved.

A scalpel is a tool to save lives; thus, it must reflect that. It is a blade formed from Chinese steel, engraved with the symbols for appreciation etched on the sides, a surface to reveal Kit's face as if they are thanking her. A handle crafted from Chinese wood, polished to a jade smoothness, a fox head carved at the end and its tails.

He wipes his brow with his sleeve and sets it nicely into a wooden box. He stuffs the inside with hay and wraps it in packing tape to keep it from rattling inside.

"There." He sets the box on the table and slides it over to me. "You can leave now."

"Thank you." I carefully take the box.

"No need." He wipes down his tools and cleans his workbench. Right before we take our leave, I look behind me to see him look at me one last time before heading out the door. His face is still disgruntled and resentful, but he has at least put down his knife and isn't threatening me.

We leave the foundry and get into the car before anyone starts talking again. "I can't believe that you got that from him." Feather starts the ignition.

I clutch the box. "Well, you just have to reason with people sometimes."

"Shooter isn't someone that can be reasoned with, especially by a human."

He seems to know something about him; maybe I should just ask him outright. "Why?" I go for the obvious answers first. "Is he an Evol?"

"Shooter was an illegal Chinese bred Prime. He used to work for the Triad as their gunsmith before they split." The Triad was the criminal organization that ran most of China's streets and casinos; they also dabbled in the Chinese government and local business manufacturing forgeries of fashion designer bags and jewelry, and the occasional prostitution ring. They were shut down once the US, with the help of the Primes, stormed through China during World War III and uprooted the entire organization. However, after the PLF occupation of China, with the rising anti-Prime sentiment, they grew into several sets of terrorist groups named the Fangs, who seek nothing more than kicking out the PLF and reinstating a communist party. "The US Army stormed into his house and well...you can fill in the rest."

I don't want to fill it in. I think he is saying that the US Army killed his gang. He'd have a good reason to keep a grudge against Americans then. "Shit, did I offend him?" I feel like I should go back to apologize, to tell him that I am not one of those kinds of soldiers. I would never hurt someone who didn't deserve it.

Tucker has my back; he literally has a hand on my back, shaking it. "Nah, there is no way you could have known. He is just a little prejudiced toward humans."

I wonder how many Shooters there are out there in the PLF.

. . .

They wave at me from the car before leaving. I feel glad to be back at the gym, but I then realize that the trip may have been my only chance to get outside of this facility for quite a while. Even so, I still enjoyed the time I spent with Feather and company. They seem really nice. Of course, a rabid badger seems nice compared to Lupine. With my gift in hand, I head inside to see if Kit is still around to receive her scalpel. I shouldn't worry about Lupine being around. It's past five o'clock, and the facility itself remains empty besides possibly a janitor or a straggler putting in some late hours.

I go through the doors and see Kit just about to leave with her doctor's bag and a backpack. She has her white doctor's jacket on and seems to be in a hurry. She notices me and stops dead in her tracks. "Ghent, what are you doing here? Have you been here this entire time?"

Remembering that Kit might tell Lupine I went outside, I have to make sure not to get busted for disobeying his orders. "Please don't be mad at me, and please don't tell Lupine this: I went outside of the facility with—"

"You went outside?" she says, alerted.

"Feather, Borne, and Tucker," I finish.

"That fucking rat." She curses under her breath.

"Listen, I know I was told not to go outside." I feel a little shy giving her the gift. "But I went out there to get..."

"I don't want to hear any of it! You know you could have gotten hurt, kidnapped by Evols, or killed! I don't want to start picking bullets out of you as well—" She doesn't see the present until I hand it over to her.

"Something for you."

"Wait..." Her hands hesitantly retrieve the box. "You risked your life to get something for me?"

I hope I am not blushing. "I just wanted to thank you for helping me with Lupine and taking time out of your schedule to take care of my health. I mean, without you I would surely be a corpse by now."

"Well... I... You know you could have just told me 'Thank you.'" I see her cheeks turning a different shade of red beneath her fur.

"Words don't mean much—that's what Lupine taught me," I joke.

Kit carefully opens the box and unwraps its contents.

"I didn't really know what to get you so I just thought you could use it."

She sees the scalpel and holds it in her hands.

"Shooter engraved it especially for you. I just…"

She remains motionless and just stares blankly down at the scalpel.

I don't know if I offended her somehow. "You okay, Kit?"

She snaps out of her trance and packs it back into the box quickly. "Thank you, it's…nice…of you to think about me." A pulse of sadness comes over her as she chokes on her words. "See you around."

I get no hug or anything, just a glance back as she pushes through the door. I mean I wasn't expecting anything in return, but…well…at least she said thank you. Kit deserves this, and hey, maybe after today I should get the gang something too for risking their tails to bust me out of here. I have to remember to thank them for that somehow.

"You're welcome, and I hope that it works great for you!" I shout back as she exits the building and heads toward her car.

I figure it is way past time that I head home. Before I go, I use the bathroom, all the while thinking of what I should have for dinner tonight. As I exit the restroom and head for the gym's exit I notice a tiger Prime standing in civilian clothes, a black T-shirt with some sort of Prime band called Roaring Tide written on the front. He is modestly built and has several piercings on his ear and his tail. He pushes himself off the door entrance.

"Hey, you're that human that everyone is talking about!" He seems welcoming and friendly, but there is something off about him. Besides, I have to watch out.

I decide to brush him off and try to get away as quickly as I can. "I am the only human here. Mister…?" I attempt to sidestep him, but he mirrors my movements to block me from the door.

"Taiga."

Never heard of him. "What rank are you supposed to be?" I look for any distinct markings or badges, yet he seems only to be a civilian. That's what scares me the most—that someone like him has access to a place like this. "I don't see a badge. How did you even get in here?"

"Oh, damn it, did I forget my badge again?" He taps his forehead with his palm. "I swear I would forget where it was if I sewed it into my skin." When he lifts his hand I notice several tattoos embedded into his fur like images on a rug. "I am part of Sagittarius."

I don't remember Lupine or anyone ever bringing him up. "Weird..." I take another step back. "...because Lupine or Gores never mentioned a tiger."

He leans into the arch of the doorway and puts his feet onto the other side, relaxing but still blocking my exit. He examines his claws and starts to pick at his fingers with his thumb. "Well, I am not part of the squad like Feather, Borne, or Kit." He obviously knows their names, and even that Kitsune is called Kit. "I am more of a supporting role. Paperwork, public relations, cleaning up Lupine's messes, and even being on a couple missions with them. Kind of like Hoots."

Maybe I can test him. "Well, if you are really part of Sagittarius then tell me something that only a member of Sagittarius would know, or maybe something on Lupine."

He chuckles and swings his tail toward me. On his tail I notice several metal bands with decorative engravings on each one fitted around his tail. "I could tell you everything about Lupine. He and I go way back. I initially trained with him back when he joined the PLF."

I don't believe him. "Prove it."

"Well," he begins, counting with his fingers, "I assume you've seen him naked being in the showers with him." How does he know that? "So you've seen his lashings on his back from when he was in the slave camp." So he was in a camp. I know Primes were put in camps and forced into slave labor for criminal organizations that illegally created or imported Primes. "That's where also he got his tail smashed in with a sledge hammer and bent to the left to where it permanently stuck there." Anyone could have seen Lupine naked, especially if he did in fact know Lupine while they were training in the PLF. "He escaped from a slave camp in South America when it caught on fire when he was about five." Wait...a camp that caught fire in South America? That would explain the jungles he went to.

"Wait, how old is Lupine?" I ask hesitantly.

He smiles. "He's about twenty-something. Hard to say how old you are when you are not given a creation date."

Twenty-something... It could possibly line up, though I somehow doubt he is that young. I mean, to have that much experience at such a young age is unreasonable, even for a Prime who is said to age faster than humans. Maybe Lupine does know something about my jungle. "Umm…okay. What is his least favorite gun?"

"Python," he answers without even a thought. "He almost blew his nuts off with them while shooting with Gores one night."

Taiga seems like he is actually telling the truth. Maybe this might be my chance to find out more about Lupine, and if I do that maybe I can relate to him more, open him up. "Favorite hobby?"

He smirks. "Work."

Lupine enjoys his work? From what I've seen he hates training me. "Other than working."

He thinks quite hard on that one. "Probably listening to music while working."

Music then? Maybe I should ask him to play some music while we train.

Taiga removes his foot from the door and approaches me. "Got any more questions for me?"

"No." I feel a little more comfortable with him getting closer to me. He doesn't look armed, and I think he isn't stupid enough to try to hurt me on Pure's turf. "I just wanted to make sure you weren't lying."

He reaches his hand out for a high-five. "I have no reason to lie to you—you are part of Sagittarius after all."

It feels awkward leaving him standing there. He seems pretty chill. I give him a high-five slowly.

His hand moves quickly to my hand. When he moves forward I notice the grip of a handgun jostle at his side, holstered in his jeans. "Awesome! Say, buddy, want to shoot some breeze, get to know each other a little better?"

I slowly peel my vision away from his gun and back to his hands that are now stuffed into his jean pockets. "I guess."

He takes out his empty left hand and points over to the sofa cushions. "Want to sit down? You must be exhausted from driving around with Feather and dealing with Tucker."

I keep flickering back to his right hand while trying to make eye contact with him. "Sure."

"Oh." He reaches down and pulls out the handgun at his side. "Sorry, I didn't mean to scare you." He dangles the gun by the barrel. "It's for my own protection." The gun looks like a modified Badger. It shares the same shape but the handle is narrower and there appears to be a silencer attached on the end. Why would a PLF soldier be walking around with a silencer? "Live in a bad neighborhood."

"I understand," I claim cautiously. "Could you, um...unload it?"

He takes the gun and hands it over to me first. "Better yet, why don't you hold onto it?"

I wasn't expecting this. I mean, it would make me feel safer if I had his gun, but he could have another stashed somewhere else and is using this as a distraction. I take the gun by the grip and slide the magazine out; it is loaded and the safety is on. When I eject the magazine I can feel it almost stick to something in the slot. The gun is lighter than a Badger too, almost filed down.

"There, now let's sit down and chat a bit." He walks over to the couch and sits down closest to the window.

I put the gun at my side just like he had it and then take the magazine and put it inside my jeans pocket. "Sure."

As he sits there he seems to constantly toy with the end of his tail and a steel bracelet placed around it like someone would wear on their wrist. "So. You like being the PLF's first human soldier?"

He doesn't know I am a hybrid? Strange that someone in Sagittarius didn't tell him. "Well, I am actually part Prime. I know it sounds weird but it's true."

He is surprised by this development. "Really? Wow, that's crazy. Do you feel like a Prime at all?"

"No, not really." I feel healthier and more energetic than I did before, but nothing else.

He taps his fingers on the sofa. "We never stop discovering things about Primes, it seems. Every day we learn of something else going on." His hand motions to me with an open palm. "Did that change the choice you made in joining the PLF?"

"Well, I wasn't really given a choice, was I?" I mean, I could have said no, but the end result would have been far worse for me.

"Fair. From what I heard the choices were pretty stacked against you." He speaks the truth. "There anything you want out of this?"

160

Only one thing. "Well, when I spoke to Pure he kind of dropped that he knows where I came from." And on the off chance, "Do you know of a place called Oasis, camp in South America, by any chance?"

"I know a bar in Utah named Oasis, and the human band, that I've been to, but nothing more than that."

Kind of figured, but I never know who could have heard or read something. "Damn, well I kind of expected that." I try to laugh my disappointment off.

"Well," he smacks the top of the sofa with his left hand. "how about I give you a choice?"

I don't know where he is going with this. "What kind of choice?"

He looks at the exit doors and outside the window. "Well...through some of my contacts and friends in higher places I can get you out from Pure's thumb, out of the PLF, and give you some freedom."

"You can let me escape?" I am careful with my words. If he is telling the truth then this might be an opportunity for me to leave the PLF and get my freedom back.

"Exactly, and all I would need from you is to help me out," he offers.

Help him out? Help in Sagittarius could mean a million different things, from mowing his lawn to killing a political leader. "Help how?"

He twiddles with the tip of his tail. "Well, I have some friends of mine who want to meet you. Some pretty important people if you feel like mingling with some higher society."

The sound of that seems unnerving. "Why not just bring them here to my condo?"

"Well..." He drums his fingers on the sofa. "...I don't think Pure wants you to talk to anyone that he might not approve of, so bringing them to you would cause issues for me—and for them."

Just who would he bring to me that Pure wouldn't approve of? "Who are these friends of yours?"

"Oh, just some ex-veterans turned executives at large corporations here in Kingdom, just some friends I've met in my work. You know, suits, and Pure never has liked Primes in suits that don't have a plate of badges on them."

He seems to be pretty involved in Prime society if he is able to get this much access, but as a member of a covert operative group it's not too far out of the question. "I don't know... I mean not to offend, but I just don't want to end up being caught up in more than I am already committed to at this point."

He frowns a bit and puts his foot up on the coffee table. "It's okay, buddy, I understand. You've got a lot to think about and worry about. I am just letting you think about it. It would just be a quick meet and greet session, not even an hour long, and then you would be good to explore anywhere you wanted in Kingdom. Hell, if you wanted to go to California or Utah I got a couple of nice places you could stay if you wanted to take a trip."

"Thanks for understanding." I don't want to risk anything right now when I am being watched so closely by Pure and Lupine. "It's just that the last time I was offered something, I was kidnapped and brought here." Wait... Lupine offered me something before I was knocked out.

He chuckles and takes out his phone from his back pocket. "Fair enough, bud. I just figured you would want a little bit of time away, to get to see the world kind of thing."

I would for sure like to see the world, and I guess the PLF will allow me to do it, but it's probably going to be for work. Maybe having an option to see the world as a civilian wouldn't hurt too much. "Yeah, that would actually be really nice."

He claps his hands together. "Well, how about this then: You think about my offer, and if you are interested you can give me a call and I can set up an appointment with them, okay?"

Call him how? "I don't have a phone."

"Here." He offers me his phone. "You want my work phone?"

Oh...um. "Well, I don't think I should..."

He wiggles it in front of me like bait. "It's a new standard issue PLF phone. I had to replace mine because it broke in half on my last mission. Don't worry, I can erase everything on it and give you a clean slate. Get five gigs of internet."

Internet access in the PLF—a window outside. "Well, I guess if you think it's okay with Lupine."

"Pfft, Lupine won't care as long as you don't call him." He pulls the phone back and shows me how he resets it back to factory mode, which he explains is as cleared of data as if it was just made. Once he is done he hands it over to me.

I reach out and grab it. It feels lighter than my old phone. This one feels brand new, not a single scratch or mark on the screen. Even has a protective layer over the screen. "Thanks."

"No problem, buddy. Also, I put my name down as a contact for you."

I look under the contacts and see *Buddy* as my only contact other than an emergency dial of 111. "Here, I guess you want this back then." I reach down to grab his gun and magazine.

He holds up his hands. "Actually, you can keep those too. Its standard issue and the silencer will come in handy for your missions later. You just twist it on and off the nose of the barrel."

I understand keeping his phone, but his gun? "Why do I need your gun?"

He gets up and starts to head out the door. "When you get your freedom you are going to need to keep an eye out for Evols. I heard they are looking everywhere in the PLF for you. Have a good night, buddy."

True protection and a chance at freedom. I gather my things and put them in my sweatpants. "Thanks, Taiga. You too."

He gives me a sweet tiger smile before heading out the door and speeding away down the road toward the gates to the PLF toward freedom.

Maturity

I awake in a sauna of my own sweat and throw off the massive sheet from my legs. The alarm hasn't gone off yet; I'm up thirty minutes early. I decide that I won't be able to go back to sleep again, so I grab a towel from the drawer and drag it over to the bathroom to take a quick shower. I pass by my new phone, which I was too tired after yesterday to look at it, and fiddle with it, and I put the gun into the nightstand drawer in the back to keep it hidden. I will for sure mess with my phone and start browsing after training today.

Just above freezing, the shower feels like a hundred ice cubes smashing against me. The initial blast of frigid water causes my entire body to shrink in a quick spasm, but every second that passes, my body cools down to accommodate the change in temperature. I wipe the thick layer of steam from the shower wall. The humidity outside has created fog in the confines of the expansive bathroom; even in a shower of ice water, I can't escape the heat around me.

Dirty training clothes. The cleaning lady who does my laundry must have a day off today as she is usually here every other day to pick up my dirty clothes. Lupine doesn't seem to mind the cleanliness of my clothes, so I think I can use these one more day. The news station covered the weather: the sun decided to come a little closer to Earth hot. There have to be some shorts. On top of my drawer, there is a pair of scissors in a plastic cup with other office supplies.

I exit the apartment with makeshift sweat shorts and a pair of sweatbands around my arms. "If I have to listen to one more goddamn cicada," I tell myself as

I trek across the paved desert. The heat of the sun bounces against the cement and radiates under my feet and into my groin. I feel like my balls are being microwaved, and my legs are being roasted under a spit. Trees offer little to no shade as they are newly planted and have yet to have girth or leaves. There are no joggers or other Primes out for walks today. They are all in their cars with the AC on full blast and a concerned look on their faces as I trek on the surface of the sun's parking lot.

Through the glimmers of sweat dripping from my brow and the shimmering rays slicing the air, I peer down the road heading to the gym. This unbearable heat reminds me of a jungle—my jungle.

Headache. Every step I take is another needle in my brain. What is going on? I've been in this weather before. Why is it affecting me now? Must be just a headache from the gin from yesterday; it might be what a hangover feels like. Maybe I need to start taking my lorazepam again if the headaches come back. I should go to Kit after training today and get a prescription.

The entrance for the gym is only a couple feet away, but my body is sweating and burning. Lupine's car is parked out front. He drove to work—the bastard could have offered me a ride.

The sliding doors open up, and a gust of AC buffers my body. It may only be room temperature, but it feels colder than ice. I scramble for the couch and take a seat, look at the time: ten minutes before training, ten glorious minutes. I just hope that Lupine doesn't see me here and decides to start early. Please, Lupine, don't make today's agenda outside. I can't imagine what it's like for him today, or any Prime with a heavy fur coat. Oh, man, Borne has got to be dying today.

I look back to see that the clock has moved to T minus five minutes to training. I guess I can arrive fashionably early. If I arrive on time, he might think I didn't wake up on time today, and another twenty pushups aren't what I want today. I slip into the locker room, fit into my training clothes, and wipe down my head and arms of sweat with a sweat towel before meeting Lupine.

Lupine is hanging upside down with his legs across a push-up bar, texting on his phone even as his ears and fur dangle in front of his eyes. He seems reasonable—he isn't drenched in sweat, and his demur appears calm and collected. Unlike mine.

"Hey." I get his attention in case he didn't notice me coming in.

He barely acknowledges my existence. "Usual routine today. Make sure you practice that high kick. Don't stretch your leg out too far again, and don't want to call Kit after yesterday." Nothing outside, thank God.

"She gave you shit for stepping on my foot with your yeti feet?" I playfully taunt him.

He gazes over to me. "My feet are not that big compared to most Primes, and yes, she did." He peers back to his phone. "'Don't step on Ghent; he is fragile,'" he mocks Kit.

"Can we turn on some music today?" Taiga said that Lupine liked music, so maybe this is my chance to lighten his mood—and my own at that.

"As long as it's not trash, I don't care."

I can't imagine what trash would be to him. It doesn't look like he enjoys country music. He seems more like rap or rock kind of Prime. Wait, do Primes have American music here? I never heard any Prime bands or singers, so what passes for music over here? "What do you like to listen to?"

"No country. Everything else is fine."

There is a bulky stereo in the corner of the room that is connected to an MP3 player. The music selection on the stereo system is slim, but there are plenty of classic bands I recognize. I start listing them off by styles first to help narrow our options. "How about some punk? I think you would like that."

His eyes shoot over to me. "You calling me a punk?"

"No." I find original Linkin Park on there, their album *Meteora*—classic to any punk rock enthusiast. "It's just that you seem like a Linkin Park fan."

"Put on *Hybrid Theory*."

"You're funny."

Everything is normal. Lupine is texting on his phone while exercising, leaving me alone. I am taking my time and keeping track of my reps, and hell, there is even music playing today. I can't find a single thing wrong with it.

"So what have you been up to after our sessions?" he suddenly says.

My heart skips a beat as I finish a kick to the training dummy. "Nothing much. I've just been watching too much Prime Time TV." I need to change the subject; he is trying to sniff out a lie—I just know it. "Didn't know that you guys dyed your different fur colors. That just looks stupid if you ask me."

"I've been recently informed by a questionable source that you left yesterday." He gets off his exercise bike and walks over to me.

Did Tucker tell him? No, he wouldn't have. "I left with Feather, Tucker, and Borne—they all said it was okay."

"I will talk to them about this later. Now why did you disobey my orders to stay inside?" He begins to sound stern, and that scares me into a stutter.

"Because I wanted to get Kit—"

He steps right in front of me and the dummy. "Get her what?"

I need to make him understand it wasn't such a big deal. I was safe, and I wasn't going to be harmed. Not to mention Feather and Borne can vouch for me. "I wanted to get her a gift for helping us out. She seemed overworked and I just wanted..."

He rolls his eyes and takes his usual sigh of disappointment. "You still disobeyed an order that came not just from me, but from Gores and Brutus."

He isn't concerned about me; he just wants to keep me in here so he doesn't have to be around me except for while we train. That must be it. He wants to keep me in a cage; they all want to keep me in a cage. No, come to think of it, it's almost like a camp. "You know how difficult it is to be trapped in one spot for weeks on end unable to see the outside world just because someone told you not to go? Oh wait, I am sure that you do." It isn't until I see his fangs clench and grind that I realize what I just said.

"What did you say?"

I feel myself fall into a deep hole and at the bottom is a wolf that I just punched. "I said—"

He threatens me. His finger is very close to my face, and with a low, dark growl from his throat. "Don't you dare tell me what happened to me there!" I can feel the dam holding back his rage start to break as his tail stands straight up and furls.

He doesn't need to lecture me about this. "I know what they do in—"

"Let me guess. You read it in a book how I got whipped daily, beaten to an inch of my life, worked nearly to death!"

Still doesn't explain why he is such an ass about everything. I hold my ground. "So just because a few people whipped you and beat you, does that give you dominion over everyone else?"

He flicks out his lighter and flicks the top open. "I read your medical profile. You're scared of fire, right?"

Where is he going with this?

"Why? Got a little burned when you were a kid?" He flicks the flint sharper than his tongue.

I avert my gaze. "No."

He approaches me and moves the flame to my face, and as I turn away he follows my gaze. "Oh, did the poor baby have his camp burn down?" He mocks me. "You know, I had to burn my camp down to the ground to escape the hell I went through!" He yells into my ear. "Did you—"

Blood rushes to my hands as I attempt to reach out and push him down to stop him from talking. However, he sees my hands go out and grabs me by my shoulders. He picks me up and tosses me back off the mat and onto the hard gym floor.

I take a sharp breath in before I hit the floor, and the world around me goes into a blur before fading into a dark aura.

As my mind stirs in a bend in reality and dream, I reach out to my side and feel wet grass scrape against my hands. Birds chirp in the distance, tropical birds. I look up to the sky and see a clear-night starry canvas motionless in the heavens. I cannot move my neck as if someone is holding it in place, and my legs and arms feel pinned to the ground. Only the shimmering oblivion above can act as my guide back to Oasis.

After what seems like hours sitting alone in the grass, I feel something start to crawl up my legs and engulf my body, a sense of rage and warmth that I felt before I collapsed. Reality starts to swallow me whole and the last thing I see is one single star shooting across the sky above.

"Ghent. Ghent!"

I feel suddenly turned to my side as he strikes me with a slap to my left cheek.

I jerk up and find Lupine, who has my legs held and elevated, with Kit cradling my neck in her hands. "What!"

Kit breathes a sigh of relief and takes my vitals. "Oh, thank god you're awake."

The numbness of my voyage through my mind fades away, and I become aware of how much pain my body is in. From head to toe, I feel like my body is being crushed by millions of weights. "My entire body feels like it was hit by a car." I move my jaw and feel something isn't quite right. Did my teeth shift? I look at

Lupine, I see some minor bruises on my left arm and feel my jaw click back into place. Did he beat me unconscious?

Lupine hoists me up and lets me wobble as I try to find my balance.

Lupine's fist appears to have blood on them. "Good, now about your-"

While he isn't expecting it, I swing at his face and smack him right on the side of his muzzle. He immediately whimpers and clenches his nose, and blood starts dripping from it. "You beat me unconscious, didn't you!"

He holds his nose shut and sounds high-pitched. "Fuck, you're the one that snapped first!" He is gripping his nose tightly and wincing in pain. What is he talking about? There is no other reason my body hurts this much.

"I didn't snap first!" I don't remember anything but there is no reason that I would attack...him.

Lupine's blood seep through his fingers. "What are you talking about!"

Kit grabs me and turns me around. "Ghent!"

"What!" I get spun around facing her. I notice something odd as I gaze upon the top of her head instead of her collarbone. "Did you get shorter, Kit?" I make sure I am standing straight and not at an angle.

"No, but you got a bit taller. "She points at the mirror on the wall, and I gaze upon to see what has become of me.

My nails have turned into claws. My teeth are elongated into fangs. My feet are contorted to resemble a canine's—I guess that's where the height came from. I run my hand through my long hair that now stretches down to my shoulders, and I can feel down my neck the shorter hairs that flow down my back. I don't have fur, but I am not clean-shaven. I resemble more of a feral child than a Prime.

I take a look at my hands; the padding on my palms seems thicker. The same with my feet, which are hard to stand on with the recent changes in their structure. They act like springs, as if I am tiptoeing around. The final difference I notice is my eyes: the black iris has become obligated, seems more feline. The color has not changed. However, they are darker than before. I look around and notice no change in my vision. In fact, there may even be an improvement. I always have had a slight vision impairment, but with Prime eyes, that has vanished.

I spin around and try to find a tail. As I turn around I feel the tearing of my clothes, which have become significantly tighter around my arms and waist.

169

Sadly there is no trace of a tail. Instead, there is a small bump protruding from my tailbone. "Holy shit... I'm...a Prime." I'm excited and relieved, and I don't know if I should be excited or scared out of my mind.

I see Lupine in the mirror storm over to get a sweat rag to press against his nose. "Good! I am off to Pure to report this."

"What Prime am I?" I inquire to Kit, ignoring Lupine.

She gives me a look-over. "I'm guessing somewhere between a wolf and a panther."

I can't remember changing. Did this all happen while I was having my dream? "How did I change?"

She reaches for my wrist and takes my pulse. "Well, after you blacked out, your body started to shift around, and you were screaming in pain. Then you went dead silent. By the way your body contorted to accommodate for the change, the pain must have caused you to black out." She infers all of this without any evidence to back it up.

I don't remember anything between when I rushed Lupine and waking up. I've felt this before when I first was kidnapped. "I think I shifted when I attacked the kid at Raiden. I attacked him as a Prime." Glad I might be figuring out what brought me here, and what I might have in store if I return back.

She thinks for a moment and then nods. "It's completely possible your body triggers a trauma-preventing measure to knock you out upon any high-stress incident. Now, I want to take you to the infirmary right away to make sure you haven't seriously hurt yourself through the transformation—if that's okay with you, Lupine."

He spits out a quick single chuckle. "Well, I've had enough of his bullshit for the day," he says, throwing his gym bag over his shoulder. "Go ahead, dissect him for all I care. Besides, I need to report to Pure that he changed. I also have to have a little talk with Tucker and break *his* fucking shell open."

I can imagine that sharp tongue going straight through Tucker's shell.

Kit lets my face go and heads over to grab her things as well. "You want me to help you with your nose?"

"No, you go with Ghent and make sure *he's* okay." He gives a quiet whimper as he moves the rag to the other nostril.

I see all the blood on that rag. Maybe I shouldn't have hit him in the nose like that. After all, he is a dog and the nose is extremely sensitive. I shouldn't leave him like this—he should know that I didn't mean what I said. "Lupine."

"What?" He doesn't even turn around.

I choke down my anger and my pride. "I'm sorry for what I said."

He pauses for a split second before pushing open the door outside. "Whatever." He shoves it open and makes his exit.

I don't know if I should be proud of standing up to him or scared shitless that I made my commander angry at me. "Should I be worried about him?"

Kit picks up an opened medical kit at her side. Within are several vials, syringes, and alcohol swabs. "Don't worry about him—he's just pouting," she says, almost like she has gone through this herself.

After gathering her things and my stuff as well, we leave Highpoint in her car, a top-down ruby convertible from the early 2000s with dozens of dings and scratches. A melon-sized dent is in the driver's side back corner, and one of the headlights is popped out. She jumps right into the driver seat and starts the car. I open up the passenger side and settle into the leather, which has several holes that let loose fabric under it. I see no cigarette burns or buds inside. However, I do see several parking tickets stuffed into the cup holder. They are pinned together with a long needle.

The air is still like swimming in a pool of water, except now at least I am being cooled by the passing wind. I can barely hear the radio over the wind and can't seem to understand what they are talking about. It sounds like a National Public Radio talk show. I don't feel like I should mess with her car, so I leave it at a low volume.

We pass several places I remember from my drive with Feather, except we take a sharp neck-breaking turn onto a side road past Stronghold and head up toward the main government building. The more I pay attention to the side buildings and Primes passing by, the more I realize how jerky and awkward Kit's driving is. I haven't driven, but I know a terrible driver when I see it. She turns like the car is attached to a rubber band. She stops like a child ran in front of her, and she merges without even alerting *herself* that she is joining. The dents should have warned me of this. I can't believe it but feel like I'd be safer with Lupine right about now.

We parked down in the employee-only section of the administration building around where I was picked up by Stall originally. She parks her car a hair length in front of someone else and crawls out of the seat. I follow her down into the medical bay; the building seems nearly empty, besides some janitors and a group of patrolling security guards. Feels odd walking around as part Prime now. I feel like I don't stick out as much.

The medical bay is open and busy with commotion. Nurses and doctors in smocks fly in and out carrying pamphlets, folders, and some who are carting around medical equipment. I nearly run into a zoned-out doctor speeding by.

"What's going on?" I ask.

She nudges past a couple of Primes at the door. "Someone important is here, and all these bottom-feeder doctors are trying to submit their work." A few of them overhear her comment and snub us.

Floods of people move out of the way of Kit and me as we approach the desk. They either must notice our badges or they recognize Kit from somewhere. Yet no one says "hi" or anything.

She taps the computer screen of a badger Prime who is focused on her computer. Stacks of folders of various colors and sizes as high as her head flank her. "Honey, I need you to get us a room. It's official Sagittarius business."

Honey pushes her glasses up onto her nose and looks at Kit. I can tell she's been busy all day as her fur is a wreck and her bloodshot eyes show her lack of a coffee break. "Sorry, Kit, they are all occupied right now."

"Well, kick one of them out then."

A moment later, I notice a lot of talking coming from the right-hand side door as an army approaches the door. A large crowd of doctors bursts through the double doors, and in front of them all is Fawn from the Zodiac. Her antlers are a rich mahogany and several trinkets dangle from straps. She seems to be staring like there are headlights in front of her, as another avian Prime talks to her, but her attention is immediately destroyed when she notices Kit at the desk. She rushes toward us and shrugs off the Primes trying to get her attention.

"Kitty!" She gives her a hug. I notice a wedding ring on her middle finger. "What are you doing here? It's been such a long time since..." She looks down from Kit's shoulder and looks at me like she sees a ghost. "He shifted?!"

Kit crawls out of the hug. "Yeah, she just turned not an hour ago." All the doctors drop what they are doing and look at me like they are predators, and I am prey.

"Really?" She approaches me and takes a flashlight from her breast pocket. "Mind if I look at him?" She shines a quick light into my eyes and picks up my arm.

"I was just off to give an examination. He just started developing and I was going..." The stag pulls my arm and starts to tug me over to the double doors she just came from. "To start." I see the passing glance of several other doctors as she blows through the crowd to get away from them.

She is giggling and excited to get to meet me. Hopefully, it isn't to dissect me or open me up to see how I work. "I have so many questions for you. Where did you come from? When did you turn? Oh, all the questions this could answer! Sorry if I seem a little excited—it's just that I've been reading so many garbage thesis papers I haven't gotten to do any actual research in months."

We make a turn and head down toward a sign that reads *Zodiac Offices*, and I notice that the density of office rooms and cubicles drops down to only a couple of doors for each block.

I see Kit following closely behind us.

I just keep up to her and tug on her arm to try to get her to slow down. "Uh, Miss Fawn—"

"Fawn, Fawn Cervidae." She holds out a hand to me to shake it. Her palms are much rougher and grittier than any other Prime's I've met.

"You are the Zodiac in charge of the Department of Health, right?"

"Yes, I run all the hospitals, research, and clinical experimentation in regards to Prime biology." She turns to a section with two elevators. There are two armed guards standing in front of each elevator and a security desk in front of the sector. We are let in without a second glance from anyone.

Must be one hell of a job. I can imagine just from looking at Primes they must each have their own anatomical differences. I wonder if each Prime has the same bodily structure but just different add-ons. "Neat. Must be a hell of a job to know all about Prime biology, with so many different types."

There is not an up or down button on the elevators or on the doors that are plated with a strange brass metal that gives off a glass-like reflection. She simply places a keycard on her up to the middle of a panel on the side. It lights up green and flashes the symbol of Virgo. "You have no idea, hun, but it keeps me interested, and sure as hell keeps me busy."

"Where are we going, if you don't mind me asking?" This seems like a high-security office if there are armed guards and keycards to get in.

The elevator hums for a couple of seconds before the doors open to an elaborate gilded cage with thick bulletproof glass in between the metal rods. "The examination rooms were booked today so we are going to my office."

Her office? This is sure to be an interesting trip. I mean, it makes sense with all the security and measures to keep people out. I wonder if Gore's office can be accessed from that panel as well. "Oh, you have your own examination table?"

Kit gets into the elevator along with us. "She's got her own laboratory. It's where we did a majority of our research back in the day."

It's obvious she doesn't have access to this lab or we would have gone there first.

The elevator doors close shut and the elevator shoots down at an incredible speed before jutting to a halt. There is no floor designator; all I know is that we are underground somewhere deep in the capitol building.

The doors open to another shorter hallway made of blue steel walls illuminated by the light fixtures built into the ceiling above. The floor is a polished limestone tileset that twists and weaves itself into genetic strands; they lead up to the door on the other side, which has a single terminal on the right-hand side. Fawn goes up to the terminal and opens a flap on the top, where her eyes are scanned. Then another keycard, a different color from the elevator keycard, is inserted into the terminal before the door clicks open.

Fawn's laboratory is as vast as a museum exhibit and as expansive as an auditorium. The lab is one and a half stories, the second floor being only the back half of the room, with glass step stairs leading up to an office area, with a desk and rows of books and possibly ten computer screens all placed around the office space. The area is enclosed in glass that I didn't catch was there until a light from terminal blinked and the light reflected back. On the first floor, each wall contains either a towering bookshelf with its own ladder or drawers as wide as a kitchen table, where I imagine specimens and samples are kept. Scattered around the center floor are laboratory tables, counters, sinks, fridges, beakers, and a cavalcade of technology bits and bobs that I would only assume to be expensive. They are all kept relatively clean and organized, as if his place is cleaned three times a day. The floor, which is the same limestone, still smells of disinfectant.

Despite all the computer terminals on the laboratory tables, there doesn't seem to be any wires leading anywhere. Either they are all hidden within the laboratory countertops or they have made everything in this room wireless. It's organized and a perfect scientist's heaven, a place of absolute quiet as the only thing I can hear is the hum of a couple computers and the ventilation shafts that are jutting out from the ceiling above in between the bright light fixtures.

"Wow." I am blown away by the sure number of different books and possibilities that lie within this room alone. "This makes my science room at Raiden look like a plastic kid's oven set."

Fawn walks up to a couple of the stations and starts to pull some supplies from under the counters. "Glad you like it. It took a lot of work to get my laboratory set up."

Just to dig this room out of the ground and get it down here is impressive on its own. "How far are we underground?"

Kit helps in getting some gear out of closets and various cabinets. "A little less than a hundred feet down."

A hundred feet down! "That's crazy." So even if I were to get trapped down here and scream as loud as I can, the atomic sound waves won't make it up to the surface.

Fawn motions me over to her while she wheels over a desk chair for me to sit on. "I am a little bit spoiled, I admit it," she titters.

As I walk over to her I pass by several counters. Each one has varying sizes of cabinets and drawers under them, all labeled with different tags that read what is inside of them. Each cabinet and drawer has a specific list of items, and a record for when they are taken out and put back in.

As Fawn conducts the same physical exam that Kit did, she explains that as the head of the Animalia Research Department as well at the Virgo Zodiac sign, she did all the research and the dissections of Prime anatomy and wrote the journal that is the primary teaching guide to the Prime body. She is famous in not just the PLF but also the US, where she is regarded as the pioneer of medical research going into the twenty-fourth century.

I flinch when she hits my knee with a hammer. "It's crazy that all of this was done in such a short time. I mean, it must have taken an army to figure all this out."

Fawn looks down and spins her hammer. "There were several brilliant genetic researchers and doctors all working on collecting data and research on Prime anatomy. Since most of the original blueprint for Primes was destroyed or lost, a couple managed to continue from scraps of research." She turns to Kit. "And I couldn't have done it without you, Kitsune—I remember when you first cut yourself on a scalpel."

"That was over ten years ago," she says quietly to herself.

"I know, but it was just so cute hearing you cry over a small cut. And now look at you, saving lives and working on your own research." She sounds so proud of her apprentice.

With the final prod and a mouth swab, Fawn puts all of the samples of my blood, urine, spit, hair, and toe nail clippings into separate labeled plastic bags and vials. "All right, Ghent, I think that's enough data to get a good idea of your physical health."

I mean, with these you could almost create another of me.

Kit reaches for an additional vial from the drawer. "Fawn, I would like to do one more test on his blood." Not another... Please, I feel lightheaded enough.

"What kind of test? We are testing him for everything already."

"No, I just want to try something out."

"Okay, I will split my sample with you." Fawn takes a new syringe, cleans it off, and extracts some of her vial into a sealed empty one that Kit supplies. "Other than that, I think you are free to go. I will lead you out to the lobby and you can take it from there, right?"

I put my T-shirt back on. "Sure, I can go from there."

Kit hands me my pants. "Fawn, I will have your results within a couple of weeks; we have a backup of tests so it might be a bit late."

"Don't worry about the backup, Kit. You just focus on making Pure happy and delivering the results." She packs everything up in her doctor's bag and heads to the sink to wash her hands.

"All right, but you might have to pull an all-nighter." Kit opens the door for me. "Also, Lupine texted me. He has someone coming to pick you up. Just hang around the lobby."

I hope that something comes out of all these tests. I know they are looking out for me and making sure I am okay physically, but I do get a feeling that they know more about me than I do, and more than they are letting on.

Fawn gathers her things. "Pfft, I've done an all weeker before, an all-nighter is nothing."

I follow the signs to the lobby. The commotion has halted while Primes wait for hopefully Fawn to reappear. Or at least that's what I assume. They could be waiting for me so they can kidnap me and subject me to their own experiments. However, I enter the lobby with only a couple of looks and a low murmur of voices.

A half an hour or so passes by with me reading a newspaper article about the rising demand for housing surpassing construction supply. According to the magazine Prime families are having a difficult time finding housing in Kingdom because those home constructions that are underway are taking longer than anticipated due to the unstable foundations created from several bombings. Families are finding temporary housing outside of Kingdom, and some Primes are beginning to travel outward from the central city and repopulating the suburbs, which are also still under disrepair. It's hard to imagine that even this many years after the war they are still repairing significant cities and suburbs to make housing for Primes. Pure has directed several ex-PLF military officers to be hired as contractors for smaller companies that are setting up simple houses to help the housing shortage.

The sound of horse hooves reverberates in the glass wall next to me, and I turn around to see Stall entering the medical bay. He is wearing the same uniform as before and looks a little distressed and nervous by the look of his shaky hooves.

He looks down at me. "A little different from last time I saw you."

I put down my newspaper. "Yeah, Lupine sure beat the Prime out of me, I guess." I try to lighten the mood. I can tell something is on his mind.

"You look...like a wild child." He purposely doesn't use the word *feral*.

"So, you are going to drive..." I look at his four legs. "...have someone drive us to Highpoint?"

"Nope." He looks around the room as if he was being followed. "We are going to walk to Highpoint—Lupine's orders."

Wait, he wants me to go on the outside with him? "Walk? You mean to walk all the way there, with me, outside?"

177

"Just think about it," he says." If you can prove to him that you are safe walking around Kingdom, just think of all the places you could go."

He is right. I should see this as a way to prove myself. Just the notion of finally being able to leave Highpoint and travel around is in itself worth all the nervousness I feel right now. "Well, I guess if anything goes wrong I got you to back me up." I try to make myself feel safer.

He turns around and walks out of the bay. I follow right behind him. "I will be keeping my distance. However, this is all you."

Lupine isn't stupid. He doesn't trust me enough yet to leave me on my own. "Okay, what if I get attacked? What should I do?"

"What did Lupine teach you?"

"Beat the shit out of them."

"Correct."

Sounds reasonable, but can I really beat a Prime when I am only at half the advantage? "You think I could take one on?"

"Most Primes aren't Lupine. Most Primes can't defend themselves against you, so just do what Lupine told you to do. Think of this as a test of everything you learned so far."

Oh, sure, just take this test. If you fail, well, you might end up in the hospital or dead. Thanks.

I attempt to pump myself up to better prepare for the dangers ahead. "All right...I can do this. Besides, just how many Evols are actually out there?" I mean really, like ten percent?

"Well...just keep your head up," he uneasily suggests.

Instead of leaving the parking garage, we leave through the front door. We get dumped out onto Castor Street, an expansive four-lane road with black limos and taxi cars lined up on either side waiting to pick up Primes. Several government workers are getting in and out while other cars pass by. From the street level, I get a better feeling of how different Primes are from one another. Heights range from half to twice mine. From the mouse to the gator, there is a menagerie of animals moving around us and by us as we walk down the street to the east where this street meets up with Pollux Street. For a government building, there seems to be a lack of security. I mean, if I were in DC and at the White House there would be guards lined up and down, shoulder to shoulder with M16s. Here, all I see is one guard protecting the front door to the administration building.

Why is it that Pure deter Evols with armed forces? I get that they can set the wrong tone with civilians. I know that the police back at home can be excessive in their tactics and their equipment. But it also lets civilians know they will be safe. Maybe Primes know as long as there are no humans around there is no need to have armed guards to protect humans from Evols. No victim, no crime.

I walk right beside Stall, being careful not to stand directly behind him in case I startle him. I know he doesn't have the same instincts that horses do, but I am not going to take that bet. Each Prime that walks next to me I keep an eye on. I try to not act paranoid, but I learned from Lupine that there could be a knife or gun in every pocket. Any of them could be Evols.

I need to calm down. I am with Stall, and not all Primes are Evols. I am safe walking around these streets.

We begin to approach a pedestrian crossing. There's a human stick figure in the box: it is red, and Primes start to pile up around us waiting to cross. I look around to see a herd of Primes waiting to cross the river of cars, and with each one that approaches my eyes begin to dart more and more frantically, looking for something to concentrate on, something to think about, something to remember from my training.

Just do what Lupine taught you.

I close my eyes and take a couple of deep breaths. As I inhale through my nose I can smell some perfume from an elegant cheetah Prime behind me. I open my eyes and look to my side. She has a purse over her shoulder and empty hands, and the purse is locked. She isn't a threat. Stall is beside me. The Primes directly in front of me are all talking amongst each other. They are not paying attention to me and have nothing out. Keep an eye on their hands and their eyes. Make eye contact; let them know you are watching them.

Stall nudges me from my side and motions with his head toward a group of teenage Primes jostling with each other and having fun. "Say 'Hi' to them," he tells me.

They are not a threat to me; no one around me is. Why should I be afraid of Primes? I am stronger than I was; I can fight for myself. These are my people, and I am just a member of society.

The light turns green, and everyone begins to move behind us, pushing me forward. I am at the forefront of the pack, and the group is mere feet in front of me. I look directly into their eyes and one of them, a jackal Prime wearing Sylvester's brand-name ruby polo T-shirt and cargo shorts, notices me and nudges the other two, a coyote girl and what looks like a fox boy. All three wear the same brand. They look at me. I clear my thoughts and nod at them. "Hello," I tell them with as much courage as I can muster. They all just stare at me all the way past us, and after that, they instantly start talking. See, that wasn't that bad.

We pass the intersection of Castor and Pollux, and we head down to the intersection of Castor and Apostle. The government buildings start to disappear as more high-end apartments and small businesses rise up. Each restaurant, café, and bar are filled with suits all drinking and eating together discussing the local news on the TV. Some discuss books and movies, and some even talk politics. I hear someone complain about the lack of action related to refugees from Wasteland and China, while another debates that "it's safer here without them—we don't have to worry about letting terrorists in if we keep all of them out."

This gets me thinking. If Pure's ideal world doesn't involve humans, does he really have a need to create security features as the US has? The world I used to live in is diverse, with Primes and humans trying to live together; however, there is also a threat that either side attacks one another. I can see Pure's reasoning, but he isn't going to fix the divide if he doesn't have children of a new generation communicate and live with humans. If there is ever going to be peace between Primes and humans, they will need that. Although, even with the integration of Primes in the US, there still is a great divide. Maybe somewhere between those extremes, we can finally create a solution, both protecting the Primes living here and assuring that the invasive species live fairly and equally.

Stall pulls me by my shirt collar as I almost walk in front of traffic at the intersection. "You got something on your mind, sir?" he asks me as if he doesn't know me. I look up at him, and then everyone else who must think I am crazy. "A lot actually."

With our long walk down to the road that brings us to Highpoint, I get steadily more comfortable with being by myself. We've seen many Primes and no Evols. I guess Feather was right: Evols don't show up in public and actively hunt down humans. Maybe when he said that he meant there were no humans to hunt down. I keep looking for someone human, someone like me, but all I see are anthropomorphic people. Not a single human for blocks—not a picture, a fragment, or a single notion of one besides the one behind the mirror looking at me, and even then he's only half. What would Evols do all day if there were no humans to harass? Hunters in the US at least have something to do, someone to harass. Here they must be bored out of their minds or lurking somewhere where there are human beings.

When we finally arrive at the intersection where I remember turning to get to the administration building, I notice that Stall has slowed down substantially and has increased the distance between us. He must be proud of me. We started out shaky, but in the end, I guess everything worked out.

On the corner rests a Quickies gas station. Its logo is a black swish in a circle, and its motto must be "Rundown but functional." There are only two gas pumps, and each has a line of three cars waiting. There appears to be a small shop inside not larger than Feather's trailer. I see a group of three Primes exit the store, each holding a couple of tickets, and one has a water bottle. They all are chatting. They look like young adults, two with wifebeaters and one with a black T-shirt and black jeans. They seem a little rowdy, but nothing is off-kilter.

I approach the sidewalk next to the station and one of them. I hear Stall's hoofprints come clopping up behind me closer than usual as I approach the group to greet them. The group notices Stall appear before they even get the chance to confront me. They scamper back into the gas station without a word. He appears next to me, shielding me from the gas station and guiding me away. "Now those Primes there, I know a couple of them. They were Evols."

How the hell was I supposed to tell? "How can you tell if they are?"

He looks back to make sure they don't follow us as we leave. "It's all about looking for any sort of tattoos, jewelry, or insignia of DNA strands, or any Evol markings on them. I know them all from my work against Evols, but that is something that Lupine will have to cover with you sometime."

Mental note for later. "Weren't you supposed to stay back? I mean, I could have taken them."

"I don't want you to get in a brawl in broad daylight. It would attract too much attention, and any attention to you is definitely unwanted."

. . .

As we are heading back to my apartment, I figure I should thank Stall for bringing me around Kingdom. "Thanks a million for bringing me here."

"No problem," he tells me casually.

Maybe he wants to hang out at my place for a bit. "Say, do you want to come into my apartment and hang out for a bit?"

"No thanks. Pure is heading somewhere today, and he needs me to create a squad to protect him on his travels."

That's odd. Pure is the leader of the PLF, and he is also a lion Prime that could snap me in half. What kind of protection does he need that he couldn't supply himself? "Where is he heading off to?" I am probably going to get shut down, but I might as well ask.

"I would tell you, but that's classified. All I can tell you is that it's not work-related."

My guess is he's going on a vacation, or maybe out with his family to eat. "All right. I hope things go well for you and for him."

Stall suddenly stops right before we head into my apartment complex. "Say, Ghent, can I tell you something?" He seems nervous as he looks around to see if anyone else is close enough to hear him.

"Sure." Is he going to tell me something super secretive? Pure's plan? Something about Sagittarius?

"About Pure."

He has my full attention.

"I've noticed he has taken quite a liking to you. He doesn't let people he doesn't know into his inner circle. I've had to clear hundreds of people to see Pure, and no one ever has been this easy to get so close to him," he tells me quietly.

"Well, it's probably because I am just a high schooler from Detroit. I wasn't a threat to anyone and my criminal record is pretty short." Though I feel like if I head back now it will be a helluva lot longer.

"That is true," he confirms, "but it was just how fast he was pushing to sign you up to the PLF."

Fair. Back when I first met him he barely took a couple of minutes to come up with the decision to induct me into the PLF. "It's almost like he knew what he was going to do with me before he even met me." However, Pure was alerted of me arriving before we met, so he did have some time to prepare a decision for me before I arrived.

He nods. "Exactly. Either he knows something about you or he has ulterior motives for you."

He knows about Oasis before I mentioned it, so of course he knows more than he is leading on to. After all, it's the bait that is keeping me on his line. "I kind of figured he did, but it's just figuring out what he has on me. I need to figure out what he is really planning."

Concern passes over his face. "Just be careful around him. Ask too many questions and you just might end up *vanishing*."

I take a dry gulp. I need to take this slow and steady. If I can find out what Pure is hiding, then that might just lead me one step closer to Oasis. Keep on Pure's good side, work with him, and get that bait, but I have to be careful or I will end up being fried and eaten by a hungry lion. "I understand."

"I never said that and you never heard it from me." He begins to turn around and head back down the street to the gate.

"Heard what?" I act like I heard nothing but I remember every word said.

"Good boy." He waves farewell and disappears into the sunset.

I head back up to my apartment and crash on the couch and turn on PNN News.

"Today was an interesting day out on the town as Primes are buzzing about a new face walking around the streets of Kingdom." They show a video that someone took of me walking, with Stall just out of view. "A human that has been recently inducted into the PLF has been spotted walking around near Castor Street earlier this morning. Several Primes passed by him, unaware that he was, in fact, a fully vetted PLF soldier. This has caused calls by Evols for his removal, but even more it has grown support online for the inclusion of a human to fight for the PLF."

Who took that video? I didn't see anyone with a camera or recording me on their phone. Well, so much for staying anonymous. Now that I am known across the PLF I guess I have to get used to Primes coming up to me, asking me questions, wanting to take their picture with me. I went from an orphan who no one knew to being a celebrity in a foreign country. I should feel happy and excited to be a celebrity, but I don't. They made me famous for nothing more than what I am when I don't even know what I am for sure. How should I talk, walk? Who should I hang out with? I don't know anything about Prime society and yet they are willing to make me a figurehead of human relations.

After I cook up some spaghetti with ground beef red sauce and enjoy the solitude, I do some dishes and then take my shower before I head to bed to get up early for training. Oh God, I need to get up for training. Lupine is going to kill me tomorrow with pushups and laps for fighting with him. Well, at least I am a Prime now. Speaking of which, I look at myself in the mirror and realize that all the attributes that I had as a Prime are starting to recede. My fangs are duller than before, claws are chipping off my nails, excess hair is shedding off me, and my feet are throbbing in pain. Holy shit, my body is sore, I need to take a cold shower and lie down.

What triggered this? I didn't do anything different from every other day, and despite our spat, Lupine didn't do anything or say anything out of the ordinary. I just got mad at Lupine for mocking Oasis and lightning his stupid lighter in my face that I, just snapped. I normally shy away from him when he's lighting up a smoke, and I even cover up the flame on my stove as much as I can when cooking. I've always avoided looking at fire, it just causes me too much stress. Stress. I would have been stressed back in that alley in Detroit. When I was first kidnapped and woke up and Kit took my first blood sample, stressed. I was stressed when I was covered in blood, and Yip managed to smell Prime from my blood. When Kit was taking my second blood samples it was after I sprayed her and was stressed from that. I was stressed today from both the heat and Lupine.

Every time I've been stressed my blood changed, and just now I started changing. Fire causes me stress, I wonder.

From my bedroom drawer I noticed that there was a couple matches still left in their packet from some hotel in the PLF. I decide to take out a match and take it to the shower. I strip down, turn on the shower and wet the floor, so if the match were to drop after I feel unconscious the wet floor would put the match out. I get inside the shower and attempt to strike the match. It takes a couple of tries but I eventually get it to light. I hold the dancing flame up to my eye level and immediately start feeling the effects of my phobia scream from smoke emitting off of the match. My legs start to buckle and my heart beat goes from normal to a hummingbird within seconds. My hand quivers and I drop the match onto the wet floor, but it does not go out, it just sits there on the floor, burning away. I sink to my knees, smashing them onto the marble shower floor. I try to reach out for the railing, the glass door, anything to hold me up, but when I finally grasp the handle for the shower door, it scalds my hand and I immediately sink it into the cold water on the floor. That match still burns in front of me, and for some reason I just can't take my eyes from it. Atom by atom I watch this stick slowly burn itself into a charry black soot that washes in with the water. As the flame crawls to the end of the stick, and finally burns itself out. I feel myself relax, and my body feels the exact same from when I came to with Lupine. I slowly get myself up from the shower, I hesitate on the shower door, testing it to make sure it's not scaling hot. It feels cold, I open the shower door and grasp the towel rail to help myself out.

I turn to gaze into the mirror which is now covered in steam, I reach over to swipe away the steam to see my claws have returned. From the clear view of the mirror, I see my body shifted back into a Prime, with each feature just as it was earlier today. Extended fangs, nails to claws, longer hair and new patches of hair developing down my neck, my feet are slightly elongated just like Lupine's, senses of smell and hearing stronger, a slight vision impairment corrected.

Its stress that causes me to shift. All this time I tried to live a stress free life, but in the end it might be the one thing that will keep me alive in this world.

Exposure

A knock at my door at six in the morning could only be one person.

I open the door for Lupine, who isn't dressed in his usual attire, but in a plain red and black striped T-shirt and a pair of dark blue jeans. The jeans he wears are cut off at the ball in his heel, and a set of sandals are strapped to his feet. He looks like a bum as his jeans have holes in the side. His T-shirt stinks of cigarette smoke and has tiny tears around the neck and arm holes. His sandals are also worn out and the leather is starting to peel on the sides and straps. For someone who must earn a lot being a high ranking solider, he sure dresses like I did back in Detroit.

"Hey." He lets himself in without asking and starts searching his pocket for something.

Umm...isn't he supposed to be at the gym waiting for me? I mean, it's been a couple of days since we fought, but he seemed to forget about our little spat last time I saw him. "Aren't you supposed to be at the gym?"

"Ah fuck." He stops picking around his pockets and heads over to my stove. "Forgot my lighter in the car." He takes a cigarette out from behind his ear and heads to the stovetop. I avert my gaze from him.

It's alarming that he's at my home, in street clothes. "Are we doing some sort of home training now?"

He turns the stove off and grabs a glass to fill it up with water. "Nope, we aren't doing any training today."

What?

"It's Veterans Day and all military members have today off, including me."

I'm happy to have a day off, but I have a sinking feeling I'll be spending it with Lupine.

"Really!" I cough into my sleeve and try to calm down. "Well, I mean if you *want* to train with me today you can."

He points a finger at me. "No. This is one of my only days off and I am going to go to Pure's private spa and abuse the fuck out of my privileges."

That sounds quite nice actually. "Mind if I come?" I've never been to a spa. I could use one, especially with all of this shifting between human and Prime I have been doing. I have been testing it out with a plastic lighter that Lupine got me. I have been building up a tolerance to the pain, tracking how long it takes, how long it lasts, and how much I can do before I pass out from exhaustion.

His tail goes down and his eyes narrow as he takes a giant gulp from the glass. "No. This is a Prime-only spa off of this site."

That's a fucking lame excuse. "I am a Prime, though."

He sighs and takes out an envelope. "It's by appointment only," he says as he changes his excuse. "Also, unless you can retain that form while getting to listen to relaxing music while having some big-titted wolf Prime rub you down, and not scare the fuck out of her as you change into a Prime, be my guest." He puts the fat envelope onto the table along with his empty glass. "Also, here is your allowance for the last couple months."

My allowance? I got paid for training? "Why are you just bringing my allowance up now?"

"You didn't have a use for it before you got cleared by Gores to leave Highpoint."

That's actually a really good point...wait. "Are you giving me permission to explore Kingdom?"

He heads to the door. "You proved you are willing and able to walk outside." He grabs my arm and pulls me close enough so I can smell his smokey dog breath. "You can do whatever you want. Just don't do anything stupid that would make you or the PLF look bad. Also, be back home by six o'clock. If you are not at that gate by six, I will hunt you down."

Wow, today is probably my best day in months! "Awesome!" I run to my room

187

and find the most casual clothes I have. Maybe I should get some jeans and nice shirts while I am out on the town. Oh, I probably need to get a charger for Taiga's phone as well—he never did give me one.

Lupine opens the door. "Well, there goes my day off." The door is shut tight behind him.

I put on my PLF uniform the second day I was here with Lupine. I am making sure I look as much like a soldier as possible. If Veterans Day is anything like in the US, a soldier walking around in uniform wouldn't be too strange. Maybe if I shift a little it would be perfect. I head to the nightstand, where I put the rest of the matches, and open it up to see the matches residing next to Taiga's gun. Do I bring it?

I mean, it is for my protection. That's the reason he gave it to me. I would feel safer with it, and I would probably not use it, but...would I be able to shoot another Prime? What would Lupine do if he knew I had it? What if I lose it? But...what if I need to use it to save my life?

When I was living in Detroit, there were always people walking around with mace, tasers, or even guns holstered for their protection. However, the US had a much stronger police force than the PLF. But I guess it's going to be day and the crowds should keep the Evols away.

Still...it's my life I am risking. I take it out and ponder the decision. While I eject the magazine, I have an idea. I bring it with me but I don't load any bullets into it. That will make it so I can't fire it, but I can still flash it in case I am in trouble. That will work, I guess. I empty out the magazine and the bullet in the chamber into my nightstand and then slide the clip back in. I also take off the silencer that Taiga had attached and place it with the bullets. It would be odd to have a silencer on a self-defense gun.

The gun is now tight and close to my side on a cloth holster that comes with the uniform, luckily enough. Before I put the uniform on I decide to repeat what I did a couple of days ago. I head to the shower and use the same match trick as before. A match lights, my vision blurs, my knees feel weak, and the next thing I feel is my lungs cough up some water as I wake up sitting down on the shower floor. I get up to look in the mirror. It's not as much as the first time, the features are not fully Primal, but they are noticeable, which is all that matters.

I open the envelope with my sharp nail. Claw? No, it's still a nail.

Inside the envelope are several hundred-dollar bills. The money in the PLF shows Pure's face front and center, of course, but he is surrounded by images of each unit of the Zodiac in a grid around him, and connecting them are lines like a constellation. The back is the most intense. It shows hundreds of family names of animals stacked like bricks that build the back of the bill. They seem to also be in alphabetical order. The number is in the corners much like US currency; however, the lines are much thinner. The unit seems to be marks. Let's see, I count it out and see I have about two thousand marks, broken down into hundreds, fifties, and twenties. I decide not to take all of it and only grab about seven hundred marks. I put all my money into my sock under my foot. Reminds me of going shopping in Detroit. I then grab my keys and put them in a buttoned pocket on my shorts, nice and secure.

Lastly, I take my phone out and make sure it's charged before I head out the door. I open Safari and type in shopping centers near me. The main attraction that pops up is the Paw Mall just a couple of blocks away. Sounds like it's the best option, and has great reviews too.

I leave my apartment and lock the door behind me. It is actually an awesome day to go outside! I take a deep breath in and fill my lungs with the fresh autumn air. It's not hot, probably about upper seventies, with a nice breeze. Sun pelts the ground intermittently between single clouds roaming aimlessly in the sky above. It is still morning as I jog down to the gate. I might as well get some cardio done today; don't want to get lazy just because I have the day off.

I wave goodbye at the security camera which still has its blinking green light to let the guard know I am heading out for the day.

The jog is pleasant as I head down. I see several Primes I never saw before. Families of the upper class getting out of their houses with their kids. Rabbits, crocodiles, gazelle, weasel, a wildcat family that notices me jogging by. They see me, turn back to their kids, and then look back quickly, as if to check that what they saw is real. I simply wave to them and tell them "Good morning" before looking back ahead of me.

As I run on the sidewalk past their house I can hear a little boy Prime start to run toward me. I look back and smile at him and give him a salute before his mother strides to him and picks him up to bring him back to her side. The kid seemed pretty interested in me.

A panther Prime greets me as I get to the gates. He is armed with a fully automatic rifle; I think it's a version of the Tiger. He holds out his hand to me when I approach.

"And where," he yawns, "do you think you're going?"

I hold up my badge for him. "I am heading out. Lupine gave me permission to leave Highpoint."

The Prime, whose badge reads *Jordan Felidae Zodiac Protection Services Zeta*, takes out his walkie-talkie. His eyes squint at my badge. "Ghent, looking for clearance."

Static comes back then another voice comes over. "Clear. Lupine gave the order this morning. He is clear to go out during the day, but he has to be back by six p.m."

He reaches into the booth and flicks a switch, the gates of freedom open up to me, and he orders me to clear the gap under the gate. I look down and see a set of tire killers under the gate that point out to the street. They look like large metallic fangs, like Pure's claws.

I clear the gate and turn back to see them close behind me with the guards keeping an eye on me. I thank him for letting me through, get out of sight, and pull out my phone and map my directions.

The looks from the Primes I get as I stroll by vary widely. Of course it doesn't help that I am constantly scanning each Prime I walk by, but as long as I do it with my head held high and a smile they won't realize that I am looking for any sign of a threat. Being truly alone walking down the street in an unfamiliar city full of non-humans is just stressful enough for my bones to start to creak with each step and my nails to throb with pain. I need to look at least a little bit Prime to lessen other Primes' concerns about me walking around unsupervised.

Maybe I am overthinking this whole thing. I keep walking by Primes and they just seem to be minding their own business and not even shocked I am walking around. I guess the uniform is helping hide my humanity. A soldier walking around here wouldn't bring too much attention as Pure just lives up the road. As I pass by more Primes that do not stop me or say anything, the more I feel like I can finally belong here.

A culture so familiar. Clothes from home worn by a species once unknown to me, but now I am a part of.

I reach down into my pocket and pull out my phone to make sure I am still on track for the Paw Mall.

As I am not paying attention I bump into a cat Prime and it startles me back right into a bus stop bench, where an older badger couple are waiting for the bus. I manage to catch myself from tripping over the bench by grabbing onto the bus stop sign. It's Feline, wearing a long-sleeve red and black button-up shirt along with jeans, traveling with a group of three girls. A racoon Prime with a sweater and dark denim pants, a darker fur fox with a lighter red jacket on with her jeans, a female wolf Prime that has whiter fur than Lupine, she has what looks like a university sweater on with a giant lion's paw on the front and the words "Lion University: We Take Pride in Our Students" written on the front in bold golden letters.

The older badgers don't seem to be perturbed by what just occurred. They seem too absorbed in reading the paper to care that a human almost fell on them.

I take Feline's hand and restabilize myself and look around to see where I am. I seemed to zone out and I found myself at the intersection between Castor and Aristotle. "Um, hey, Feline, sorry I wasn't paying attention."

Feline immediately, without skipping a beat, goes over to the older couple. "Oh sorry, miss and mister, didn't mean to startle you."

The older woman lifts her palm to Feline. "Oh, it's no problem, dear, we are all good."

I turn back to them as well. "Yeah, sorry, I wasn't really paying attention either." I try to laugh it off.

The woman badger catches a look at me and notices my face and badge. "Oh don't apologize. Say are you a new recruit to the PLF?" I notice her hands tighten around her rose leather purse.

My face feels a bit red. I should have prepared for something like this before, some answers to this question. "Yes, ma'am." I am glad she didn't quite notice me as a human, the shifting must be working.

She nudges the male badger. "Bill, are you still awake?"

He stirs a bit before opening his eyes and seeing me. "Oh, well hello there." He puts his hand on what I assume to be his wife's knee.

Feline interjects by leaning next to me. "Yeah he is still a newbie, hasn't quite gotten his army legs quite yet."

I notice the bus begin to approach. "Hey, is that your bus?" I point over to the approaching bus.

The male looks around him and gathers his plastic bag. I don't want to pry into what's in it. "Oh, yes it is. Well, it was nice to meet you." They begin to collect their things in a hurry. "And who are you, my dear?"

"Feline, ma'am, future soldier in Sagittarius! I got a Fang profile and following if you are interested!"

The elderly couple get up and head toward the bus. "Well, we will think about it. Have a wonderful Veterans Day and thank you for your service."

My service? That sent a shiver down my spine hearing that from someone for the first time.

Feline waves goodbye to the couple and then turns his attention to me. "So." He swings over and sits down on the bench, legs crossed. "What are you doing outside of Highpoint?"

I have a better question. "Lupine gave me permission to leave for the day. How did you find me?"

He pats down on the side beside him, motioning me to sit down. "Oh, the big bad wolf let you free for a day!" His tail starts to wag. "That's great! Oh, and Gores let slip to me that you are clear to wander around now."

Gores told him? Why would he tell him anything regarding me? "Did Gores send you to watch me?"

He shakes his head. "No." He fiddles with the end of his tail. "But he did mention just hanging out with you for the day. Maybe show you around with some of my friends." He motions to the three Primes that were chatting among themselves. He points to each of them. "The racoon is Noir, the fox is Sylvia, and the wolf is Claire." He cups her hands to her mouth. "Ladies, come see our new friend!"

Getting a closer look at them, I can't really tell their ages because it's harder to tell how old Prime is compared to a human. However, they seem to be wearing college-branded sweaters and I notice one of them has a phone case for Lion University. They are college girls, or maybe high school girls. Raiden is called a university but in reality it was just for branding and marketing itself as something it obviously was not. They are pretty attractive, though. "Hey." I feel uncomfortable being around these Prime girls out in public like this. I've never been around a group of girls like this. "You girls in college?"

Noir tugs down her sweater so I can see the print. "Lion University is a private high school."

Private high school, so they are probably either wealthy or smart. They might also be near my age. "Cool. Say, I was going to go to the Paw Mall to get something. You girls want to head down there?" I figure it will be better if I am with a group of Primes. Less attention given to me if I can blend in with a group.

They all agree with each other and Feline then grabs me by my arm and pulls me to my feet on the bench. "Sounds like a great idea!" He seems unnaturally strong for his size and how thin his arms are. "They got some sweet Veterans Day sales going on too!"

I get up and start walking with Feline to my right and the girls to my left. I open up my phone to make sure we are going the right way.

Feline immediately notices my phone out of my pocket. "Hey, where did you get that?"

"A member of Sagittarius gave it to me." I didn't want to mention Taiga's name because I know he seems like a person that can't hold a secret to save his life, and I don't want to get Taiga in trouble.

Sylvia notices my phone. "That's a weird brand." She leans her neck to look at the screen. "What kind of phone is that?" she asks Feline.

Feline reaches over the phone and taps it with his finger to lighten it up. "It's a PLF-issued brand. You can't get them in stores."

I enter the code, which is a simple star shape on the password grid. "How is it different from any other phone?"

Sylvia opens up her phone and shows it to me. It looks mint condition and has a rosewood back case to it with a tiny cute fox plush toy dangling from a chain in the corner. On the screen pops up at least five screens worth of apps, and it looks like she has three hundred unread emails and twenty unread texts. "There is usually a brand in the corner." She shows me the Roar brand in the corner near the cellular data and six gig internet speed reader. Six gig phones are relatively new in the states, and expensive at that. "Also, the back doesn't have a marking or branding on it."

I don't feel comfortable talking about where my phone came from around Feline. Time to change the subject. "What is that?" I point to a random app on her phone.

"Oh." She opens up an app with a strand of DNA in front of an open book, and a long list of family names come up. "It's called Texonomy. It allows you to connect with Primes of different species or find ones close to you."

That's actually quite interesting. "Cool."

The racoon pulls out her phone and comes up to me on the other side. "You also have this app that shows you all the different species of recorded Primes." She opens up a book icon and a directory pulls up with the taxonomy tree that starts with Animalia.

I peel my eyes away from their screens and notice around me people are starting to stare at us. It must be because I am chatting it up with several Prime girls on the street. They walk by with a quick glance while others wait at bus stops look intently at me and talk among themselves. I try to hear some of their conversation while the girls talk about the app, but even I can't hear that well, unlike Lupine.

They start showing me various apps that they recommend I put on my phone. They tell me to install a GPS app that recommends restaurants, shops, and bars.

They don't look of drinking age. "You girls go to bars? You seem too young for that."

Claire shuffles to my right and replaces Noir and giggles at my question. "Did you hear him? He thinks we are young."

They all laugh among themselves. Did I just accidentally flirt with them? "Well, isn't there a drinking age?"

Sylvia goes up to my left. "Nope, you can drink when your parents think you are ready."

That seems risky. "There are a lot of Primes your age that drink?"

They tell me that the PLF doesn't like to tell kids how to act. They tell them that if they want to drink, smoke pot, or party they let them. It's up to the individual Prime to watch themselves and for their friends and family to help them make personal decisions.

Claire's tail brushes up behind me. "But there is an age of consent. How old are you?"

Umm... I can feel my face heat up like someone smacked me with a hot iron. "Well, I am about seventeen, I guess."

Feline manages to bump Claire aside. "Hey, back off. Hands off the human." He defends me, or maybe he is claiming me. Never thought that Feline could be gay and just attracted to me.

Claire pouts. "Oh, come on, he's pretty hot for a human. Besides, Feline is so boring—she's as flat as a board."

Wait, Feline is a girl? I mean, it is hard to tell with the way she looks but I assumed that if she was in the army, she was a guy. I can barely tell with the lack of any breasts or obvious feminine features.

I can't help but notice Claire and the rest of these girls are showing far more of their breasts than Feline, who is conservatively wearing her shirt over her flat sternum.

Claire smirks. "See, Ghent's even more interested in us—right?"

Shit, did they see me? "Well, I don't think it's right for me to *like* a Prime." It's forbidden in The States; I wonder how it is here.

"It's not liked by most Primes, but it's legal," Claire highlights, "and it makes it much more *interesting*." She runs her finger on my chest.

I don't want to be rude around these girls, but I just don't think I should be flirting with them. "Sorry, but I don't think it's natural for me to get with a Prime."

She giggles. "Then what is natural for you?"

I... honestly don't know. Would human girls find me attractive knowing I am half Prime or would they reject me? Same goes for Prime girls. Even though these girls seem interested in me, I don't know if either side will actually find me attractive. If society doesn't look highly upon hybrids then I don't have a chance anywhere at finding anything long term. Maybe it is for the best that I try to act more like a Prime and flirt with these girls to test the waters, and get some experience talking to Primes, especially a department I severely lack in, women. After all, they seem nice. "Well, I think it's natural for both, right? 'Cause I am half of both."

Feline manages to nudge Claire from getting any closer to me. "Seems right to me! Just make sure not to get too attached to Claire, though. She's got a bad history with men."

195

Sylvia gets to my other side. "We all do." I can feel her tail come up behind me as well. "But Feline has told us you're cool."

Cool? As in okay or is someone actually calling me cool for once? "Well, I don't think I am that cool." I am just a freak of nature after all.

Noir jumps while walking backwards in front of me. "You are a human in the PLF, though. If that isn't cool I don't know what would be!"

They continue to fawn over me and ask me questions while we walk. The more I talk with them, and the more I gaze at Primes walking past, the more I seem to grasp a concept of being one with them. I am walking down a street surrounded by Primes being escorted by four good-looking Prime girls. Six months ago I could never imagine that I would be here, let alone wanted to be talked to, wanted to be around other people, wanted at all. Countless nights would pass while I rotted in that orphanage hoping to be a parent's wanted child, to be someone that would be picked up and whisked into friends, siblings, a pet, a home. A family, a society that I could be a part of.

I am walking taller than I have ever been in my life. Pure gave me this life and a chance to start over. I am damn well using this chance to stop being an orphan and start to finally be a teenager, be an adolescent and have some fun with my life.

For the first time I think I finally feel like I am a part of a clique, and it feels great.

I can tell we are getting closer to the mall as more and more parents and kids emerge in the crowd. All the while, PLF military members, dressed in their uniforms, are intermingling with the civilian population. Pop music can be heard around us. The mall is curved at the entrance and stands tall above the smaller stores around it. The amphitheater feeling of the festivities outside makes it seem like it's a tailgate party. I ask the girls if there is a festival or a fair going on today. They mention that since its Veterans Day there are celebrations around the entire city, and the Paw Mall is one of the busier festivals that the center holds every year to commemorate the PLF.

"Why is it called the Paw Mall?" I ask them while keeping close so as not to get separated.

Noir points to the flag in front of the center's entrance, which displays a banner of a golden paw. "The building is shaped like a paw, and the smaller bits above the main paw print are different shopping centers that sell different stuff."

That's really cool! "How long did it take them to build all of this?"

"Only a couple of years. This used to be a crater in the city from the bombings, so they leveled it and built a facility to commemorate the fallen soldiers who fought for Kingdom." She points to a statue just out of sight, but I can see an arm of a Prime hoisting up a PLF flag in the air. "They built a memorial inside the mall."

A memorial for veterans in a mall? "That's kind of weird for a war memorial to be in a shopping center."

I can feel Feline's hand brush against my pocket with my phone in it. "They put it in there so more people would go and see it. Not many people would constantly see and be reminded of it if it was just a memorial."

That's not too unreasonable.

We approach the entrance to the mall. No one seemed to notice or care about me. Maybe blending into the group wasn't such a bad idea. Also, with how busy it is here and all the PLF soldiers, I doubt that any Evols are wandering the fair. I might as well get a little loose and enjoy myself; I shouldn't be stressing out on a day like this. Everything is going well. Everyone seems to be enjoying themselves.

We are let in without any checkpoints, no metal detectors, no security. Community members throw down flower petals from above onto the soldiers passing by. It's almost surreal how different it is here compared to the US. From just getting into a mall the change is palpable. Even though there are no police or soldiers armed with M16s to watch over us, I am feeling safe. The police back there did not show a vibrant atmosphere, but instead instilled a sense of force over us and that someone is always watching, protecting. The air here, on the other hand, is welcoming, and most importantly a happy feeling fills the entire mall. There is nothing more I need than experiencing something like this with possibly new friends, girl ones.

A massive open space carries the echoes of shoppers all around each floor. The floors are layered like a pyramid all the way up, with each layer forming an empty egg-shaped center that hangs a giant glass, rotating crystal that is bearing each flag of the Zodiac as it spins in air, almost as if it is floating. Natural sunlight fills each floor, and the shops are bustling with shoppers. In between the outer rings reside several smaller carts with wares, benches, fountains, and Primes admiring the beauty that is all around us. Stairs are positioned all around in the center and on the outer edges.

The air is filled with the scents of a candle shop, spicy dishes from the restaurants immediately to our right, and thousands of animals all blending together. This is all too amazing. Detroit mall, eat your heart out. You got nothing on this place.

The girls grab me by my shirt and pull me toward a coffee shop down to the right side. Feline takes the lead and pulls me to the entrance past several large elephant Primes. "Come on, let's get some coffee to start off!"

Despite all of the noise around me I can hear her words fairly well. Maybe it's my hearing getting better, or maybe it's just how this building is built that amplifies sound in one direction. As I am led to the shop I can't help but glance at a band performing in the center on the south side of the center. It looks like it was making music from outside. It's not that bad, but I was never into pop music. I also see what looks like a newscaster crew setting up next to them, maybe reporting on the activities of the day. I know they are newscasters because I've seen them on the streets of Detroit, which usually only meant a murder or crime.

The line to the coffee shop is fairly long. We get at the end of the line and each one of the girls pulls out their phones and talks amongst themselves. From a reflective glass window that extends down the outside of the cafe I can see myself. I look human, but with a hint of a Prime scratching from under the surface of my skin. My mouth is hurting more than usual. As I open my mouth to check to see if my teeth have changed, I feel a light hand from behind me rest on my shoulder.

"Excuse me, sir, but I just noticed..." I turn around slowly to see an older female falcon Prime dressed in a teal and white thin dress. She immediately sees who I am and lets go of my shoulder. "Oh! I am sorry, I didn't know that you were..."

I remove my finger from my mouth, prodding my canines. "Oh, sorry... I was just checking a tooth." Maybe that's rude in Prime society to show your fangs.

"No, I didn't realize you were part of the PLF," she kindly apologizes. I can see that she motions with one hand to my badge. "You know official PLF soldiers can cut in line today as part of the celebration."

Feline thanks her and tugs me by the shoulder on my shirt. "Come on, let's get some fast coffee!"

"Umm, girls..." I try to stop them from displaying me to the rest of the line and to the cashier taking orders in front behind a display stocked with baked goods. "I will stay here. actually I..."

I don't really want anything now. I don't think I have the right to be considered a soldier. It just doesn't feel right.

"Sorry, I am just a soldier in training," I confess to the confused bunny cashier behind the till.

I start to move back to the end of the line. As I turn around, I notice the Prime behind us that we cut in front of is an elderly lizard Prime. He is dressed in a badgeless uniform and looks at me with a stern look. Everyone is gracious about him cutting in line, but all he does is point to my badge with one of his talons, and I can feel his skin flake as his jaw moves. "You are good, son. Take your time," he assures me.

Claire is tugging at my shirt to get my attention, but all I can do is stare at this old lizard and wonder what he could see in me to say something like that. I peer past the other customers in line and notice they are all too absorbed in what is going on to really care what I did. I am a human walking around in Kingdom. Why aren't they all freaked out that I am calling myself a soldier but cutting in line in front of the elderly, who are far more deserving than I am?

I feel Sylvia's hand rest on my shoulder as she leans in to talk to the rabbit. "I recommend the mocha with extra caramel," she suggests with a smile and a sniff.

I look at the bunny Prime who looks distressed and exhausted. In the gleam of the silver till in front of me I can see myself, and I am in the process of shifting. My eyes are getting thinner and my face muscles are twitching. I probably look like a freak right now. "S-sure, I will have that then." I shakingly get out a hundred-mark bill and hand it over to the cashier. "Please put these girls orders on mine." It will be easier to break down the bill, and I don't really need the money for anything.

Once I have put in my order and put the money on the table I scoot over to the side to get away from everyone. Once I see Sylvia get done with her order she and Claire walk me over to a booth near the back towards the bathrooms.

Claire sits down and scoots over to let me sit. "Say, you okay back there?" She motions back to the line.

I guess I did have a freakout there. "Oh, I just thought that I didn't deserve to cut in line. I just don't think that I should have gone up there like that."

Noir joins us with Feline who sets the change down on the table. She points at my badge. "You're a soldier, though. You have the badge and you were inducted by Pure himself."

I don't think she gets what I am saying. "I know, but it's just that I don't think I have done anything deserving of it."

"You are sitting with a bunch of random Primes off the street." Claire scoots a bit more toward me. "And you are walking around in public as a human. That takes some big balls." Her hands get closer to my leg.

I feel Sylvia slide over on the other side of the booth and kick Claire under the table and look scornfully at her. "Hey, hands off Ghent." Claire moves to the edge of the booth.

Noir giggles and puts her phone away. "Sorry about that. Claire must be in some serious heat to try to cuddle up to a human."

Claire kicks Noir under the table. "Oh really, *I* am in heat. Bitch, you were dumpster diving a week ago behind the school's locker rooms with those filthy jocks."

She kicks her back. "Hey, at least I can find something digging in the trash."

Feline manages to quell the infighting between them. I know that they are teenagers and everything, but I wish they would lay off hitting on me so much. Its uncomfortable for me, and I don't know what I should tell them to make them stop without upsetting them.

I decide to keep quiet and to myself, only nodding my head and occasionally putting in minimal input into their conversations amongst themselves about various topics they bring up, mostly about their classes and teachers. We all eventually finish off our coffees and as soon as I am the last to finish mine Sylvia notices and collects her purse.

Sylvia taps Noir to move out. "All right, let's move out, trash panda and horn dog."

. . .

We leave the coffee shop and ascend up to the second story, where the girls head into a fancy clothing shop. I can tell it's fancy and high priced as the less they have displayed the more expensive it usually is. I decide to skip that and tell them I will meet them here later. I have to go find an electronics store and get a charger, and maybe some other accessories for my phone.

Feline decides to stick next to me as the others stroll in. "I will keep an eye on Ghent. You girls head in and I will catch up later."

I guess it's good to have Feline around with me. She seems more focused on my protecting my ass instead of trying to touch it. Maybe she knows what kind of charger I need to get. "Hey, Feline, I need to get a charger for my phone. You know of a good place to get one?"

She thinks for a moment and then looks across the skyway just to our right. "There is a Wired store just over there. They should have one."

"Awesome—lead the way," I ask like a gentleman.

"You didn't get a charger when you got the phone?" she asks as she starts leading the way.

Taiga never did give me a charger. I guess he didn't carry one with him and wasn't expecting to give me his phone. "I guess they forgot."

She smiles. "Stupid PLF, always forgetting the small details." Her hand comes out and she puts her hand out in front of me. "Can I see the phone? I need to see the phone jack."

I take out the phone and pass it to her.

She takes the phone with her right hand, before she looks at the charger port. "Looks like a standard multi-purpose Core phone brand."

"Got it. How do you know that's the brand?" It doesn't sound like Feline to know that; sounds more like Tucker.

She flips the phone over and looks at the back. "It's the same as mine!" She reaches in and takes out her phone from her back pocket and compares the two. They are identical in every way except that Feline's has a smiling red fox cartoon sticker on the back.

Makes sense if all the PLF phones were the same brand and model. "That's a cute sticker on the back," I point out.

She smiles and puts her phone into her back pocket. "Oh, thanks! A friend of mine got it for me!" My phone is still in her left hand as she heads over the railing and looks out and points out to the center. "Wait, is that Instinct?"

I've heard of that band on TV. They are a pop band that is newer and has quite a large following online. I head over to the side with her and she points to the band forming on stage. There is quite a massive crowd growing.

Several event attendants are funneling people in and organizing them as to not swarm the stage.

"It is!" She begins to run off toward the stairs. "Come on, Ghent!"

As soon as Feline makes a bolt for it, I notice she still has my phone in her hand.

"Feline! You still have my phone!" I shout at her to try to remind her.

I attempt to chase after her but she swiftly maneuvers her way through the crowd at the bottom of the stairs. Her body just squeezes between the people in the crowd like a furry liquid, and her agility beats my strength-based training. I try to keep my eyes on the top of her head, but through all the cats, lions, and other felines in the crowd it is hard to keep her on track. As soon as the music starts going and the crowd has turned into a sea of Primes, I decide to surrender and head back up the stairs out of the mess of people and up to a higher vantage point where it is safer for me to walk around.

Maybe if I head up to the Wired shop she will meet me there later.

I head toward a shop with a sign with the word *Wired* written in what appears to be wires with lights inside them all lit up red and black. I can't seem to see them outside the store; maybe they are inside. There are shelves stacked with computer parts, phone chips, phone repair kits, and a younger adult owl Prime behind a workstation protected by a glass shield in front and sides fiddling with a smartphone that was opened up. He doesn't seem to notice me entering. I peek between the shelves of parts to see if I can spot the girls, but they don't seem to be in here. Then where the fuck did they go? Well, while I am here I might as well get my charger, for the phone I don't have.

I approach the man behind the glass shielding. "Umm, excuse me, sir."

He peeks up from screwing in a processor into the phone. Once he looks up at me I can see his eyes zoom out as if he was zooming in on the phone before I approached. "How can I help you today?"

"Oh, I am just looking for a phone charger."

He rolls back from the stool he was sitting on and rolls down to the other side of the counter, which holds a register and a shelf with phone accessories dangling behind him. "What kind of phone is it?"

"A standard multi-purpose Core phone brand." At least Feline managed to tell me what I was looking for before she stole my phone.

He stands on the stool to reach the top shelf and takes down the cardboard box. "You in the PLF?"

Idle chitchat I guess. "Yeah, I joined a couple months ago."

"Great, it's always nice to see the army's funds finally trickling down to us normal folk." He pulls the box back. I notice that the chair is starting to slide a little too far forward. He is going to fall if he keeps pushing like that. I walk around the register and just as I reach him the chair gives way and he falls back, but I manage to catch him and the box that he has in his arms. "Fuck me! Thanks, man, I almost blew it." He looks in shock.

I let him get to his feet. "You've got to be more careful. You could have seriously hurt yourself there."

He sets the box on the table with the register. "Well, if I hurt myself I would get the time off I wanted." He jokes as he opens up the box and takes out a locked silver briefcase. After entering a combination on both sides of the front it pops open to reveal several packets of silver bags all labeled with serial numbers. He peruses inside the case and grabs a silver pack and takes it out, relocks the case, then opens up the pack. "This should charge your PLF phone." Inside is a charger with a coiled cord and a port that has several exit points on it.

I guess they keep the PLF gear off the shelf, but I have to wonder if they are supposed to have that briefcase or if I am buying illegal hardware as a member of the military. "Great." I reach down and take some money out of my shoe while he places the case back into the box and covers it with some other junk. "How much?"

"I will give you a save-my-life-discount along with a veteran discount." He rings up three dollars, marks, whatever currency they use here.

I had him a hundred-dollar bill. "Do you take hundreds?"

He opens the register and counts the bills inside. "Yes, I will take hundreds but it doesn't mean I can break it down."

"Okay." I take back the hundred and hand him a twenty. "Sorry, I just want to break these down."

He puts the twenty in and gives me change. "No problem. I wish I had that problem of having too big of bills."

Well, I am not used to having this much money on me at a time. This is the first time I've ever had a hundred-dollar bill on me. "I know the feeling; I was a bit poor before living in Detroit."

He smiles and hands me a receipt in a bag with the charger. "Glad the PLF could give you your American dream."

The irony makes me shiver hearing that. "Well, thanks for your help." I say my goodbyes and he smiles back before heading back to his station.

Feline is still not around. I even look down at the crowds to see if I can find her. Nothing. The mall is getting less busy as the day marches on. I don't have a way to tell the time. Maybe there is a clock somewhere around here. I peek back into Wired to look at the clock behind the clerk. It's two, so I have six hours to make it back to Highpoint. Maybe if I just walk around I will find her.

With my charger in a bag, I decide to browse around, trying to look into stores that girls would normally flock to. Perfume stores, which are surprisingly less pungent than those back home, makeup stores, clothes stores... Wait...while I am here I might as well get some new clothes. I walk up to a store that markets to my age group, with pumping music inside and what I assume to be teenagers working part-time jobs managing the counter. There's an overall sense of rebellion as the clothes are all designed with either bright vivid colors or depict various unfamiliar brands.

I should just get some casual clothes, especially if I am to walk around Kingdom more. I need to wear what kids my age are wearing. It feels weird, shopping here and looking around and seeing new clothes with prices above five dollars. I grew up on thrift stores, hand-me-downs, and donated clothes. I've gotten more out of the PLF than I ever did back in Detroit. I feel independent even though I am dependent on the PLF's money, training, and protection.

A blue T-shirt with claw marks across instead of stripes... Prime fashion is so strange. I've seen advertisements and what high society Primes wear on TV and it's all so bizarre. I guess a society wants to make an identity for itself instead of borrowing from The States, so experimentation is the name of the game around the PLF.

I have no idea what the hell I am looking for. Once I see a wandering employee, I go over to her. She's an antelope-looking Prime wearing the store's merchandise and has earrings that smack against her black antlers as she walks around. I get her attention and ask her to help me pick out a wardrobe. She seems hesitant at first, but once I make some small chat she seems to loosen up a bit. I guess not every Prime knows who I am. Some are just too focused with their own lives to pay attention to the news, I guess.

She helps me pick out several sets of clothes, and also throws in some socks. There is a sale going on for veterans, and she doesn't believe I am a PLF soldier initially. However, a coworker of hers has seen me on the news and confirmed I am in fact a PLF soldier.

"He's been all over the news. How haven't you seen him?" the male squirrel Prime remarks.

The antelope brushes him off. "The news is so boring, though. There is nothing ever going on to pay attention to that I can't just get on my phone."

God damn it, I wish I had mine. Feline, what the fuck did you do with it?

He laughs despite her uninterested mood. "Oh, come on, you're getting fed a bunch of shit...I mean crap...from Fang again. It will rot your brain."

I finish up my purchase and thank the attendant for helping me out. She lets me know of a survey app I can use to give her a recommendation. I would, but no phone. She understands and hands me the business card with her phone number on it...kind, but not very bright.

Still no Feline or company in sight... fucking why? She couldn't have just ditched me, and the other girls seemed interested enough in me to stick around and find me. I head back to Wired to look at the clock again. It's four o'clock. I should get going now...except I don't know where the back is. I was expecting my phone to guide me back, or at least Feline or the girls to direct me back to Highpoint.

This day turned from one of the best days of my life to a nightmare.

Bounty

All right, let's start by finding my way back out the way I came into the mall. I pick up my bags of purchases and move back to the south entrance of the mall. While I am leaving I am combing over the crowd trying to find the girls. Despite all the different races of Primes, the sizes of larger Primes make it difficult to see past them. I am also trying not to trip on smaller Primes prowling around beneath my waist. The last thing I need is to step on someone's tail or child to attract attention to myself. I need to get outside and find someone to take me back. I can take a taxi.

I leave the mall. There is a coating of flower petals on the floor as I leave that are kicked up into my bags I am carrying, one with each hand. I set my bags beside a busy road and scan for a taxi. I don't know what taxis look like here, but I assume they will have the word on them or the symbolic taxi hat on top of the roof of the car.

I wait some time for one to show up, but after about ten minutes without any luck I am starting to think that either they don't exist in Kingdom or they all use an app on a phone for ride sharing. Maybe a PLF officer would know, so I look for a badge. Come on...there has to be someone here...a Prime in uniform...ah! I catch a fleeting glimpse of an eagle Prime wearing a soldier's cap and supporting a fledgling.

I squeeze past and shift my way through the crowd and approach the soldier along with his family, a female hawk Prime and two kid Primes about half their

206

height, one on his shoulder while the other is holding the mother's hand who is wearing civilian clothes and wiping some ice cream from her son's feathers under his chin.

I approach the father, who immediately notices my badge. I set my bags down and wave to him. "Hello." I see his name on his badge. "Wingens sir, can I ask you a quick question? I am kind of lost, and I was wondering if you could tell me if there is a taxi service I can use."

He puts down his son from his shoulders and tells him to go to his mother. He turns back to me with an unreadable face. "You are human that everyone is talking about in the PLF."

I notice past him that the mother notices me and corrals her kids back toward a nearby bench near the monument. "Yes, sir." He outranks me; I have to be polite.

He looks around and notices several Primes are looking at him before walking on. "Umm... There is an app called Stork you can use."

Shit, and I can't use it because I don't have my phone. When I get back to Kingdom I am going to tell Lupine about my phone so he can track her down. "Do you know the fastest way to get back to Highpoint? I am kind of on a curfew."

"You can head down that street." He points to a street going diagonal from the main street that everyone seems to be using. It is pressed between an apartment high-rise and a grocery store resting under a set of medical professional offices. "That should take you right to Highpoint."

"Thank you, sir!" I salute him and pick up my bags and rush down to the street so I can make it back before curfew.

The street that cuts down diagonally is named Division Street, and appears to consist mainly of middle- to lower-cost apartments. They are not nearly as bad as what I had back in Detroit, but these are not even close to the condo I have back at Highpoint, or that are closer to the mall. Primes are still avoiding me as they continue with their own business. A lot of Primes are heading back from the mall, so I stay blended nicely in the crowd to avoid any encounters with Evols. Speaking of which, I haven't seen the hair or tail of an Evol or Evol group since I left. They must be keeping to themselves today as a national holiday. With all the PLF soldiers out, they wouldn't want to get in trouble harassing other Primes. I am still on alert for any signs of Evols, but I am no longer scanning every Prime

I come across fearing they will jump me. It's strange, really. I feel safer confined among Primes than I do back in Detroit surrounded by my own kind.

The brick apartments with grocery stores, or mom and pop department stores, fade away and end with a fork in the road with a peace sign shape. Let's see, if I need to go diagonally west, I need to follow the setting sun, which should get me to Castor Street, and from there I can make it back to Highpoint. I make my way across to a crosswalk heading south on M. Division Street. Wait, this is Division Street as well.... Well, I can't say that these streets were laid out conventionally. I mean, the city was rebuilt from rubble after the war, so maybe the people here just forgot what the streets were named.

I seem to be left alone as I cross the crosswalk with a green light. The rest of the crowd seems to head north toward...Division. Wait, is that the street I should be taking? No...that would take me west of Castor Street and north of where I would end up. I think it would be shorter if I took the south road and just followed it all the way to Castor or Pollux. Besides, it's nice to finally be able to breathe and move around now that I don't have a herd of Primes beside me.

Sunlight is becoming dimmer and my shadow is crawling farther onto the cracking cement ground as I track down the street. Words on buildings retreat into shadows, and the buildings seem to grow darker. I can tell a bad neighborhood just by the number of houses or apartments that look all alike, and the number of bars on the windows. I seem to be getting deeper into a ghetto, and I am a human carrying goods. I am a literal caravan that is traveling down bandit territory. I guess I should pay more attention around corners, and behind me, as I walk down here. It's strange—the only ghetto I have been to in the PLF is the one I stayed at on my first night here. Other than that there seems to be a distinct lack of any poor neighborhoods around here. Besides, most of the slums and ghettos were for Primes back in Detroit; the poor just managed to creep in on their ghettos and meld with them. I mean, I lived in a relatively safe neighborhood in Detroit, but go any farther down south from my house and I would be entering Chinatown and some of the worst slums just east of Chicago.

The lights on all of the apartments are covered in heavy blinds and curtains that block every gleam of light. Several bars are placed on the first two floors of each building, and there doesn't seem to be a single soul outside walking around.

Where is everyone? It's a holiday and it's so nice out. Even for a slum there would be some kids roaming around or some gangsters talking smack to each other. The sound of rocks being kicked up from loose asphalt as I walk down these shitty roads is the only sound I hear. It's a ghost town in the middle of the PLF. Maybe I am in a district that is pending demolition. There are plenty of areas in Detroit that are pending to be demolished as they have been havens for drug addicts or criminals. They just might be doing it here, but then why are there lights on inside?

The street abruptly takes a hard left turn without a connecting street. Instead, an alleyway goes straight into the void between two taller apartment complexes that are covered in laundry lines, potted plants, and balconies supporting unused patio chairs. The turn will take me going east, which is what I want, so I take the turn and make my way down...M. Castor Street... What the fuck is going on here? I am parallel to Castor Street, but what does the M mean?

Just as I look up to the sign above me, I hear a new sound: someone's heavy footprints coming from behind me. I brace myself to be mugged, then I spin around to see no one. There was someone behind me, not too far, but not close.... I am being followed. I pick up my pace heading down M. Castor, keeping an eye behind me as I continually look behind me every twenty steps or so. I keep seeing no one, but the strangest thing is that I keep hearing those footsteps behind me. Why am I getting a sense of déjà vu?... I've been in this situation before—someone following me.

The sound suddenly moves down to the north. The sound is becoming faint, but I can still hear the footsteps. It sounds like they are down less than a half-block away.

I make it a couple more blocks before a trash can pops out from an alley, as if someone has thrown it. Trash spills out onto the street and the lid rolls out onto the side of the street.

Okay, someone has to be there. Right before approaching the alleyway I set my bags aside at the staircase leading up to the front door of an apartment complex. I put my body against the wall and peer around the brickwork to see down the alley.

Immediately, a buffalo Prime approaches me. I reach back and take out the empty gun, undoing the safety, just in case he knows the safety is on. I point the gun directly at him. "Get back!" I demand.

He ignores my threat and keeps approaching as I step back deeper into the alley. Work, dammit, I don't want to fight him—he's huge! "I am part of the PLF. I order you to step down!"

The buffalo does not stop moving. He advances without any fear of the gun in my hand. There is no way he knows it's not loaded, so either he knows the gun won't stop him or he doesn't care if I shoot him.

My back hits a fence. I am out of stalling time. I can't get over the fence in time—it's too high. I can maybe get around him and grab my stuff and run. My only option is to fight or run, but I should be able to beat him. I was trained to fight him. I decide to put the gun away and fake him out by running left, but then jump to the right to squeeze between him and the building. His eyes track my movement and anticipate me. His right arm slams against me and sends me flying back down.

I try to grab the dumpster before being flown, but the sure strength of this Prime is too much to resist. I manage to keep myself on my feet as I nearly stumble down the dark alley behind us. I get a look at the Prime. He is a buffalo Prime for sure as his beard and his mangled hair cover nearly his entire face and most of his eyes. He is a head shorter than Borne, but taller than Lupine. I notice he is wearing a workman's overalls stained with brown splotches and worn work jeans that are coated in a fine dusting of sawdust and splinters coming out from the fabric. Work shoes stomp down the alley as he begins to approach me. That was the sound that was following me this entire time.

I look around me for anything to use as a weapon, but I only see a dumpster to my right, and a fire escape hanging just out of reach for me to climb up to get to. He attempts to reach out to grab my collar. I step back out of his reach, but he manages to take a quick step forward to cover the distance. I take a quick sidestep closer to the right wall and throw away his hand; however, when I attempt to push his arm away I feel like I am pushing against a statue. His hand does not give way and he spins with his other hand and tries to grab my left side.

I decide to close the gap between us and punch his face. I lunge forward and land a punch right onto his fur, but when I make contact it feels like I am punching a down pillow due to the amount of fur on his face and body. He simply laughs. I am immediately put into a vice by his dry, furry arms around every bone in my body. I can feel the breath escape my lungs. I can't even scream as my bones creak under the pressure of a trash compactor squeezing me dry.

I need to get out of this! I manage to squeeze my leg close to his genitals and wind up for a kick straight to his balls. With all the force I have left in me I give one hard kick. I make contact with the denim he is wearing, but I can only feel my foot bounce off his fluff and buff.

This is bad! I am starting to fade out as he squeezes me like a child to a teddy bear.... He lifts me up right to his neck.

I hear nothing but my wheezing and my heart racing. Faster and faster it beats, faster it thumps in my ears, in my chest, in my veins, in my eyes, on the soles of my feet, until suddenly...it all stops. For a millisecond, my eyesight is covered by a crimson filter and the only instinct I have is to lunge forward with all my remaining strength. The next thing I feel is the taste of blood on my tongue or the bones grinding against my teeth.

The buffalo Prime yells in pain and releases me from my vision and loses his grip just enough for me to breathe in the scent and taste of his blood and pry myself free.

He drops me as I scramble backwards. He immediately grabs under his chin where I bit him and rushes toward me with a haymaker with his right hand. He winds up on his last punch downward to finish me off before he suddenly stops as I hear the sound of a melon being struck by a bat.

As the buffalo topples in front of me, I see a hare-looking Prime holding metal rebar splattered with blood at the tip. He isn't a PLF soldier this time. He sports a black long-sleeve shirt, strange for mid-August, patterned with red stripes radiating from the collar, which is flipped up to cover his neck, which has several impressions embedded in his skin. The rebar drops to his side and the blood smears onto his dark blue jeans. He kicks the buffalo Prime right in the stomach with his white and black sneakers. Getting closer, I notice he has a short gray fur length and his hair isn't much longer—almost finger length down the entire front and back. His bunny ears don't seem long, almost stunted at the base and bend to an arrow shape at the top. He is wearing a crimson scarf that is wrapped around his entire lower jaw. A pair of black tinted glasses cover his eyes. I can only notice, though, that his mouth sticks out much more than a rabbit Prime's should. It almost reminds me of...

"Beating up points in the gutters again, Bufford?" He smacks him in the back with a quick strike. The buffalo grunts heavily in pain. "You should know better than to fuck with our..."

He looks directly at me and freezes in place.

I pick myself up from the floor, wipe my sleeve on my mouth to remove the blood, and move back toward the street away from the unconscious Prime on the floor bleeding from his head and neck. "I can't thank you enough...umm...mister..."

As soon as he gets a better look at me, his flight instinct kicks in. He breaks his frozen stance and bolts down the street away from the scene with a blood trickle from the rebar trailing behind. I scramble to see where he ran off to but as I get out of the alley he is already gone.

The buffalo Prime is clenching the back of his head while a thin outline of blood seeps from in between his fingers. I can't just leave him.... I mean, I am a PLF soldier, not some thug like he is. I reach into my bag and pull out one of the white T-shirts I got and rip it into two sections. I've seen Kit do this enough times that I should be able to create at least something of a bandage. I cautiously approach the beast, who is fading in and out of consciousness. "Hey, you have two choices: let me wrap your wounds and get out of my sight, or bleed out here."

His left eye looks at me from the side and he nods his head before putting his hands down on the ground behind his back.

I approach right up to him and move his arms, clenching his neck. I see a trickle of blood coming from puncture wounds in his neck. Did I really do that? "All right."

He shifts his hand away from the wound and manages to get up and sit upright. I first wrap the cloth around his neck and press down where the wound is, then I tie a knot tightly around his neck—not to choke him, but enough to keep it secure. As I bandage him up and move the fur away from his wound, I can see several braids along his hair. Each braid is done with a criss-cross pattern, like strands of DNA. As I reach around I do also see that his back is shaved in an oval shape and a tattoo, or at least the top of the tattoo, of a panther Prime holding up a rifle. No doubt about it, he is an Evol. But as I treat his head next, I wonder what is going through his head right now, other than the ringing from the rebar. He is sitting down like a defeated man, breathing in deep and picking the ground with his hands. Even when I press down on his wound he just sits there with a low groan.

While I am attending to his wounds I might as well ask, "Why did you attack me?"

He breathes deeply but then only to lurch in pain. "We—I was told there was a bounty to bring you in to the Evols alive. There is a ten thousand mark reward for you."

There is a bounty for me? I can at least breathe a sigh of relief that it requires me to be alive, I guess. "Who set up the bounty?"

"Pantheon." He calms himself down from the sharp pain. "He has some weird fascination with you."

I have to make sure to tell Lupine of this. If Pantheon's true goal is not to get me killed but meet me and talk, then that would explain the lack of Evols trying to harm me. The real question is: What changed all of a sudden? "Why try to kill me before if you want me alive now?"

He winces. "I don't know. Pantheon never said anything about killing you, he just wanted you out of the PLF, at least until a couple of days ago. Once you came to the PLF everyone just saw you as a threat to the natural order, which is why they wanted you out of the PLF. Some Evols took that as killing you, some took it as simply scaring you to leave. Sorry if I hurt you; I was only trying to knock you out."

My bones still ache from his squeeze. "Well, I got lucky that someone showed up, I guess." There is an awkward feeling I have. I am talking to an Evol like just some passerby, but this Prime was trying to kidnap me not just a couple of minutes ago. "Last question, then I will let you go. Why are you talking to me like this and telling me this stuff? I thought you Evols wanted all humans' dead."

"Not all of us are in it for the teachings. I honestly just wanted the ten grand. I could use the money to help my son get through school or maybe get a better house. I only joined the Evols because I live in a cesspool of them, and they needed some muscle. Honestly, they are all a bunch of fucking ferals."

As I finish, I back up from him. I can tell I at least stopped the bleeding, and he should be able to walk to a hospital or a clinic to get help. "All right, get going. You should check at a clinic if you need stitches or something." It might get infected if he doesn't get it treated by an actual doctor.

213

He slowly gets up and starts shuffling away down the alley, then suddenly stops, looks back at me, then without another word continues to move into the darkness.

I gather up my things and continue my journey back down the road, heading back to Highpoint, keeping a better eye out for anyone behind me.

The guard who let me out isn't there when I arrive back at the gate to Highpoint, but instead it's finally a familiar face resting against the wall just beside the gate, eyeing me as I walk up to him.

"You made it back—late." Lupine pans his eyes over me.

I am just glad I made it back alive. "Sorry."

He takes out his phone and peeks at the screen. "I was just about to go after you."

I don't feel like apologizing more will help any, but it's all I got right now. "Sorry, I got a little bit lost and sidetracked."

He leans off the wall and heads up to the terminal outside the gate and swipes a card from his neck. "Walk with me back. I need to talk to you about something."

The sun has set and the streetlights flicker on as we walk back to my condo. I noticed Lupine's car just parked inside the gates near a visitor parking lot. Why is he walking with me? If he wanted to scold me then he would have just done it in the car as he drove me back to my condo.

He keeps right beside me as I dredge my way back. "I know you think I am still mad at you for hitting me and attacking me. Well I am, but I am not going to get in the way of training you." Lupine sounds different. It's a calm and collected voice that I haven't heard from him. "You managed to go out into the PLF on your own, meet Primes, and overall looked like you enjoyed your time. That is something in itself."

Is he praising me for something? Well, maybe not praising but telling me I did something right? He must have gotten the best blowjob of his life from that masseuse. "Well I was...until Feline and the other girls ditched me."

He flicks out his phone. "Feline should have never approached you. She was told to monitor you, and that you were to be left by yourself today as a test to see how you handle yourself alone."

So, they were watching me this entire time, I should have assumed the PLF didn't entirely trust me walking around without some sort of protection. I don't want Feline to get punished for failing her mission to keep an eye on me. "Hope she doesn't get in trouble; she seems really nice."

Lupine is surprised by my humility. "Well, don't worry, Feline is a wild cat, has done stupid things, but she is a good solider. Gores will talk to her, but she will be fine." He opens up his text message app. "So what happened after Feline lost you?"

No sense lying to him. "Well, I asked a PLF soldier for directions, and he pointed me to M. Division Street to head back to Highpoint."

He sighs heavily and rubs the temples of his head with his fingers. "He shouldn't have told you to go even near that area. It's a ghetto infested with Evols and criminals."

Well, I know why now! I reached back to see if I still had my gun, but it was starting to fall out as I was running back here. "Well, I kind of found out about that the hard way."

"Why?" he asks concernedly.

God, here is the part where I will sound like I failed to fight off that buffalo. "Well, I was heading across and I got jumped by a buffalo Evol. I tried to fight him off but..."

He stops dead in his tracks and pulls back my arm. "When it comes to what I taught you, I told you how to fight-"

"And it didn't seem to work. I mean, he was too big and my punches and kicks did nothing." I tell him disappointed in myself.

"If a Prime is bigger than you, and you feel like you can't beat him, run. Even I would have a hard time taking down a big Prime like a buffalo."

Makes me feel better even if he says he couldn't do it.

Then I realized just how close I was to actually dying. I didn't know if he would have killed me, but I guess it would have been better than to be brought back to Pantheon.

"I used to spar all the time with Primes back in my day. I floored them all, but there were two Primes that I could not beat. Borne and Gores. I've sparred with Borne over fifty times and I only beat him once, and that was only because I bit him."

Borne is that powerful? Man, I should train with him so I can get that strong.

I still feel nauseous from filling my mouth with the buffalo's neck. "That's what I had to do to beat him, and even then I lost." Even with all my efforts he just shrugged off that bite like any other bruise.

215

He grabs me by both arms. "Don't bite Primes ever." He looks sternly at me. "In the PLF it is against the law to bite other Primes as a carnivore." I guess it makes sense, but Pure said we have lighter restrictions on the law. Is shooting a Prime and killing them better than biting them? "I will let this one slide because you didn't know, but that would have gotten you kicked out of the PLF."

I take a heavy gulp and a taste of blood travels down. "Well, I only lived because I bit him. Some Prime wearing a face mask came up and beat him with a section of rebar." I would have been crushed if I didn't bite.

He lets go of me. "Well, you got super lucky then, but don't expect someone to come and save you next time. If you absolutely have to fight a larger target, a tip is to go for the nose or muzzle, it's a weak point. Speaking of which..." He spins around and punches my nose.

The impact is heavy and I hear the cartilage in my nose twitch and feel it bend as I fall back on my ass. My nose ruptures blood from both nostrils, it doesn't hurt as much as I expected, but I try to imagine how much it hurt Lupine when I hit him.

He takes out a handkerchief from his jean pocket and tosses it on my face, and puts out a hand for me to pick me up.

"All right." I grab the cloth and put it to my nose, within a couple of seconds the cloth is dyed crimson. "I guess I deserved that. We are even now." As I reach out to grab his hand I notice my right hand compared to his.

"What is wrong?" He gets me up on my feet and notices me stare at his hand.

"Lupine, will I ever be able to fit in?"

He picks me up to my feet by my hand. "You've done great so far. A little misguided, but overall I think you will fit right in here. Besides, whatever race you are, or face you wear, wear that face with pride." He fixes my hand into a salute and puts it back up to my face.

I guess I keep looking at myself as a human. I see myself in the eyes of a human—a pasty, white-skinned, normal ape. I am a Prime. I need to look at myself as just that, and as a Prime I am going to fit into society even if I do look a little feral. It's just that...I don't want to scare my parents when I see them. I don't want them to turn away from me after everything I've done to find them just because of what I am or what choice I made. "Thanks, Lupine. Say...why are you being so supportive of me today after what I did to you?"

I never thought I would ever see him smile, but that strange sight of him smiling makes me feel like there is some form of humility there...however faint it might be. "Let's just say I did some thinking while getting a full rubdown today. I blew my cool and did not act professional. I kind of do that on occasion, if you haven't noticed."

Is he...apologizing? "It's okay—you've worked your ass off for me. I guess we just needed to let off some steam, that's all."

"Let's leave it at that. Oh, speaking of blowing steam, Pure wants to talk tomorrow morning. You will be meeting him at an undisclosed coffee shop for morning coffee. There will be a set of clothes at your apartment to wear."

"All right.... Do you know what he wants to talk about?"

"Probably just to catch up with your progress. Good luck tomorrow, buddy." When he calls me buddy it's almost exactly like how Taiga did. "Oh..." He stops and turns around and points at my bag. "Gores wanted me to check what you bought, just to make sure you're not bringing anything dangerous into Highpoint."

Damn it, he is going to ask about the phone charger. "Sure." I hand it over. Please don't ask about it.

He takes the bag and takes out the clothes, unfolding and feeling around each one, giving my entire wardrobe a shakedown. He then puts his hand over the silver package from Wired, sniffs it, opens it, and pours the charger onto his hand. "Your phone?" He looks like I just stepped on his tail.

I am treading on rough waters but I needed to cross them eventually. "Yeah, I went to get a charger for a phone that someone..." Maybe he won't ask who. "...gave to me to use."

"Who gave you a phone?" he asks intently.

"Your friend Taiga. He stopped by after training—"

His face tenses up. He snarls, and I heard the crunching sound of the charger in his hand as it breaks. He drops the shattered charger to his side and grabs me by both shoulders. "I need you to tell me everything that you told him and everything that he told you!"

Why is he freaking out over Taiga? They were best friends! "Well, um..." I am scared by Lupine's sudden change. "He stopped by the training facility to say hi."

I begin to tell him everything that we talked about, about Lupine, but I leave out his offer to take me away. But as an exchange for keeping that out, I give him the gun. His face doesn't seem to relax, and by the end of the story he has pulled out his phone and has rung up someone. I can hear the phone ring several times before Gores' voice echoes over the phone.

Lupine starts pacing back and forth. "Gores, it's me. I know it's late. This is an emergency—code red. Our *buddy* got into Highpoint and talked to Ghent, gave him a phone and a gun after talking with him about me.... I understand.... I know but.... No, I will hunt this motherfucker down if I have to and.... No, I understand.... No, I won't.... I will talk to you tomorrow morning.... Tonight? Sure I will go to your office. Be there ASAP.... What do you want me to do with Ghent?... Okay, I can do that. He is talking with Pure tomorrow. I won't let Pure know either.... I will let him know. Thanks.... Bye." He hangs up the phone and then turns his attention to me. "Why didn't you tell me about this earlier?" He is trying to calm down.

"Well, he said he was with Sagittarius. I just assumed that he was cool. He knew a lot about you and thought he was with you guys."

He lets go of me and scrunches his fingers between his brow, takes a couple of deep breaths, and looks up, cursing to the sky. "Taiga Panthera *was* with Sagittarius, but he got kicked out after Gores purged the department of Evols."

Wait...Taiga is an Evol! "He was an Evol?"

"He still is," he corrects me. "He's Pantheon's right-hand man. Obviously you're aware he is really good at deception."

Well, if he got into Highpoint undetected and managed to make me believe that he was in Sagittarius, he has to be good. "How did he get into Highpoint then?"

Lupine looks back toward the gate. "That's what I would like to know."

He looks down at Taiga's gun that he had set down on the ground beside the crumbled phone charger, reaches down, and picks it up. He slides the gun back and notices it's empty. "Wait, you brought an unloaded gun with you?"

"Well..." I scratch the back of my head. "I didn't want to shoot anyone. I just wanted to flash it to scare them."

The gun gets taken apart in front of me, Lupine examines the inside parts, I imagine for any computer chips or toxins. "Well, we can get you a standard issue Badger for you. Just please make sure that you carry it loaded. The next time you might be fighting for your life, and I don't want you to get hurt."

I guess Lupine has finally trusted me enough to carry a gun on my own. Despite the fact that I could use it to escape, he knows that I deep down inside have no goal to escape, or maybe he actually cares more about my safety than me staying in the PLF? "Thanks."

"Just remember, this is a right to carry a loaded gun. Just don't go firing it off for no reason. Fists over fire—remember that. Also, I will get you a phone you can use while in the PLF to call me in case of emergency." He looks down at the charger. "And a charger."

I remember back to what the buffalo told me before he left. "The buffalo Evol also mentioned to me that Pantheon has put out a bounty to kidnap me alive and bring me to him."

Lupine seems confused by this development. "That doesn't make sense. Why would Pantheon want to meet you? He gains nothing from inviting, what he presumes to be a human, into his home." He immediately takes out his phone as to take a statement.

"The bounty has only been out for a couple of days, before that Pantheon only wanted me out of the PLF." It all seems a bit strange that Pantheon changed his mind only a couple days ago. Nothing really changed since then, I mean I transformed into a Prime, and before that I met Taiga and talked...

He pats me on the back. "Thank you for telling me this. You did a good job. I will make sure this gets to Brutus so he can do some digging into this shitshow."

That single pat to my back easily is the highlight of my day, if not my entire time I've spent here. Finally getting recognition for doing something right from Lupine is a syringe of dopamine straight to my brain, something I needed after today's exploits. I think even him, with his seemingly desolate empathy notices how much it means to me.

He might be a sentient animal raised to kill for his country, but he just might be the closest thing to a friend I've ever had.

"Just doing my job." I tell him with a grin.

I am allowed to keep everything except the gun and the charger from today's shopping. Lupine said he will take the confiscated gun and make sure it wasn't tracked with a GPS chip, and to store it for evidence if they do manage to find Taiga. Lupine tells me before I head up to my room to get a good nights sleep for my meeting tomorrow morning, and tells me to not mention Taiga at all when talking with Pure.

"This issue is between me, Gores, Brutus, and the Evols. There is no reason to get Pure involved in something that he has no control over." Lupine doesn't even want to say Taiga's name, goes to show how much bad blood is between them.

I understand not including Pure, not talking about it also gives me more time to talk about my experiences in the PLF, future plans, and reminding Pure about Oasis, just to keep my reward fresh in his mind.

Lupine takes his leave, walking back to his car by himself. He does take his phone out and starts texting away like always does. There never seems to be a moment of relaxation for him, like a hamster trapped in his wheel.

I climb up the staircase to get to my condo, as I get up to the top the overhead street lamps come to life and illuminate the balcony leading to my door. I've never actually seen Highpoint late at night, never had a reason to leave my condo this late. I notice in the corner of the balcony the security camera is not blinking its usual green light. The key is still in my pocket, thank God it's still there, I almost forgot to check to make sure it was still in my pocket after the scuffle with the buffalo. The wind picks up a strange scent and delivers it to my nose, from in front of me. It's a rotten smell, like the garbage was left out in the sun. The garbage man must have not picked it up today cause of the holiday.

As soon as look to see my door to put the key into the doorknob, I see a letter stuffed in-between the door and the frame. The note never made it into the door, so the door was never opened, its just neatly pressed in the fold of the frame. I look around to see no one around me before taking the note. There is no envelope for it, and it is stuck together with an adhesive film. There is my name written thinly in cursive on the front. I first shake it close to my ear, there doesn't seem to be any powder inside. I hold it up to what light is left outside, nothing inside. I carefully lift the adhesive and unfold the letter.

Ghent,

I found something about Oasis. If you want to know more just give me a call whenever you get a chance. I tried to call you, if the Big Bad Wolf took your phone just call me at my phone number below on your landline, just be careful, your line is tapped.

Will talk to you soon.

Your buddy.

Taiga

ABOUT THE AUTHOR

Daniel Becker grew up in Northfield, Minnesota, diagnosed with high-functioning Autism at an early age, he has had to overcome challenges of belonging, acceptance, and social barriers. Upon graduating from Gustavus Adolphus College, he became intrigued in politics, history, and forgien cultures. Overcoming societal barriers and political identity both heavily influenced his first fiction series *American Feral*. When he is not writing, he enjoys being absorbed into the world of video games, rocking out while on nature walks, or at the bar with his friends discussing topics of the day. *American Feral: Imprint* is his first science fiction novel.

Contact me at!
Email: americanferalnovel@gmail.com
Twitter:@MeatBeast4